ALSO BY ALI STANDISH

The Ethan I Was Before
August Isle
Bad Bella
How To Disappear Completely

The Mending Summer

ALI STANDISH

HARPER

An Imprint of HarperCollinsPublishers

Library of Congress Control Number: 2020950474
ISBN 978-0-06-298565-1

Typography by Laura Mock
21 22 23 24 25   PC/LSCH   10 9 8 7 6 5 4 3 2 1

First Edition

For Dad,
who taught me there is no need
to move mountains
if you can find the strength to climb them

Chapter One

~~~

Some summers are just meant to break your heart.

Georgia had heard those words last summer, on a sweltering July day—the kind that sticks to your skin like honey—and she remembered them still. It had been rest hour at Camp Pine Valley, and Georgia should have been dozing in her bunk, but it was far too hot. So she'd snuck out to the lake and dived in, letting the mountain water seep the sun from her skin. When she saw two counselors approaching on the shoreline, she ducked beneath the nearby dock.

Two pairs of tanned legs presently appeared, their toes skimming the water just inches from Georgia's nose. She was surprised to hear that one of the counselors was crying.

"How could he?" she said. "Why would he do it, Jen?"

Georgia treaded water silently, feeling guilty for listening but equally unable to do anything else without getting caught.

The second counselor was quiet when she answered. Her voice was little more than a whisper, but it wriggled its way through the cracks in the rickety dock planks and into Georgia's ears.

"Oh, Annie. I'm sorry. It seems like some summers are just meant to break your heart."

All the rest of that afternoon and into a night still too hot for sleep, Georgia couldn't stop thinking about those words. She couldn't say how she knew, but she was certain—could feel in her bones—that they were true.

In the days that followed, Georgia imagined heartbreak to be a sudden and violent thing. Like when she had accidentally knocked over the Wedgwood vase that her grandmother had given to her mother on her wedding day. A single crash, a shattering into a thousand pieces.

Georgia should have been at Camp Pine Valley this summer. Today. Right now. Throwing her arms around the shoulders of old friends, racing them to claim a top bunk. Now that she was twelve, she would have finally been in a cabin in the Upper Girls camp.

Instead, she was leaning against the trunk of the crepe myrtle that grew in front of her house, listening to the rain pattering down around her. Thinking.

And she thought, as she folded the paper she was holding into halves, that perhaps she had been wrong about heartbreak. Perhaps heartbreak was something that happened bit by bit over time, so slowly you almost didn't know it was happening until it had.

Georgia considered the puddle that had formed in front of the tree, between the street and the curb, where water always collected during a good rainstorm. It would be the perfect size for the paper sailboat she was constructing.

From inside the house came the sound of shouting.

Georgia looked down to consult the guide to origami that she had bought at the school library's end-of-year sale. It was splattered with rain. She pulled the book closer to her, deeper under the branches of the blossoming tree that sheltered her like a giant pink umbrella. She needed to concentrate on folding the edges of the paper into just the right size of triangles, or she would have to ball this one up like her last two attempts.

And the book made it look so easy.

A muffled *clap*—a door being slammed inside the house. Georgia winced.

And just like that, she had botched the triangles again, so she crumpled up the paper and pulled a dry sheet from her backpack. The crease in her brows matched the neat creases she made in the paper as she pinched it together between her fingers. Harder, perhaps, than was necessary.

But perhaps some things needed a hard touch, because soon the paper began to resemble the picture of the boat in the book. She felt a tiny lurch of triumph as she held the thing up and inspected it. It looked entirely seaworthy.

Georgia leaned over the puddle and caught sight of her rippled reflection. Brown hair untidy over a narrow face. Green-gray eyes wide and flighty. She ran her finger through the water, down the long line of her nose, splitting her reflection in two.

Gingerly, she set the paper boat down in the puddle— probably she should call it a very tiny lake, because what respectable boat wanted to sail in a puddle?

For a few moments, she watched as it bobbed in small satisfying circles. Imagining it might be a pirate ship loaded with cursed treasure, or an explorer's vessel heading for icy, uncharted lands.

For a few moments, she left the tree and the house and the shouting behind.

"Having fun?"

Georgia's head whipped around. She hadn't heard her father approach.

She looked up at him for a moment, taking in his black, slicked-back hair and his smile. Her father had a nice smile; people said so all the time. He was tall and long-limbed, like Georgia. Her heart filled with the sight of him, like a ship taking on water.

"Hi, Daddy," she said. "I made a boat."

"I see that," he replied with a wink. "Well done, Captain. You better get inside, though. It's almost suppertime.

If you're lucky you can sneak past your mother and change before she sees you're sopping."

The smile flickered.

"You aren't staying?" Georgia asked. Though she already knew he wasn't. He carried his car keys in one hand and had one of his nice suits on.

"Can't, sweetheart," he said. "I've got a set." His fingers flexed and curled, as though already feeling for the piano keys. "But I'll see you tomorrow, so no long faces, all right?"

He didn't wait for her answer. He was already halfway in his car.

Georgia thought of the countless afternoons she'd sat right here on the sidewalk—or perched up in the crepe myrtle—waiting for him to come home. It was always the best part of the day, when he emerged from his car and stooped down as she ran to him, lifting her in his arms. Wondering if he might suggest making pancakes for dinner so Mama could have a break from cooking, or going to the Chargrill for milkshakes, just the two of them. If he might pull a new book from his briefcase and hand it over, telling her he'd seen it and thought of her.

Watching his car drive off through the rain, she wondered if he was thinking of her now, or if she had faded from his mind as soon as she'd disappeared from his rearview mirror.

She could almost feel her heart break a little bit more.

Chapter Two

Georgia's mother was sitting at the kitchen table, poring over one of her textbooks, when Georgia clattered through the door, cradling her boat in one hand. It would dry overnight and then she would put it on her bookshelf, where it would live between *Stuart Little* and *Peter Pan*—books she and Daddy had read together—until the next storm.

Her mother looked up, then did a double take.

"You're soaked," she said, sighing.

Under her reading glasses, her eyes were red rimmed.

"I was playing outside. I didn't realize it was raining so hard," Georgia lied.

"I didn't either. Hang your things to dry off a little and then put them in the hamper. What do you want for supper? Turkey? Chicken? Beef?"

Before Georgia's mother had gone back to school, she used to make all their suppers herself. Now most nights they ate frozen dinners. Georgia didn't mind. They weren't bad, especially the turkey, and she wanted Mama to have the time she needed to study.

She didn't even mind that paying for Mama's school meant that there wasn't enough money to go to Camp Pine Valley this year. That is, she minded not going—minded a *lot*—but she didn't mind Mama using that money for her college.

Mama was studying to get her degree in biology. She wanted to find a job in a lab somewhere. She wanted to "contribute to something bigger." But she was the oldest one in her program, and one of the only women, which she said meant she had to study extra hard, because she knew lots of people were just waiting for her to mess up.

"Chicken," Georgia said, because that's what Mama liked most, and Georgia liked to eat the same thing as everyone else. It felt more normal that way. Like when they all used to eat together.

The trouble was, nothing *was* normal anymore.

For as long as she could remember, everything had been normal, and then one day she woke up and realized all the normal had disappeared, and she couldn't think when it had gone or how she'd failed to notice it slip away.

Normal was having dinner with both of your parents and

listening to Daddy play the piano while you did your homework. Normal was being read to before bed (even if you were "a bit old" for that sort of thing).

"Georgia? For goodness' sake, you're dripping all over the floor!"

A small puddle had indeed formed at her feet, as if she had begun to melt. "Sorry, Mama."

"It doesn't matter," said her mother, her voice worn. "Just go get changed and dry off. Summer colds are the worst kind, you know."

Georgia nodded and walked away into her room, shutting the door behind her. When she looked down, she realized her fist had clenched around the little paper boat, crushing it into a useless soggy ball.

Chapter Three

That night, Georgia lay in bed, not quite awake but not asleep either. Not dreaming but remembering.

A warm night that was not quite spring but not yet summer either. A slow song was playing from the radio in the living room and the party guests were laughing. And then there was the sound of the door being opened wide, the sudden light. Bleary-eyed, she turned over to see Daddy's silhouette in the doorway. He knelt beside her bed and smiled her favorite smile—the one he reserved only for her—the one that made his eyes crinkle at the corners.

"I've got something to show you," he said.

He scooped her from the bed as though she were made of feathers, held her against his chest with one hand and his glass in the other. He swept her through the living room, where the last party guests were still dancing, their dinner jackets and heels long since abandoned, drowsy smiles spreading on their faces as they caught sight of Georgia.

Mama was standing at the sink, hips swaying gently to the music as she worked her way through the stack of silverware and dessert plates. Daddy put a finger to his lips as they snuck behind her toward the front door.

It had always been this way. Always been Georgia and Daddy who shared secrets and adventures, who had traveled to distant lands and new worlds in the stories they read together. They hadn't meant to make Mama an outsider, but sometimes it felt like that's what she had become. She was just too quiet, too serious to join them in their games. Better at helping with homework than planning adventures.

Georgia felt snug and sleepy against Daddy's chest as he spirited her past the camellia bushes, past the garden beds sprinkled with weeds and with seashells collected from Mama and Daddy's honeymoon many years ago.

"There," Daddy said, hoisting Georgia higher on his hip and pointing to the sky. "See that?"

The full moon loomed above them, silver and certain, casting a veil of pale light over the world. She nodded.

"That's a strawberry moon," he said. "That's what you call a full moon in June."

"It doesn't look like a strawberry," Georgia said doubtfully.

"But it's ripe for the picking," Daddy said slyly. "What do you think, huh? Should I pluck it right out of the sky?"

"You can't do that, Daddy," said Georgia, giggling. Old enough to be in on the joke, young enough to be pleased by it. "It's impossible."

"I would do anything for you, sweetheart," he replied. "Even give you the moon."

He set down his drink, reached his hand up toward the sky, and pinched the moon between his thumb and pointer finger. Then, suddenly, he really was holding something between his fingers, something silver and shiny, and he swept her in a half circle as he placed it in her palm.

"Told you so," he said.

The object was perfectly round and cool in Georgia's warm hand. And even though she knew it wasn't the real moon, even though the light of morning would reveal it to be a nickel rubbed to a shine, she didn't mind.

Because Daddy was the moon. And she was safe in his arms.

Georgia could still feel her arms around Daddy's neck when suddenly she was pulled away from him, from the memory, like a flower being uprooted from the soil by rough hands. She opened her eyes and lay blinking in the darkness.

The shadows were too heavy for her to read the time on the round clock that squatted, gnomelike, on her bedside table. The only light in the room was the golden pool that had spilled in from the living room and collected on the floor in front of the bedroom door.

As Georgia watched, fully awake now, she saw two sets of feet dancing back and forth across the crack beneath the door. Her mother. And him. The man who looked like Daddy but walked just a little wobbly. Who sounded like Daddy but spoke a little too loud. Who smelled like Daddy but just a little sour. Who had arrived in Georgia's life just as all the normal had left it.

He was her father, certainly. But not Daddy.

He was the Shadow Man.

The words he and Mama spoke did not dance. The words—not quite whispers—simmered and seethed and hissed. On and on they went, two pots left to boil and forgotten far too long. The floorboards creaked beneath their feet. Ice tinkled against glass.

A stifled sob came from beyond the door.

Georgia crept from her bed as if pulled by an invisible string. She didn't want to see him, but somehow tonight she *needed* to.

She turned the handle and opened the door just wide enough to peer through.

Daddy was slumped at the kitchen table like a doll, his suit rumpled. In his hand was a glass, which he swirled round and round over the table, making the ice chime as if with laughter. His eyes were two dark coals. Mama stood across the table, looking down at him, misery etched into all the lines of her face.

Georgia's throat tightened. Something sharp rustled in her belly. She had made a mistake. She didn't want to see either of them like this. But as she pulled the door shut, she thought she saw Mama's head turn in her direction.

She dived back into bed, burrowing deep under the summer quilt. Hoping to forget what she had just seen.

A moment later, the light from the living room was extinguished. The sound of footsteps, followed by quiet. And then Georgia's door opened. She shut her eyes, pretending to be sleeping.

The bedsprings squeaked as someone sat beside her.

"Georgia?" whispered Mama. "Are you awake?"

Georgia did not answer. She didn't want Mama to know that she'd heard. That she'd seen.

Mama brushed her fingers over her hair and dropped a gentle kiss on her head.

Then she was slipping back through the door, and Georgia was alone once more. Lying awake, her body stiff as a starched sheet.

Chapter Four

The next morning began with a pie and a suitcase.

Georgia could smell the pie before she even opened her eyes—warm, buttery, sweet. It was both familiar and foreign. It had been a long while since her mother had had enough time to make a pie.

Georgia's eyes fluttered open to find the room flooded with warm July light. The kind that is bright but not hot, that you got in North Carolina only for a few hours in the morning before the summer day began to harden and grow stale.

A square of light illuminated the open suitcase at the foot of Georgia's bed. She blinked and saw that it was full of her things, folded and tightly packed.

Where was she going?

For a second, her stomach fluttered with hope. Maybe

she was going to camp after all! But that didn't make sense, because camp had started already, and Mama would have packed her things in her footlocker, not her little suitcase.

Daddy had been known to rouse her early some summer mornings for a surprise beach day. Mama would pack a picnic of sandwiches and lemonade for the three of them, and Georgia and Daddy would spend the whole day running through the surf while Mama watched from under her umbrella.

But Georgia wouldn't need a suitcase for a day-trip. Besides, who took pie to the beach?

Still groggy, she padded to the kitchen in her nightgown. The neatly latticed cherry pie was cooling atop the stove next to a skillet of scrambled eggs. Georgia's mother sat at the table in her apron and slippers, taking notes on the textbook in front of her.

Daddy was nowhere to be seen.

"Your father's got a headache this morning," said Mama, looking up as Georgia approached.

Georgia didn't need telling.

"I'll be quiet," she said.

She meant this in more ways than one. She would not talk about the night before. They never talked about the night before.

And Georgia never told Mama about the feeling she had carried around with her, deep in her stomach, since everything started changing. The one that was always there but felt worst on the mornings after the Shadow Man came. The dark one with burrs and thorns that could stick you if you weren't careful.

She didn't know how to talk to Mama about things like that. It was Daddy she would have turned to once, Daddy who would have understood.

But Daddy had a headache and was not to be disturbed.

"I made eggs," said Mama.

"And a pie."

"Yes." Mama stared out the window as Georgia moved around the kitchen, careful not to make too much noise as she served herself eggs and poured her orange juice. When Georgia sat down, Mama smiled.

Mama didn't smile as often or as wide as Daddy, and there was something tired at the edges. Where Daddy's smile came easy, Mama's was a smile you had to work for. A shabby prize to be won, like a blue ribbon with tails that had begun to fray.

"Why is my suitcase packed?" Georgia asked, sinking her fork into the eggs.

Mama looked at her for a long moment before speaking, as if *she* had been the one to ask a question. As if she might find the answer in Georgia's face.

"I'm taking you to stay with your aunt Marigold," she said.

Georgia's face widened in astonishment. Her aunt Marigold—actually great-aunt Marigold—existed only as the vague memory of a strange adult presence at a handful of Christmas dinners and birthdays. She had been to Aunt Marigold's country house once several years ago for some kind of occasion, but she had spent most of the time playing in the chicken coop.

"Why?" Georgia asked.

The question hung between them.

"It will only be for weekdays," her mother said. "I'll pick you up every Friday for the weekend. My summer course schedule is so busy, and with all the—hours—your father is putting in, there will be more for you to do at Marigold's. It will be fun, don't you think?"

Again, the question lingered, inviting all sorts of answers that were best left unspoken.

"Sure, Mama," Georgia replied finally. But she didn't meet her mother's eyes. She glanced at the bedroom door where her father was sleeping and willed him to open it. To come out and ruffle her hair and say there had been a change of plans. That he hoped she was up for some fun today, because he had an idea.

"How about a little adventure?" he'd say with a wink.

Life with Daddy was always such a wonderful adventure. But the door stayed firmly shut.

Some summers are just meant to break your heart.

"Good," said Mama. "Then after breakfast, go get dressed and make sure you don't need anything I haven't packed. We'll leave in an hour."

And an hour later, they did. Georgia sat in the passenger's seat, the wind in her hair, the pie on her lap. In her pocket was a silver nickel that shined like the moon.

Chapter Five

〜

As they traveled east, the houses grew farther apart and the trees closer together. Red clay gave way to loose, sandy soil that clung to the car bumpers and gas pumps in the one-light towns they drove through. Georgia recognized some of the sites from their trips to the coast—a redbrick main street with American flags yellowing in the windows of the Piggly Wiggly, a clapboard church in the shade of a lightning-struck oak tree.

The car's air conditioning was broken, so they kept the windows rolled down for the hot breeze that swept in. The drive was only an hour, but halfway there they got too hot and pulled over at a gas station for Dr Peppers. Georgia wanted a bag of M&M's, too, but Mama said they'd only melt and get chocolate everywhere.

Once they were back in the car, Mama reached into her

handbag and pulled out a set of flash cards. She handed them to Georgia. "Want to quiz me?"

Mama sometimes asked Georgia to test her before her exams. Georgia didn't understand most of the questions—could hardly pronounce some of the longer words—but it always made her proud when Mama got the right answer, which she usually did.

Besides, Mama was better at quizzes than she was at conversation.

So they settled into a comfortable rhythm. Georgia listened as Mama spoke about mitochondria and plasmolysis until she turned off the highway.

"Here we are," Mama said a few minutes later.

She stopped the car at the end of the driveway, giving Georgia time to stare at the house. Mama and Daddy always spoke of it as "the country house." It had belonged to Daddy's granddaddy, and Daddy had grown up visiting for summers and Christmases.

It was white with a red roof, two brick chimneys, and some kind of vine snaking up its sides. The house looked tired, like it needed a break from all that standing. Staring at it, Georgia suddenly felt tired, too.

An overgrown pasture swept from the porch to the road. Within the rusting fence, a lone cow stood, staring in their direction with neither suspicion nor interest.

Finally, Mama guided the car onto the dirt driveway.

Sunflowers lined the drive on one side, tall and bowed as lampposts, their bright petals like rays of electric light. Beyond them, forest swallowed everything.

As they pulled up, a screen door slammed and a woman appeared on the porch.

"Hello, Marigold," Mama called, stepping out of the car.

If Aunt Marigold answered, Georgia didn't hear it. She got out of the car, suppressing the sudden urge to hide behind her mother's skirt the way she used to when she was small.

"You'll track dust in if you keep dragging your feet, Georgia," Mama scolded.

But her eyes didn't scold. Her eyes looked uncertain.

Georgia stepped onto the porch and, summoning her courage, looked up at her great-aunt. "Hello, Aunt Marigold," she said. "We brought you a pie."

Aunt Marigold was a tall woman. She wore men's denim overalls with a white shirt underneath. Her hair was brushed into a neat braid—silver twisted with rust. She had a sloping, dainty nose that seemed out of step with the rest of her, especially the sharp green eyes above it. Those eyes studied Georgia, and she wondered what they would find.

"That was kind," she said, taking the pie. Her voice was deep but soft, like velvet you couldn't help but run your fingers over. "Y'all come in."

She held the door open for Georgia as Mama went back for the suitcase.

Inside, it was not as dark as Georgia had pictured. Sun poured into the kitchen, where a long wooden table took up most of the room. A covered serving bowl sat atop it.

The house was silent, though. Mama had grown up with a heap of brothers and sisters and always said if she didn't keep the radio on, the house felt too empty.

There was no radio that Georgia could see in the country house. No television, even. She had never met anyone who didn't have a television. She thought it must get lonely—all that quiet. Suddenly she didn't want Mama to leave her here on her own.

"You'll be hungry," Aunt Marigold said, setting the cherry pie on the table. "I made chicken and dumplings."

"That sounds wonderful," Mama replied, putting down Georgia's suitcase by the stairs. "I'd love some before I get on the road."

Aunt Marigold nodded in approval, then pulled three plates and three glasses out from a cabinet and handed them to Georgia. Her great-aunt's hands were shaking slightly, and Georgia wondered how long it had been since she had had guests.

They ate the chicken and dumplings off smooth gray plates with blue rings running round them and a delicate flower painted at the center of each one ("These are beautiful," Mama had said, and Aunt Marigold had thanked her), and poured their iced tea from a matching pitcher.

"Is this chicken one of yours?" Mama asked, gesturing to the slightly soggy dumplings.

"No. Fox got in the coop summer before last. It wasn't pretty. None of them survived, and I haven't kept any since."

Mama changed the subject, but Georgia felt a spark of interest. She didn't know many adults who spoke about things like death in front of children. Without hushed tones or arched eyebrows.

"And this new college course of yours?" Aunt Marigold said later as Mama served up slices of cherry pie.

"It keeps me busy," Mama said. "But I like it."

"Do people think it's odd? A woman your age—a mother—going back to college?"

Mama chewed slowly. "Not as odd as it used to be," she said. "But yes. I'm sure plenty of people think it's strange."

"Well, I say let them think whatever they like," Aunt Marigold said, pointing her fork at Mama for emphasis. "You just show them all."

Mama smiled at that, even laughed a little as she tipped her glass toward Aunt Marigold.

"Georgia, why don't you go upstairs and settle in while I talk to your aunt," Mama said once Georgia had finished her pie.

"Second door on the left," Aunt Marigold added.

Georgia held the banister in one hand and her suitcase in the other as she climbed the creaking stairs. At the top, she found a dark corridor with two doors on either side.

The second door on the left was open. A mahogany bed reigned over the room within, so tall that there was a little step stool pushed up beside it. Otherwise, the only furniture was a bedside table with a lamp, a little desk, and a stout chest of drawers. Between the heavy curtains, the window was open to let in the fresh air, but the room still smelled of mildew. Cobwebs glimmered in the corners of the ceiling.

Georgia heaved her suitcase onto the bed. As she unpacked her things, she could hear Mama and Aunt Marigold speaking in low voices. She put her clothes in the drawers and then pulled out a framed picture she'd taken from her own bureau at home.

She wasn't sure why she'd brought it. She'd never brought pictures to camp. She wasn't even *in* the picture. It had been taken before she was born, when her parents were on their honeymoon on Tybee Island, Georgia.

They were standing on the beach, hair swept back by the wind. In the distance, you could see wild ponies behind them. Both of their smiles shined like they were brand-new.

Mama and Daddy had named Georgia for this trip. For the state where they had honeymooned. So, in a way, she supposed, she was in the picture after all.

She set the picture down next to a small collection of dusty books that looked as though they had not been opened in many years. *Classic Poems for Children* read the gold writing on one of the spines. It sat next to an old copy of *Peter Pan.*

She pulled *Peter Pan* out, ignoring the musty smell as she opened it to the first page. *All children, except one, grow up . . .*

She had lost count of the books she and Daddy had read together. Books where magic was real, and anything was possible. But *Peter Pan* had been Daddy's favorite book to read aloud. They'd read it so many times that they both had large parts of it memorized. Year before last, for Halloween, Georgia had been Peter, Mama was Wendy, and Daddy went as Captain Hook. He'd made a wonderful pirate.

And then one night last winter, she'd held the book out to him when he'd come to say good night. Though they hadn't read together in a while, she knew he wouldn't be able to resist *Peter Pan.*

But a strange look had crossed his face, one that made her curl up her toes.

"Aren't you getting *a bit old* for that sort of thing?" he'd said.

Then he'd turned and left, forgetting to say good night at all.

But no. It hadn't been Daddy who had said those words, turned his back on her.

She had smelled the drink on his breath.

It had been the Shadow Man.

Georgia looked around her new room. It still looked bare.

What would she *do* here?

She went to stand by the window, which looked out over the woods. That, at least, was something. There were no woods to play in at home, not for miles. The view made her feel almost like she was back at Camp Pine Valley.

She crept back into the hall. Mama and Aunt Marigold were still talking downstairs. Beside her room, there was a bathroom with a claw-foot tub. Across the hall were two closed doors.

Of course Georgia knew she shouldn't open them. But the house was old and interesting and sure to be full of secrets. She didn't know when she would next get a chance to explore it.

The first door revealed another bedroom, this one obviously lived in. There was a book and a pair of reading glasses on the bedside table, framed pictures, a pair of slippers sitting under a chair in the corner, and papers stacked up on the desk.

Closing the door to her great-aunt's room, Georgia moved to the last one and was just about to turn the handle when she heard chairs scraping the floor below. She nearly jumped when she heard her mother's voice calling up the stairwell.

"Come on down, Georgia. Time to say goodbye."

Chapter Six

A few minutes later, Georgia and Aunt Marigold stood side by side on the porch, watching the green car rumble down the drive.

"Well, then," said Aunt Marigold.

She cast an appraising eye over Georgia, as if only really noticing her for the first time. Georgia realized that she hadn't spoken a word since handing over Mama's pie.

"Your mama didn't give me much notice you were coming," Aunt Marigold said, folding her arms and hooking her thumbs through the overalls' straps. Their silver buttons made Georgia think of the coin she had in her pocket. Her fingers clutched it tightly.

"Me neither."

"Humph," muttered Aunt Marigold. "I don't look after children much these days, you know."

"Me neither."

She narrowed her eyes, then gave a snort of laughter. "Well, then," she said again, opening the screen door, "we'll just have to get along the best we can this summer. But this ain't a hotel, and I'm no maid. You'll have to pull your weight."

Mama never let Georgia say "ain't," even though other kids at school did. She liked that Aunt Marigold said it.

"Yes, ma'am," she replied.

"Starting with the lunch dishes. You wash and I'll dry."

They stood next to each other at the sink, washing and drying in silence. Georgia paid special attention to the little flowers painted at the center of each dish—a daisy, a tulip, a yellow rose. But even these couldn't distract her from the quiet. She had never heard so much silence in her life, and it was already driving her a little bit crazy.

"Don't you have a TV?" she asked finally.

"No," Aunt Marigold said. "Does that bother you?"

"A little. It's too quiet."

"Maybe you just don't know how to listen right."

Georgia considered this doubtfully. "Well . . . I *guess* that could be it."

"Go on," Aunt Marigold said, lifting her chin toward the door. "I'll finish here. You go explore. Keep your eye to the ground for copperheads, though. And if you see a black bear, let it be, hear me? Even if it's a cub. The mama's never far behind."

Georgia didn't need to be told twice. Shaking her hands free of suds, she ran out of the house, letting the screen door slam behind her.

The cow had come to stand on the close side of the pasture, so Georgia waded through the grass toward the fence. To her surprise, the animal took a few steps toward her, sticking her head over the wire.

There was a dull spark in the cow's eyes as she considered Georgia.

"Hi," Georgia said. "I live here, too, now. But only during the week. And only for the summer."

As she spoke, the cow's black ears perked up.

"Do you like living here?"

The cow gave a long sigh.

"Well, I guess there's not much to do. Maybe cows don't like fun anyway."

Georgia stroked the matted hair beneath the cow's ears. The animal tolerated this for a moment, then turned and flapped her lips against Georgia's palm. Georgia jerked her arm back, not wanting to be bitten, before she realized what the cow wanted.

"Oh. A treat, huh? Well, I didn't bring anything."

The cow gave a scornful snort and promptly walked away.

So much for that, then. Georgia felt like a kite that had been cut loose from its string, floating aimlessly. She realized that the feeling was loneliness.

If only Daddy were here, he would know what to do. He always did. Or had. When she was with Daddy, she was certain of herself, because he knew her better than anyone else in the world.

If only, if only . . .

Georgia turned and noticed a tin-roofed barn poking out from behind one side of the house. On the other side, cicadas called out from their perches in the knotted trees.

Georgia followed their summons.

As she stepped into the trees, it was as if someone had drawn a curtain over the world. Sunlight became shadow, and shadow became darkness. Georgia crept forward, listening to the sounds of the leaves rustling against the forest floor as she walked. Underfoot, the ground was soft, slightly sinking.

She could recognize some of the trees. Loblolly pines that stood stiff as soldiers, and sweet gums with their star-shaped leaves. She had learned to identify them at camp. Looking ahead, she could see several oases of dappled sunlight, yet the forest seemed to go on forever.

Spotting something on the ground, she froze, remembering Aunt Marigold's warning about snakes. But it was only a stick. Georgia picked it up and waved it in the air like a sword, pretending to be Wendy in Neverland. Only *this* Wendy wasn't content to stay back and wash dishes while Peter and his Lost Boys went out to fight. This Wendy was brave and ruthless and kept a scabbard slung around her waist.

When she had vanquished all the enemies she could imagine, she let the stick drop to the ground.

Had her father played make-believe in these same woods when he was little? she wondered. She had heard him talk about coming here in the summers with his own father—Aunt Marigold's brother—who had died before Georgia was born. But she couldn't remember what her father had said about the place. What he had done or where he had played.

It was a strange sensation to think of her father as a child. Almost like thinking of him as a ghost. She shivered.

Then, suddenly, she had the slightly queasy feeling that she *wasn't* alone. That she was being watched. She looked around, squinting into the trees.

"Hello?"

The cicadas hummed on.

It was probably her imagination, Georgia thought. Her teachers were eternally scolding her for daydreaming, losing the thread of reality in favor of picking up another, brighter thread that led to places unknown.

Still. Georgia decided that she'd had enough forest for one day.

The problem was, she had spun around so many times she no longer remembered which way she'd come from. She chose the direction that looked most familiar, but found herself hiking up a hill that she certainly hadn't climbed before. She went back and tried another way, but this one took her over a shallow creek.

She spotted a place up ahead where the shadows weren't as heavy and headed in that direction.

It was the colors she noticed first. The splashes of pink, purple, and orange dappling the little glade of clover and moss. Coming closer, Georgia saw that they were flowers. Some she recognized from Mama's garden, though she didn't know their names. They weren't quite wild but not exactly a garden either.

There were stones in the grass, too, forming a rectangle about twice the size of Georgia's suitcase. The flowers had clearly once been planted inside the tiny stone walls but had long since spilled beyond them. Weeds shot up between the blooms, slowly racing for a spot in the dappled sun. Clearly, no one had tended them in a long time.

So overgrown was the patch of flowers that Georgia nearly missed the statue. It stood at the far end of the stones, wearing a delicate veil of green moss.

It was an angel. Her head was bowed, her hands clasped, wings folded neatly behind her.

But what was an angel doing out here in the woods? Or these flowers, once so carefully planted, or these stones, so neatly arranged?

"Oh," Georgia said, suddenly backing away, her heart

giving an unpleasant jolt. "Oh!"

Georgia had not spent much time in graveyards, but she had visited many in the books she and Daddy read. She knew people planted flowers over graves, that graveyards were full of angels like this one, placed there to watch over departed souls.

But *this* was not a graveyard. This was a forest. And if these stones marked a grave, it was a grave for someone small.

Mind racing, Georgia took a single step forward, wondering if she might be able to decipher a name written at the angel's stone base. But then she felt a sudden ghostly chill in the air. Her breath caught in her throat.

She backed away and began to run, eager to leave the mossy glade behind.

Chapter Seven

When Georgia finally emerged from the forest, she had circled around the back of the house and come out on the other side, near the tin-roofed barn that was being ever so slowly smothered by ivy. It looked like someone might have once painted the barn the color of cardinal wings, but the hue had faded away to a dull copper.

"You're back. Good."

Georgia turned to see Aunt Marigold standing in a large vegetable garden. Much like the flowers in the woods, this garden's occupants had been allowed to grow a bit wild. Butter bean vines had outgrown their trellises, rows of cabbage had been invaded by enormous summer squash vines, and the okra and cornstalks shot up tall and straight as ladders fixing to reach the sky.

Aunt Marigold wore a straw hat that shaded her face, and

she carried a basket on one arm. Her feet, Georgia noticed, were bare. Her toes scrunched up and down against the sandy soil. They looked younger than the rest of her, almost childlike.

"You can pick the corn and the sweet peppers," her great-aunt said, squinting up at the sun, which squinted right back down at her. "There are more baskets by the door. Mind you only pick the ripe peppers. Shuck the corn before you come in and take it to the sink to wash."

Then she slipped between two cornstalks and was gone.

Georgia found her way to the back door of the house, passing an old water pump. There was a stack of baskets, just as Aunt Marigold had said. And there were fruit trees around somewhere, because one of them was filled with peaches.

Suddenly very thirsty, Georgia took one of the peaches and bit into it, savoring the tart, warm sweetness that ran down her chin. She wiped her mouth, picked up an empty basket, and started back through the grass before stopping to wriggle free from her own shoes.

Aunt Marigold tutted at the husked corn Georgia had deposited in the sink, showing her how to pull the silky white strands from the rows of kernels. They even discovered a tiny green worm clinging to one of the ears. Georgia shivered, but Aunt Marigold said it was a harmless earworm and threw it out the open window.

Next, Georgia shelled the butter beans while Aunt Marigold washed the potatoes and cut the corn from the cobs. She seemed to concentrate hard on every task she put her hands to, and as soon as Georgia was done with one thing, Aunt Marigold had something else for her to do. Finally they were sitting across from each other at the table, steaming plates of succotash and red potatoes in front of them.

Georgia bowed her head and waited for Aunt Marigold to say a blessing. Instead came the sound of her fork clinking against her plate. Georgia opened her eyes. Aunt Marigold had already begun to eat.

"Do you eat succotash at home?" her great-aunt asked.

"Sometimes," said Georgia, looking down at the mixture of corn, beans, and sweet peppers. It was colorful, like a finger painting. She had never seen it before, but she didn't want her great-aunt to know this.

Nor could she quite summon the courage to ask Aunt Marigold about what she'd discovered in the woods. Among the cornstalks, with the heat of the sun baking into her skin, she had almost convinced herself that she had imagined the chill she had felt as she'd leaned in toward the angel statue. The sudden certainty that some deep terrible sorrow lingered in the little green glade.

She didn't know how Aunt Marigold might react if she asked about it. If she might laugh or lie. Aunt Marigold was an unusual kind of adult, which made Georgia like her. Want to be *liked* by her.

But it didn't mean she could trust her.

"Does your father still play the piano?" Aunt Marigold asked, breaking the silence.

"Yes, ma'am. He plays most nights. In clubs and hotels and things like that."

"I see."

Play made it sound like a game. Something small and silly.

But anyone who'd ever heard Georgia's father on the piano knew it was a serious business. Knew that he belonged on a big stage somewhere, not in an office like the one he went to every morning. Daddy never even used sheet music.

"It's all right here," he'd say, wiggling his fingers at Georgia. "My music is all in my hands."

Hearing Daddy play the piano at home was Georgia's favorite sound in the world. When she closed her eyes and listened, his music sparkled just like his smile.

"What do you think?" he'd ask her after he finished playing. "Good enough for Nashville? Maybe even New York?"

Those places, Georgia knew, were where people got discovered. Where they could see their names up in lights.

"Yes, Daddy."

"Well, we'll see about that, won't we?"

Then, before closing the piano lid, he'd play one last

song. It was always "Georgia on My Mind." Georgia knew he hadn't written it himself, but it felt like he had. Like he'd written it just for her.

But since Daddy had started playing shows more and more, he played the piano at home less and less. Came home later and later and sometimes not at all. And when he did come home, most nights he wasn't himself.

Georgia felt the thing with thorns stirring in her belly. She wasn't hungry anymore.

Aunt Marigold was looking at her again in that piercing way she had.

"And I suppose you like it?" she asked. "Living in the city?"

Georgia thought of her street, lined with neat houses, green lawns, and cars that were washed every Sunday. Had it really only been this morning that she'd woken up there? It felt like so much longer.

"I like it fine," she said. "Do *you* like it here?"

"It suits me," said Aunt Marigold. Her fork clattered loudly as she ate, or maybe it was just the silence that made it sound loud.

Georgia tried to imagine living by herself out here, in this big old house. She couldn't.

"But don't you ever get lonely?"

Aunt Marigold stared at her for a moment, so that Georgia saw the gold flecks in her eyes. "Everybody gets lonely," she said.

Georgia remembered the feeling of someone watching her in the forest. "Does anyone else live around here?"

Aunt Marigold leaned back in her chair, causing it to groan. "The Boatwright place is about half a mile east," she said. "Other side of the forest. It's empty, though. For sale. Then there's the Norman farm down the other way. And there's Ruby, of course."

"Ruby?"

"The cow. She keeps me company."

Aunt Marigold got up and returned with two bowls of stewed peaches with cream. She placed one in front of Georgia—who had picked around the butter beans, which sat in a small unappetizing heap at the edge of her plate—and ate her peaches instead. Aunt Marigold glanced at the beans but said nothing.

"Thank you for dinner," she said. "And also—for letting me stay here."

If Mama were here, she would give Georgia a little smile, nodding approval at Georgia's manners.

But Mama would have long since made it home. Was she eating her frozen dinner by herself while Daddy went out, or was he home with her? Would they be silent or fighting?

Aunt Marigold nodded. "It's late," she said, not unkindly, though it was only twilight. "Time for bed. I'll do the dishes tonight."

Truthfully, Georgia did feel tired, and she could tell that her great-aunt wanted to be alone. Maybe it was as odd for her to have Georgia staying here as it was for Georgia. "Good night, Aunt Marigold," she said.

"Good night."

She heard the tap from the kitchen sink turn on as she climbed the stairs. She stepped into the dark hallway with its four heavy doors. Her eyes turned instinctively to the one on the left—the only one she had not yet opened.

The sink was still running below. Georgia knew she would have time to open the door, peek inside, and close it again before Aunt Marigold could even make it up the stairs.

Except that when she tried the handle, the door stuck. It was locked.

There was a large keyhole—the type that needed an old skeleton key to open it. Georgia bent down and pressed her eye to it. The room was dark and small, and she could only make out the shape of a narrow bed shoved up against the far wall, a rocking chair beside it like the one that used to be in Georgia's room. Where she knew Mama had sat and rocked her to sleep when she was a baby.

She stood and walked swiftly down the hall to her own room, closing the door behind her. Why, she wondered, was that room locked when all the others were open? Whose room had it been?

It took her a moment to realize what the little room reminded her of: the little rectangle of stones in the forest.

Both of them tucked away, hidden in the shadows.

Both of them just the right size for a child.

Chapter Eight

The husky songs of the katydids echoed so loud that night, Georgia couldn't believe she'd ever found the country house quiet. Long after she heard her great-aunt creak up the stairs and into her own bedroom, her thoughts circled around the grave in the forest (for she felt sure now that it *was* a grave) and the locked bedroom down the hall.

But she was careful not to let them stray too close.

It seemed she had only just drifted into an uneasy sleep when she woke with a start.

What had stirred her?

Ice tinkling against a glass. A stifled sob. A door slamming.

Georgia's hands had formed fists around the edges of her sheet.

But no. That hadn't been it at all. The noise had been more of a clanging. And besides, she was not, she remembered, at home. She was at the country house with Aunt Marigold.

She felt as though she were a world and a day away from home. But the dread had followed her anyhow. It was always with her, but it was worst in the mornings. That foggy fear of something approaching that she could not name.

Her fists unclenched. Dawn was breaking outside, watercolor light tickling the curtains. There had been no arguing last night. There would be no heavy silences this morning.

Knowing she wouldn't be able to sleep again, Georgia threw back the summer quilt and climbed from her bed. When she had gotten dressed, she went downstairs. Aunt Marigold was just putting a cloth over a plate of biscuits. Her hair was plaited in a long braid, the same as it had been the day before. She wore yesterday's overalls, too, but a different shirt.

A baking sheet lay on the floor by the stove. It was still warm when Georgia picked it up. Aunt Marigold glanced over her shoulder.

"Oh," she said. "You're up."

She took the baking sheet from Georgia's hands. "I grabbed it when it was too hot," she said shortly. "Silly."

The sound of the tray hitting the floor must have been what had awoken Georgia so suddenly.

"Well, it's good that you're an early riser," Aunt Marigold went on. "It's better to do the outdoor chores early in the summer. Before it gets hot as Hades. Did you sleep well?"

"Yes, thanks," lied Georgia.

They sat across from each other, eating their biscuits with blackberry jam and their scrambled eggs with salt and pepper sprinkled on top. Neither of them said very much. Aunt Marigold sipped her cup of coffee as Georgia traced the blue rings that went round the gray plate.

After breakfast, Georgia washed and dried the dishes while Aunt Marigold swept the floors. Then Georgia was sent to weed the vegetable garden and take the mail to the box at the top of the dusty drive. Ruby made a point of ignoring her when Georgia clicked her tongue and beckoned to the cow. Apparently they really had gotten off on the wrong foot. Or hoof.

When she returned to the country house, Aunt Marigold was already sitting at the table once more, a bowl of leftover chicken and dumplings in front of her, a book propped up behind the bowl.

She looked up as Georgia appeared. "I kept some warm for you in the oven," she said. "Wash your hands first."

Georgia scrubbed the dirt from under her nails with a brush by the sink, and when she was satisfied they were clean—clean enough, anyway—she fixed herself a bowl. Aunt Marigold had set her a place and poured her a glass of cold, thick milk.

She kept reading her book, which was by someone named William Faulkner. Georgia thought she'd heard the name before. The book was called *As I Lay Dying*.

"Are you a reader?" Aunt Marigold asked, seeing Georgia studying the book.

"Yes," Georgia answered. "I read a lot."

Her great-aunt lifted her chin approvingly. "Must run in the family, then."

"Daddy used to read with me all the time," Georgia blurted.

Used to.

But if Aunt Marigold noticed all the heartache packed into those two flimsy words, like elephants into milk crates, she didn't say so.

"And I used to read to him," said Aunt Marigold. "When he and his daddy came to visit. Every night, until he fell asleep."

"Really?" Once more, Georgia pictured Daddy as a boy, being tucked into the big bed upstairs. His eyes closing slowly as he listened to Aunt Marigold read. She remembered the books she'd found on the bureau upstairs. "Did you read *Peter Pan*?"

"Sure," said Aunt Marigold. "It was one of his favorites."

"It still is," said Georgia. But she wasn't sure if that was even true anymore.

"What's it about?" she asked, suddenly needing to change the subject. "Your book?"

Aunt Marigold chewed slowly before answering. "Family," she said. "The things we do for family, mostly."

Once again, Georgia found her mind circling back to the narrow bed upstairs, the little grave in the forest. They had to be connected, didn't they? She couldn't bring herself to ask the question she wanted, but curiosity was like a gnat buzzing in her ear.

"Do you ever wish you had a family?" she asked suddenly. "Like, kids and stuff?"

As soon as the words left her mouth, she knew that she had crossed an invisible line, and there was no tiptoeing back to the other side. Her great-aunt's mouth was suddenly thin, and her eyes pierced Georgia with a hot gaze.

"And just when," she said, "has wishing ever done anyone a lick of good?"

Before Georgia could respond, Aunt Marigold stood and swept her bowl into the kitchen. She must have thrust it into the sink with too much force, because Georgia heard it shatter. She winced, squeezing her eyes shut. All those smooth blue rings—the beautiful flower in the bowl's center—broken into little pieces.

"I can clean it," she said in a small voice. "I can help."

"No," said Aunt Marigold. Her voice was firm, but it shook, too. "No, you can't. Go outside, Georgia. Find something to do. Be back by five."

Then she turned her back on Georgia and began to pick the pieces of the ruined bowl from the sink.

Chapter Nine

Storm clouds were beginning to gather overhead when the screen door slammed behind Georgia, but she didn't care. She couldn't go back to the house. Her feet pointed her toward the safety of the trees, and she shot through them like an arrow.

She brushed her palms against their rough bark as she darted between them but did not stop.

Instead she flew.

Sycamore sapling. Holly bush. Mossy oak.

She had wanted her aunt—who walked barefoot through the garden and read William Faulkner at the table and wore overalls like a man—to like her. And now she had ruined everything. Aunt Marigold might even tell Mama on Friday that Georgia couldn't come back.

Creek bed. Fox hole. Thicket of dread growing thorns in her stomach.

She felt the silver nickel turning in her pocket as she ran. *I would do anything for you, sweetheart. Even give you the moon.*

She imagined Daddy as a boy racing alongside her. For a moment she thought she glimpsed him. Could almost believe he was real.

Black hair. Freckled cheeks. Mischievous grin.

Tree root.

Her foot caught on a gnarled root. And then she was tumbling to the ground, her hands stretched wide. As she fell, pain shot through her knee.

She sat up to see blood beading through her capris. She began to cry, but there was no one around to hear her, and so she cried harder.

It was only a scraped knee.

Well, it was and it wasn't.

It was bedtime without books, and the silent piano, and the feet dancing outside Georgia's door at night.

It was Mama's worn-out smile and the suitcase that had been packed while Georgia slept and the green car disappearing down the dirt road.

It was the little grave in the forest and the locked room upstairs and the shattering of the bowl in the sink.

More than anything, it was that she wished she didn't

have to be so alone anymore.

Georgia had just lifted her hands to wipe her eyes when she heard a twig snap nearby. She looked around and could just make out a silver flicker of water through the trees. Seeing no one else, she lifted herself from the ground, wiped the dirt from her hands, and walked toward the water.

She stepped through the narrow gap between two enormous oak trees to find herself standing on the sandy bank of a lake.

Its waters were still and smooth. And it seemed to be perfectly round. It looked like an old mirror—a looking glass, wasn't that what they were called? Dull and bright at the same time. There was a little island in the very center of the lake, with one tree growing upon it. Perhaps it was a trick of the cloudy light, but it looked as if its leaves were white as snow.

Around the water, a ring of tall oak trees guarded the shores like a giant fairy circle. And tucked up by the trunk of the closest one, there was a wooden rowboat that gleamed like an acorn in the sunlight. Like it could have simply fallen from the branches of the great tree above.

Georgia blinked, half expecting that everything before her would simply disappear. But when she opened her eyes, she was still staring at the glassy lake.

"Hello."

Georgia spun around, her heart spinning with her.

Almost expecting to see that black-haired boy she'd envisioned a moment ago.

But on the bank behind her stood a girl. She smiled, her hazel eyes curious as she looked at Georgia. She wore a yellow top with jean shorts, and her dark, shining hair had been tied back in a perfect ponytail.

"Did you follow me?" Georgia asked.

The girl's smile faltered. She shook her head. "No. Well, yes. I mean, I heard you crying," she said. "Then I saw you walking this way. I just wanted to make sure you were all right."

"Oh," said Georgia, her heart finally slowing its dizzy dance. "Do you—do you live around here?"

"I just moved in nearby," she said, pointing through the oak trees in the opposite direction of Aunt Marigold's house.

Georgia looked across the lake. She couldn't see any house. But hadn't Aunt Marigold said something about a place that was for sale?

"I was kind of relieved to see you, actually," said the girl tentatively when Georgia didn't respond. "I thought I was the only kid for miles."

"I live over there," said Georgia finally, pointing back in the direction of the country house. "With my aunt Marigold. But only on weekdays. Only for the summer."

The girl looked crestfallen for a moment, but then her smile brightened. "Well, summer is a long time, anyway. I'm Angela."

She held out a pale, slender hand, which Georgia took in her own dirt-crusted palm. Angela didn't seem to mind. "I'm Georgia. Do you know what this place is?"

Angela shook her head. "I've never been here before. I didn't know it was here until I followed you just now. It's . . . pretty, isn't it?"

Georgia nodded, although "pretty" didn't feel like the right word. "It's perfect is what it is," she said. But perfect wasn't really the right word either. It was something *more*.

Angela's gaze landed on the boat, and she gasped. "Did you see this?" She darted over to examine it. Georgia was surprised at how quickly and lightly she moved—like a cat or a rabbit.

"Yeah," said Georgia, stepping closer. "Who do you think it belongs to?"

Angela bent down to examine the polished wood.

"I think right now it belongs to us," she said.

"You mean you want to take it out?" Georgia asked.

"Well, I've never been on a boat before. Have you?"

Georgia nodded. "Lots of times at camp."

Angela clapped her hands together. "Then you know how to row! Come on, say you'll come with me. Please?"

Georgia glanced at the sky. The storm clouds were still huddled there, but there was no sign of thunder or lightning.

"Okay," she said, and Angela bounced onto her toes. Seeing the other girl's excitement loosened something in

Georgia's chest. "Help me pull it into the water."

Georgia rolled her capris up to her knees, doing her best to staunch the blood from her fall. After she had pulled off her shoes and put them in the bottom of the boat, she grabbed the prow and pulled while Angela pushed from the stern until the front half of the boat was floating in the shallows. The water felt cool against Georgia's ankles, the lake bottom silky against her feet.

"Now you get in," she instructed, "and climb to the front."

Angela did as she was told, and again, Georgia was impressed by how nimble she was, barely rocking the boat. When she was seated, Georgia pushed the boat the rest of the way into the water and climbed aboard herself. She drove one oar against the lake bed, sending them gliding out over the little waves.

When she rowed, the oars cut through the water like hummingbird wings through the air. She hardly had to try at all.

"So, why are you staying with your aunt?" Angela asked over her shoulder.

Georgia didn't answer right away. She studied her fingers wrapped around the oars.

"My daddy has to work," she said finally, "and my mother is studying for a biology degree."

Angela's ponytail bobbed. "Is it just you staying there?"

"Yep. What about you? Do you have brothers and sisters?"

"No," she answered distastefully. Georgia imagined her wrinkling her nose.

"Me, either."

Angela turned around, lifting her legs over the wooden bench so that she could face Georgia. "I hate it sometimes," she said. "I always wanted a baby brother or sister I could dress up and play with."

"I just wanted someone to have adventures with," Georgia replied, "like in books. Kids always have brothers and sisters to play with in books."

Angela gave Georgia a long, thoughtful look. Then she leaned forward. "I have an idea," she said, amber sparkling in the pools of her eyes. "What if you and I decide to be summer sisters? We'll have adventures together, and neither one of us will have to be lonely. What do you think?"

Georgia hesitated. *Sisters.* She wasn't sure if she wanted to be sisters with Angela just yet.

But then, hadn't she been wanting to feel less lonely? And hadn't it been Angela's suggestion to take the boat out on the lake, which Georgia could now see had in fact been a very good idea? She might make quite a good sister, actually. A *summer* sister, at least.

"Well, okay," she said. "Summer sisters, then. As long as you don't want to dress me up like a baby, I mean."

Angela beamed at her. "Summer sisters. And no bows. I swear."

Both girls jolted as the boat slid up onto the pebbly shore of the little island. A giggle escaped Angela's lips.

She stood and jumped onto the island. Georgia scrambled behind her, pulling the boat more firmly onto shore.

The island was only as wide as the tree canopy above it. Georgia could see now that she had been right about the tree—its leaves really were white, its bark gray. A wizard of a tree. Angela took one of its leaves in her hand without tearing it from the branch.

Beneath the tree grew a perfect circle of green clover, and an even band of stones ringed around that. Gentle waves curled against them.

Angela plopped down in the clover and ran her fingers over it. Georgia sat down next to her, their knees knocking together gently.

"It's kind of weird, isn't it?" Angela said, a thoughtful frown tugging at her mouth. "The white tree. How the lake is so perfectly round and all hidden away."

Georgia had been thinking the same thing, afraid to say it aloud in case it broke the spell. "It feels like ours."

"Maybe it *can* be," said Angela excitedly. "We can spend the summer here, swimming and rowing and exploring."

Georgia nodded in agreement. It wasn't camp, but it was better than spending the summer with just her great-aunt for company, especially considering their last conversation.

Georgia stood and picked up one of the stones—a flat,

gray disk—and clenched her hand tight around it. Then she raised her arm and flicked it from between her thumb and her forefinger. It had been a while since she'd skipped a stone, but it seemed to understand what she wanted it to do, and she watched as it glanced across the surface of the lake: once, twice, three, four times before disappearing into the water.

"Wow," said Angela. "You're good at that, huh?"

"My dad taught me."

It was the day Mama and Daddy had dropped her off for her very first summer at Camp Pine Valley. She had been nervous to be away from home, and scared to talk to the other girls. Daddy had suggested they walk down to the lake. He'd picked up a stone and shown her how to flick it across the water.

"There you go," he'd said, once she'd gotten the hang of it. "Now you have something to teach the other girls. To make a start with them."

She had, too. And by the time she was done teaching them, they had become friends.

"I wish I could do that," Angela said now.

Before Georgia could respond, thunder snarled through the sky overhead.

Georgia sighed. She picked up another stone and let it fly from her hand.

"*I* wish the storm would go away so we could stay longer,"

she said. The second stone skipped five times before dropping into the lake for good. "Then I could teach you."

"So you won't teach me now?" Angela asked, coming to stand next to Georgia.

"Maybe tomorrow," said Georgia. "It's not safe to be on the water in a storm. We really should go."

"But look!"

Angela was pointing up, where the clouds were suddenly pulling apart from one another. Here and there, blue sky began to peer down at them, and then all at once the sun broke through the clouds, and the lake became spangled with silver so brilliant the girls had to look away.

Chapter Ten

~

Georgia and Angela stared at each other. The glittering
lake made Angela's eyes bright as she grinned.

"How cool was that?" she asked. "You wished it, and then
it came true! Almost like magic."

Aunt Marigold's voice ricocheted in Georgia's head. *And
just when has wishing ever done anyone a lick of good?*

"*Almost,*" she murmured, squinting up at the sky suspi-
ciously, as though it might have been a trick of the light. But
the sky was blue as far as the eye could see. "But I guess we
can stay now."

She twisted around to look at the white tree. It forked
into two about five feet up, then forked again on each side.
Near the top, she could make out the thatch of a bird's nest.

"Come on," she said. "Let's climb the tree. I want to know
what you can see from up there."

Angela didn't need telling twice. She was up the tree before Georgia could say, "Race you," and Georgia found herself equal parts impressed and annoyed at being beaten to the punch. Ignoring the dull throb of her scraped knee, she clambered up, too, deciding to take the left fork where Angela had taken the right. The left fork held the bird's nest.

The nest was empty except for two halves of a robin's egg, but it was easy for Georgia to pretend that she and Angela were birds themselves. She perched on her branch and stretched out her arms, pretending they were feathered wings.

In one direction, Georgia spotted the twin chimneys of Aunt Marigold's house. In the other, she glimpsed a solitary rooftop in the distance, which looked to belong to a large blue farmhouse. Before she could ask Angela if the farmhouse was her new home, Angela spoke.

"What's that?" She was pointing to the eggshell halves Georgia had taken from the nest. Georgia held one half out to Angela.

"A bird's eggshell. Half for you, and half for me," she said.

"Much better than one of those friendship necklaces," Angela said approvingly.

Georgia laughed. Angela suddenly reminded her of the girls she liked best at Camp Pine Valley. The ones whose mouths were always twitching with a smile, whose eyes always gleamed with adventure. Who seemed so bold and easy in the mountains that they might have been stitched from the balsam boughs and the river rocks. Angela made Georgia feel easier in her own skin. Easier than she had in a long time, in fact.

And, suddenly, she was very glad that she had met Angela.

After that, they stood on the stony beach as Georgia showed Angela how to choose the right stone and make it skip. It took her a dozen or so tries before she was able to skip one twice across the lake. She jumped up and down and cheered when she did, then bumped her hip against Georgia's.

"Hey!" she exclaimed. "You're a good teacher!" Then she bent down to choose another stone and closed her eyes, her brows furrowed tightly.

"What are you doing?"

Angela opened one eye a crack. "You made a wish when you skipped your stone before," she said. "And then the storm went away. Maybe it'll work again."

Georgia couldn't tell if she was joking or not.

"I wish . . . ," Angela said, "I wish for a giant ice cream sundae, with extra sprinkles and chocolate sauce."

Then she opened her eyes and skipped her stone across the lake. This time it only skipped once and sank with a heavy *plop*.

She looked up at the sky, as if waiting for an ice cream sundae to fall from it. But nothing happened.

Georgia felt the tiniest sadness drop into her stomach, as if Angela's stone had landed there. Magic, she reminded herself, was for books.

"Oh well," Angela said, grinning. "I tried. A sundae would have been really good right about now, though. My parents never let me have ice cream before dinner."

Dinner.

As she squinted out at the lake, Georgia noticed that the light had taken on that golden hue that meant afternoon was turning to evening. It would be getting close to five o'clock.

"We should probably go," she said. "I'm supposed to be home soon."

Angela took one last longing look at the sky before helping Georgia push the boat back into the water.

Back across the lake they rowed, Georgia's oars cutting easily through the water once more. By the time they reached the shore, her arms weren't even the slightest bit tired.

"See you tomorrow?" Angela said hopefully, after she and Georgia had dragged the acorn boat back to its spot under the oak tree.

"Definitely," said Georgia, flashing a smile at Angela, who reflected it back at her before bobbing off into the forest, silent as she'd arrived.

Georgia turned to go, too. But as she passed between the two oak trees she'd come through, she felt a change in the air. And no sooner had she stepped out from the shade of their branches than the rain began to lash down on her, finding its way through the forest canopy and churning the ground to mud.

The storm must have decided to come after all.

Georgia pumped her legs hard as she ran back through her own side of the forest, cupping the robin's eggshell in her hands and careful to watch where she was stepping this time. Before long she was dashing across the overgrown grass and up onto Aunt Marigold's front porch. She hesitated, wondering if her aunt was still angry at her.

Aunt Marigold opened the door before Georgia could, and the answer to Georgia's question was written clearly on her face. If she hadn't known better, Georgia might have thought it was Aunt Marigold herself who had brought such a fierce storm down upon them. Her expression was thunderous.

"Where have you been?" she demanded, pulling Georgia into the house.

"I—I was in the woods," stammered Georgia. She wanted to shrink away, to become a mouse and scurry off into the darkness unnoticed.

"Look at you," Aunt Marigold said. "You're soaked to the bone."

She looked Georgia up and down, catching sight of the blood on her capris. "Have you hurt yourself?"

"It's only a scraped knee."

"Well, go upstairs and get out of those clothes. I'll run you a hot bath, and then we'll clean that knee." Aunt Marigold started for the stairs, but Georgia didn't move. She felt rooted to the doorway.

"Come on, Georgia," she said impatiently.

Georgia hesitated. Her great-aunt had softened when she'd seen Georgia's knee, but the sharpness of her earlier words—the surprise of them—stung like a slap.

They made her think of the Shadow Man.

"What on earth's the matter, child?"

"I didn't mean to upset you," Georgia said. She stared at her sopping shoes, the white laces stained brown with mud.

"I'm not upset," said Aunt Marigold, stepping closer to Georgia but not touching her. "I was worried, that's all. You were out in the rain for so long."

Georgia glanced at her great-aunt. "How—how long?" she asked.

At this, Aunt Marigold's silver eyebrows shot up. "It's been howling rain all afternoon."

Chapter Eleven

After she'd left Georgia to soak in the bath for half an hour, Aunt Marigold knocked on the door and told her to come down to the kitchen. There, she sat Georgia at the table and poured out a tablespoon of rubbing alcohol.

"Hold on now," she said. "It'll burn."

And it did, but not as much as when Georgia had fallen in the first place. Aunt Marigold bent over Georgia's knee, fanning it with her hand and blowing cool air to help the alcohol evaporate. Then she put a large Band-Aid over the scrape. She had a look of concentration on her face as she worked, moving slowly. She treated Georgia's knee as gingerly as Georgia had cradled the robin's eggshell in her hands.

Georgia stared on in silent surprise. She didn't understand where or why the angry Aunt Marigold with the flashing eyes had gone. Was she hidden away somewhere beneath all this gentleness?

At least with her father, Georgia could tell right away which man he was by the way he walked and talked and smelled. But how was she supposed to know with Aunt Marigold?

"There," her great-aunt said, sitting back in her chair. "Better?"

"Better," said Georgia, glancing up into her great-aunt's furrowed face, then quickly away again.

Supper was tomato soup and corn bread, which Aunt Marigold had finished cooking while Georgia had been in the bath. The soup was hot and salty going down Georgia's throat, and she soaked her corn bread in it, devouring her food in silence.

As Georgia was sopping up her last bit of soup, Aunt Marigold cleared her throat.

"I'm sorry if I was hard on you at lunch," she said, leaning back in her chair and brushing a silver strand from her face. She had barely touched her own supper, and Georgia noticed now that she had a bandage around one of her hands. Had she cut it on one of the bowl shards?

"It's okay," Georgia said.

"I understand your being curious about me," her great-aunt went on. "I must seem awful odd to you, living like I do. But I don't want to be gawked at, and I don't want any pity."

"I don't pity you," Georgia protested. "I don't think you're odd either. I—I like how you live. You can do whatever you want whenever you want to. I wish I could."

Aunt Marigold let out a little bark of laughter. "Well, children see things differently than adults do, I suppose. You look at the world and all you see is possibility."

"But not you?" Georgia asked.

Aunt Marigold tore off a corner of corn bread and dipped it in her soup. "Life doesn't always go the way we expect."

Georgia already knew this, but she didn't say so.

She had not expected Daddy to turn into someone else. Someone she didn't know.

And, apparently, Aunt Marigold hadn't expected to end up living in this old house by herself. Had it been Georgia's imagination, or had her great-aunt glanced toward the window—toward the forest where the little stone angel hid like a pearl within an oyster—when she'd spoken? Georgia burned to know what unexpected thing had happened to her, and who was buried in that glade. But this time she knew better than to ask.

When she went upstairs to get ready for bed, she glanced to where her half of the robin's egg now sat on the bureau, next to the picture of Mama and Daddy. Standing beside it was another new addition—a tall clay vase with a narrow neck. With a single, bright sunflower set inside.

Chapter Twelve

～

Rain beat down against the windowpanes the next morning. Disappointment settled over Georgia. She knew there would be no going to the lake or seeing Angela until the weather cleared.

She went down for breakfast but stopped short on the bottom stair. Sitting at Aunt Marigold's table was a stranger, a plate of biscuits and jam in front of him.

He wore jeans and a flannel shirt rolled up to his elbows, and he had an untidy silver beard that hung from his face like a clump of Spanish moss. It was impossible to tell how old the face above the beard was. The man's nose was round—almost comically so. His face was sun-browned and his cheeks speckled with even deeper brown spots. A scruffy baseball cap lay on the table beside his plate, and a pair of enormous muddy boots sat just inside the door.

Georgia made a little noise at the back of her throat, and the man turned.

"'Morning, little lady," he said, his haggard face brightening. "You must be Georgia."

It was the second time in as many days that a stranger had appeared, seemingly out of thin air. Georgia nodded slowly, then turned her eyes to Aunt Marigold, who was brewing a pitcher of tea in the kitchen.

"Well, don't just stand there," she said, waving Georgia into the kitchen. "Sit down and eat some breakfast."

"Mighty pretty state, Georgia," the man said as Georgia hesitantly took a seat. She couldn't imagine a man like this in Mama's kitchen. "Ever been to the Okefenokee Swamp?"

He said the name slowly, drawing out each syllable. Oh-kee-fen-oh-kee.

She shook her head. "I've never been to Georgia," she said. "It's just my name. Is that where you're from?"

For some reason, this question summoned a booming laugh from deep in the strange man's chest.

"No," he said. "I ain't from Georgia."

"Then where *are* you from?" Georgia asked hotly, not liking the way he'd laughed at her.

The man leaned in to look at her and settled his elbows on the tables. "I never understand," he said, "why that's the first question people always ask. Seems to me the more important question is: where are you going?"

Georgia took her time picking a biscuit off the plate and slathering it with jam. She didn't want to give him the satisfaction of her curiosity.

"All right, all right," said Aunt Marigold, setting the tea down. "Enough with your teasing. Georgia, this is Hank. And he's from right here, to answer your question. He used to work on the farm back when it was still, well, working. He stops in some days to help with what needs doing."

"Pleased to meet you," said Hank, holding his broad hand out across the table.

Feeling her aunt's eyes upon her, Georgia held her own hand out and shook. Hank's grip was gentle, and he sent her a wink so sly she almost missed it.

She sat a little deeper in her seat, allowed herself to enjoy the sweetness of the jam and the crumble of the biscuit as Aunt Marigold and Hank began talking about the tasks that needed tackling.

"Georgia will help you," Aunt Marigold said. "She's earning her keep here this summer."

Georgia didn't know what exactly it was she was going to be helping with, but she figured she'd find out soon enough. When Hank unfolded himself from the table and rose to his feet—and kept rising and rising, until he was nearly as tall as one of Aunt Marigold's cornstalks—Georgia took her dishes to the sink and followed him out into the gray day.

As she sat on the porch to do up her laces, Hank walked

straight toward the pasture, where Ruby was making a beeline for him. Her head was swinging to and fro as she hustled over. She let out several long *moos*.

Hank, who didn't seem to be bothered by the steady rain, met Ruby at the fence. He reached into his pocket and handed something to her. Ruby's eyes went wider than silver dollars as she lowered her nose to his palm. When she was done eating, Hank stroked her beneath her ears and even planted a kiss on her head.

Ruby had wanted nothing to do with Georgia. What had Hank given her that had made the cow such cozy company all of a sudden?

Hank grinned as he threw a glance over his shoulder and saw Georgia marching toward him. "She's a good girl, ain't she?"

"She doesn't like me. What did you give her?"

He reached into his pocket again, pulling out a handful of peppermints. "She'll like you just fine if you give her one of these. Food is the way to every cow's heart, you know."

"I didn't know cows ate peppermints," said Georgia doubtfully.

"*That* cow sure does," Hank replied. "Go on—try."

Georgia took the peppermints from his hand and held them out to Ruby. Without hesitation, the cow plunged her nose into Georgia's hand. Georgia giggled as she felt the rough tongue licking up the candies. She was careful to keep her palm flat, her fingers close together, like she did when she fed the horses at camp.

Ruby gave Georgia's palm an extra lick, then let Georgia pet her under the chin.

"Looks like you made a new friend," Hank said, smiling down at Georgia.

Georgia couldn't help but agree.

It turned out their task for the morning was to paint the porch, which Hank said would be fine to do in the rain. They laid down a tarp to protect the floor, and then Hank instructed her to do the door and the shutters in red paint— in honor of Ruby.

"So," said Hank, "how's a girl get a name like Georgia if she's never been?"

"My parents went there on their honeymoon," Georgia explained, thinking about the photo on her bureau. "On Tybee Island. Have you been?"

Hank shook his head. "Nope," he said. "But I been most everywhere else."

"Like where?"

When the farm stopped running, Hank said, he'd hopped the first train he could find and hadn't looked back for a few decades. As they painted, he told her how he'd done odd jobs to work his way from San Francisco all the way up to Washington. Then he'd caught a fishing boat headed for

Alaska and lived there for a while, where land met glacier. He told her about billy goats and brown bears, lakes so clear you could count every little fish and mountaintops forever covered in white.

"Why'd you come back?" Georgia finally asked.

He shrugged. "Home is home," he said, gesturing to the fields behind them. "After a while, it came calling."

If Hank had spent his youth working on her great-grandfather's farm, Georgia thought, he must think of *this* place as home. He would know plenty of stories about it, too. Might even know something about the grave in the woods and the locked room upstairs.

Just as she was wondering how she might approach the subject, the screen door creaked open. "Lunch," Aunt Marigold announced.

Georgia felt her cheeks go hot, though she knew Aunt Marigold had no way of knowing what she'd just been thinking. Still, she couldn't quite look her great-aunt in the eye.

Instead, she stepped back to inspect her morning's work and saw that the shutters were much improved. Shiny and red as rooster feathers. *Good*, thought Georgia. The old house deserved something to crow about.

Chapter Thirteen

~

After a lunch of cold ham, collard greens, and lemonade, Hank left for the day, promising he'd be back to finish painting soon. Aunt Marigold and Georgia did the dishes together, and then Aunt Marigold said it was time for her nap.

"What do I do?" Georgia asked. She shot a dark glance outside. It was still raining.

"Read or sleep or think, I suppose," said her great-aunt. "But no going out in this weather."

As she watched Aunt Marigold retreat up the steps, Georgia thought about sneaking out. What if Angela were at the lake waiting for her? Georgia needed to talk to her, to tell her about the strange thing Aunt Marigold had said yesterday. *It's been howling rain all afternoon.*

Georgia didn't understand it. How could it have been

raining at the country house when there had been nothing but blue skies over the lake?

But if she got caught sneaking out, Aunt Marigold might decide she couldn't go into the woods on her own at all. And besides, her arms ached from all that painting, and she was a bit tired herself.

So Georgia followed her great-aunt upstairs. She pulled *Peter Pan* from the bureau and lay down on the bed with a sigh, opening the book to a dog-eared page. It was the beginning of the chapter called "The Mermaids' Lagoon."

If you shut your eyes and are a lucky one, you may see at times a shapeless pool of lovely pale colours suspended in the darkness; then if you squeeze your eyes tighter, the pool begins to take shape, and the colours become so vivid that with another squeeze they must go on fire. But just before they go on fire you see the lagoon. . . .

Georgia must have fallen asleep, because the next thing she knew, her eyes were fluttering open, and the book had fallen to the floor. She picked it up gently, slotting it back into its place on the bureau.

When she went downstairs, the kitchen was empty. She thought perhaps Aunt Marigold was still asleep, but then she heard a noise coming from the other side of the staircase.

She crept past the kitchen table and into the parlor with its empty hearth. There was a door in the corner of this room that she hadn't noticed before. It was half open, and Georgia heard a whirring sound and caught sight of a flash of denim inside.

"Hello?" she called.

After a moment, the door opened wider. Aunt Marigold stood there, her hands covered in gray, as if she had dipped them in the storm clouds outside.

"Oh," she said. "Hello."

Georgia looked over her aunt's shoulder into the room beyond. It was a small room with a tile floor. Shelves climbed up the walls, filled with stacked buckets, piles of brushes and sponges, books on pottery, and big flat bags with "CLAY" written across them.

In the middle of the room, there was a table with a stool next to it. On top of the table was what looked like a large round basin with a wire snaking out its side and a plate in the middle of it. A misshapen lump of wet clay sat on the plate.

"Is this a pottery studio?" Georgia asked.

"Yes. I bought all this after my father died," said Aunt Marigold, moving to a sink at the corner of the room and washing her hands. She wore a white, paint-splattered apron over her usual overalls. "He left me a bit of money. A silver lining, I suppose."

"So, you're a, um, potter?" Georgia asked.

Her great-aunt shrugged. "I don't come back here so much

anymore. Just thought I would try to make a replacement bowl, but I don't know what I was thinking. The time's gotten away from me. I need to get dinner started."

"You made all those bowls? The ones with the flowers?"

"And the pitchers and the plates and the cups, too," Aunt Marigold flicked the extra water off her hands and dried them on her pant legs.

"And the vase in my room!" Georgia said. She'd never known anyone who could make something like that before. "You could sell stuff like that."

"I used to."

"So why don't you anymore?"

Her great-aunt just sighed and rubbed her hands. "It's complicated."

Georgia fought off a scowl. "It's complicated" was what her mother would say when she didn't want to explain something. She expected more from Aunt Marigold, even if it was to shoo her out from the studio.

Which is exactly what she did next, shutting the door behind them.

Georgia set the table as Aunt Marigold put the water on to boil. She studied the plates as she laid them out. She had so many questions. Like how did her great-aunt get the rings so blue? And paint the flowers so delicately? And why did the plate shine under the light and feel silky under her touch?

Most of all, she wanted to know what it felt like to make

something perfect and whole like that with your own two hands.

She was so tired of broken things.

She wished she could go back, even just for a few minutes, to a time when things were good and normal again. A time when Daddy was just Daddy, before the Shadow Man had arrived.

Because it wasn't just Daddy who was broken. Without him, Georgia couldn't be whole either.

"Aunt Marigold?"

"Mmph?"

"Could you teach me?" Georgia asked. "How to make something like this?"

Aunt Marigold did a funny thing with her head, like she'd seen a spider about to drop onto her nose and had to jerk back to avoid it. But she didn't look upset. Only surprised. "Well, I—I'll have a think about it," she said. It was the only time Georgia had ever heard her sound uncertain about anything.

"Okay," said Georgia.

"Okay," said Aunt Marigold.

And then they went on making supper.

Chapter Fourteen

Thursday morning dawned bright and blue, and by the time Georgia made it outside, Hank had already worked up a sweat from painting.

"'Morning, little lady," he said, handing her a brush.

Hank talked all morning and didn't seem to mind whether Georgia was listening or not. Mostly she did listen, because his stories were interesting—especially the one about the earthquake—but then thoughts of the lake would take over, and she would catch herself staring toward the forest. Counting the minutes as the sun rose in the sky and sweat beaded her own forehead.

By the time she finished lunch a few hours later, Georgia's legs were itching to run despite the heat. It had been two whole days since she'd visited the lake and seen Angela.

"I want you back by five again," Aunt Marigold said

when Georgia asked if she could go. "And sooner if it starts raining. Am I clear?"

"Yes, ma'am," said Georgia. Then she took off before her great-aunt had time to change her mind.

She liked the hush that came over her when she entered the trees. It was a bit like entering a church. Even the birds were quieter the deeper in she ran.

Her heart beat hard. What if she couldn't find the lake again? What if it had all been a figment of her imagination? Or if she stumbled upon the glade with the grave again instead? It wasn't the grave itself that scared her so much as the feeling of sorrow that had come over her as she stood in the hushed little glade.

She ran up a small slope covered with pine needles and down into a little leafy glen. Just as she was feeling uncertain about which way to go next, she spotted the enormous tree root she'd tripped on before.

And then there it was. The lake. Glittering through the narrow gap in the oak trees. Georgia hopped through them, landing on the sandy beach.

"There you are!"

She jumped—startled—and turned to see Angela already sitting in the sand, leaning back on her palms, dressed today in shorts and a polka-dotted shirt with red buttons. Her cheeks, too, were red with heat.

"I was worried you weren't coming," she said, standing

up and brushing off her hands.

"I got away as soon as I could. You didn't come yesterday, did you?" Georgia asked.

Angela shook her head. "The rain," she said simply.

"Yeah. My aunt wouldn't let me come out either."

Georgia cast her gaze around the lake. Blue, sparkling water. Little island with the white tree. Ring of oaks hiding them from the world. It was all just as she had remembered. She felt a wave of giddiness rise in her chest.

"Angela," said Georgia slowly. She didn't quite know how to say what she wanted—to *ask* what she wanted—without sounding foolish. "When we left the other day—"

"It started pouring," said Angela before Georgia could even finish. "As soon as I crossed through the trees."

"Me, too. And when I got home, my aunt was really mad. She said it had been raining—"

"For hours?" Angela finished.

"Yes! But how could that be possible? How could it be raining at both our houses but not here?"

"You think your wish came true," said Angela, wide-eyed.

Georgia shook her head. "You didn't get *your* wish. Remember?"

Angela squinted up at the sky. "Maybe there are rules about what you can wish for. Maybe you just get one wish a day or something."

"Or maybe it was a coincidence," Georgia said.

"Maybe. But there's only one way to find out, isn't there? We have to go back to the island. We'll do everything just like you did last time."

Where was the harm in that? Georgia thought.

Soon they were back in the boat, which shone proudly in the sun as it nosed through the waters. Georgia had the oddest feeling that she was making the little vessel happy by giving it a purpose.

She handed Angela one of the oars and showed her how to row with it. How to dip the blade all the way into the water. To paddle on the left if she wanted to turn right, and the right if she wanted to turn left.

"I think I'm getting the hang of it now," Angela said, moving the oar in a graceful circle, into the water and back out again.

"Then we'll row like we're in a canoe," Georgia replied. "You row on the left and I'll row on the right. I'll keep time with you."

So they rowed together, and in a few minutes, they were beaching the boat on the island again, both sweating beneath the bright sun.

"We make a good team," said Angela happily, stepping out of the boat.

Georgia smiled. She liked being on a team with Angela.

When she looked into the clear water, she saw that it was full of more smooth pebbles. Hundreds and thousands of them. Were they all wishes just waiting to be made?

You look at the world and all you see is possibility, Aunt Marigold had said. But this—a magic lake—was *im*possible.

Only, what if it wasn't?

The two girls hastily pulled the boat up farther onto the beach, into the shade of the white tree. Then they stood side by side on the pebbles, barefoot and panting, staring out at the water.

"What now?" Angela asked.

"You try," Georgia said. "I made the wish yesterday. It's your turn."

Angela bent down and searched for a good skipping stone. Finally, she settled on a pink one speckled with brown.

"Do you know what to wish for?"

Angela thought for a moment, wiping the gossamer glaze from her brow, then broke into a grin. "I know." Closing her eyes, she said clearly and slowly, "I wish . . . for *snow.*"

She opened her eyes and cast the stone from her hand, watching as it skipped three times over the lake.

Georgia held her breath. She didn't move, both afraid the magic wouldn't work and afraid that it would. She and Daddy had long ago discovered that books could be magic—portals to other times and places. Escape routes from the real world.

But a book's magic was contained between its covers. It was certain and knowable. But *this*—magic unbound by pages—was something altogether different. With the flick of a stone, they were summoning something wilder. Something that could change everything.

Only, nothing *did* change. Nothing happened for so long that Georgia had to let her breath go.

When she did, it came out in a frosted cloud.

The air had gone suddenly cold against her skin. She turned to Angela, but before she could say a word, the wind began to whip her hair so that she had to close her eyes. When she clawed her hair back enough to open them again, a curtain of white had risen up from the lake, blocking her view of everything.

"Angela!" she called.

"I'm here!" Angela cried back. "I can't see anything!"

"Me either," Georgia said, though as soon as the words left her mouth, she realized they weren't quite true anymore. She could just make out the shape of Angela's figure standing next to her.

Ever so slowly, the white curtain faded away until it was a veil of fine lace over the world. A softly falling snow.

Angela held out her hands, catching the flakes in her palms, and began to laugh.

"It worked, Georgia!" she cried. "It really worked!"

Georgia said nothing, but uncurled her hands, too, and

held them to the sky. When the first snowflake landed there, white and cold, she watched it melt into a tiny puddle in her palm.

And then, finally, she smiled.

Chapter Fifteen

Snow covered each branch of each tree. And the lake must have frozen over, because a thick layer of white covered it, too. Dove-feathered clouds roosted overhead, turning the sun into a shining, ivory egg.

Georgia studied the snowy mantle that sat atop the rowboat's sides. "It's got to be four inches of snow," she said. Was that what the curtain of white had been? A blizzard? Was all this snow the work of a single moment?

Angela stepped tentatively out onto the ice. Just a toe at first, then a foot, and then both feet.

"Be careful!" Georgia said. "You could fall through."

"Hand me that stick, will you?" Angela asked. "I'll use it to test the ice."

Georgia handed her a long stick from the ground, which Angela plunged through the snow before taking each step.

She was right: the ice held. It didn't so much as creak.

"I . . . I can't believe this is real," Georgia murmured, following in Angela's footsteps, savoring the crunch of fresh snow under her sneakers.

"I can," Angela replied. "I knew from the moment I saw this place that there was something magical about it. Didn't you?"

Hadn't Georgia felt something stir inside her when she'd seen the lake, so perfectly round and calm? Hadn't she wondered when she'd seen how the oak trees grew like an enormous fairy tree around it, and the white tree that stood like a gnarled old wizard at its center?

"Yeah," she said now. "Maybe I did."

It was strange, but even with so much snow all around, Georgia didn't feel very cold. Angela was bending down, packing snow into a ball with her bare hands.

"Why did you wish for this?" Georgia asked. "You could have wished for anything."

"I guess it was the first thing I thought of," she said. "It's so hot today, and I love the snow. Don't you?"

Georgia didn't answer. She had just caught sight of a flash of red on the nearest shoreline, and now her eyes were scanning the trees. Sure enough, she picked out a cardinal perched on a branch that stuck out over the lake.

The bird was silent, but it seemed to call to something in her memory. Another cardinal on another snowy branch, this one outside the kitchen window at home, staring in.

"He's got the right idea, don't you think?" Daddy had said, pointing to the bird and handing Georgia her mittens. "Nothing better than fresh snow."

It was Christmas Eve two years ago, and it had snowed all morning. Mama was in the kitchen making a start on their dinner, and Daddy was shrugging on his winter coat. "Come on," he said. "How about a little adventure?"

Georgia had thrown her own coat over her shoulders, wrapped her scarf around her neck, and followed Daddy out into the sugar-glazed afternoon. He held her hand in one of his and dragged a rickety wooden sled in the other. They sang "We Wish You a Merry Christmas" as they made their way to the hill one street over, where other families had had the same idea.

Most of the parents were gathered at the bottom to watch while their children shrieked their way down the steep hill, but Georgia was frightened, so Daddy got on the sled behind her.

"You can do it," he said softly. "I know you can."

Daddy's words made her feel strong and brave. If he said she could, then she could. So together, they whizzed down the hill together, over and over, until Georgia wasn't afraid anymore. Then Daddy watched her from below, cheering her on as she did it on her own, laughing all the way down.

Not until their cheeks were whipped with cold, their

throats hoarse, did they turn back toward home. It was getting dark, and the colored strands of lights began to wink on one yard at a time. As they neared home, they could see that the bright kitchen window was empty. Perhaps Mama was setting the table.

"Quick," Daddy said. "Let's give her a surprise for the morning."

They'd worked fast, packing the snow into a squat little snowman who faced the kitchen window. Except that Daddy wanted him built upside down, with the smallest snowball on the bottom and the largest one on top. "What are we doing, Daddy?" Georgia whispered.

"You'll see. Go find some arms, will you?"

When Georgia returned with the branches, she began to giggle so loud, Daddy had to shush her so Mama wouldn't hear. While she'd been gone, he had found pebbles to make eyes and holly berries for a mouth. He had given their snowman an upside-down face, so that his eyes were nearly touching the ground.

"He's doing a handstand, see?" Daddy said, taking the branches from Georgia and slotting them into place so that the snowman looked like he was balancing on his new wooden hands. "Perfect!"

"Wait," Georgia said, an idea coming to her. "One more thing!"

Then she'd taken the boots from her feet and, hopping

from one freezing foot to the other, had set them on top of the snowman's rounded bottom, so they were sticking up in the air. "Now it's perfect."

"Genius," Daddy had said, pulling her to him and kissing her on the head. "Now let's get you inside before your toes fall off."

Ouch!

Something hit Georgia in the shoulder. She looked up to see Angela grinning at her, throwing a snowball up and catching it. "Bet you can't catch me!" she said, launching the second snowball at Georgia, who just barely dodged it. Then Angela was off, running through the snow and laughing.

After a second, Georgia chased behind her, bending down to pack a snowball of her own as she ran. She threw three before one finally found its target, hitting Angela on her back. She let out a cheer as Angela threw her hands up in defeat.

They chased each other back and forth until they were out of breath. Angela collapsed and began stretching her arms up and down and legs side to side.

"Come on!" she said. "Snow angels!"

Angela's pale skin almost glowed next to the snow. She *did* look a bit like an angel, or a snow maiden from the fairy tales, who might transform into a snow goose and take flight into the sky. Georgia suddenly shivered. Perhaps she was finally feeling the cold after all.

"Come on," she said, holding an arm out to help Angela up. "I have another idea."

Angela laughed at their upside-down snowman, almost as hard as Mama had when she'd come into the kitchen that Christmas morning and seen him from the window.

"Merry Christmas," Daddy had said, sneaking in behind Mama, picking her up in his arms and whirling her around while Georgia laughed, too. Mama had seemed so pleased to be part of the fun.

The echo of their laughter felt so close she could almost reach out and grab it, like a snowflake in her palm. Georgia suddenly felt full and warm again, as though her belly were full of hot chocolate. Just like she had that long-ago morning.

And, she realized, it was because of Angela she felt this way. Angela had made the wish. Angela had looked at the lake and seen an adventure, just like Daddy would have.

Once.

When it was time to go, Georgia said they'd better walk back across the lake to shore and tug the boat behind them like a sled. There would be no rowing over all this snow.

"Angela," she said as they crunched toward the shore, "I don't think we should tell anyone else about this place."

Angela nodded. "If we did, they wouldn't believe us. Or they would all come, and the magic might not work any-more."

That was exactly what Georgia had been thinking. And now that she'd had a taste of the magic, she couldn't let it slip away.

"How *does* it work, do you think?" she asked.

"Maybe the stones are magical? Or the water?" Angela mused. "Maybe it's wishing water."

"Maybe this lake is . . . a wishing lake."

And out of all the people in the world, they had been the ones to find it. It seemed pretty miraculous. An idea was forming in Georgia's mind.

"Can you meet me here tomorrow?" Georgia asked as they reached the shore. "In the morning? My mom is coming to get me for the weekend after lunch."

Angela nodded. "It'll be your turn to make a wish. Do you know what you'll wish for?"

Georgia closed her eyes. She was still savoring the sound of Mama's laughter. The feeling of Daddy wrapped around her on the sled. Memories of the past tangling with the present. Imagination all tied up in reality.

If the lake could turn a storm away, if it could transform summer into winter, why couldn't it do what Georgia wanted more than anything else in the world? It was a wishing lake, after all.

Why shouldn't it give Daddy back to her?

She and Angela hugged goodbye, and Georgia wished they didn't have to part. She was nearly between the oak trees before remembering something.

"Angela?" she called. She wanted to ask whether Angela had seen the cardinal, too. Or whether that bit of the magic had been just for her, to remind her of a day long past.

But when she looked up, Angela was nowhere to be seen. The snow had vanished from the lake, which shone its usual blue.

And Georgia was all alone.

Chapter Sixteen

~~~~

"You seem a bit distracted tonight," Aunt Marigold commented over supper.

Georgia snapped her attention back to her aunt, who wasn't wrong. Georgia's thoughts were back at the wishing lake. Back with Angela.

When she'd doubled back to the lake that afternoon, there was no sign of the recent winter. The tree frogs chirruped, the cicadas purred, the muggy heat smoothed the goose bumps from her arms.

And Angela had disappeared.

Georgia had called for her but gotten no answer. As if, in the seconds she had been gone, the forest had swallowed Angela up completely. It had given her an uneasy feeling—how her friend could simply vanish like that.

And then, on her way back to the house, she had had

the feeling again of someone's eyes upon her. Someone following her just a few paces behind. But when she'd turned around, there had been no one there.

"I'm sorry," said Georgia. "I was just thinking about something else."

Aunt Marigold pinned her with one of her searching stares. "What did you do all afternoon?" she asked.

"Just . . . played."

Aunt Marigold made a tutting sound. "I don't know if your mama would like it," she said. "You spending so much time out there alone. How would I find you if something were wrong?"

"But I'm not alone," Georgia blurted.

At this, her great-aunt raised an eyebrow. "Oh no?"

Georgia had no choice but to carry on. Better to tell Aunt Marigold about Angela than to be banished from the woods. "I met a girl," she said. "Her family just moved into that house you said was for sale."

Aunt Marigold went on staring at Georgia before giving a small nod. "I didn't know the Boatwright place had been sold," she said. "But I suppose that shines a different light on things."

Except that Angela had never exactly told Georgia that she lived in the Boatwright house. Only that she had recently moved in nearby.

She thought of the way Angela had moved so lightly on

her toes—the way her skin had glowed against the snow as she had carved her arms and legs through it.

It wasn't until she was lying in bed that night that Georgia realized why it had given her a funny feeling, seeing Angela making a snow angel.

Because she had reminded Georgia of another angel, one made of stone.

But that was silly. Angela had nothing in common with that statue. Angela was warmth and laughter, not coldness and sorrow. And besides, Georgia had more important things to wonder about.

Like the feeling she'd had twice now of being watched in the forest.

Like the wishing lake. How its magic really worked.

And if it would be strong enough to do what she needed it to.

The next morning, after she and Aunt Marigold had eaten their pancakes with butter and maple syrup dripping down the sides, Georgia took the dishes to the kitchen without being asked and began to wash them.

"What's gotten into you this morning?" asked Aunt Marigold, reaching for the drying cloth.

"I'll do that," said Georgia, snatching the cloth away. "And then . . . maybe I can go play for a while before lunch? I told my friend I would meet her."

Aunt Marigold's eyebrows lifted. "Uh-huh," she said. "I see."

Georgia waited, eyes pleading. She needed to get to the wishing lake. To make her wish before Mama came and took her home.

"I s'pose," relented her great-aunt. "Don't need help with lunch anyway."

"Thank you," said Georgia, throwing her dripping arms around her. "Thank you so much!"

When she pulled away, her aunt looked stiff as barn wood, and the surprise was naked on her face. Georgia flushed.

"Well, go on, then," said Aunt Marigold, blinking away her shock. "It's not like I can't dry my own dishes."

Without another word, Georgia slipped out of the house and into the dewy morning.

Georgia didn't have long to wait for Angela once she reached the lake. She only had time to cast an eye over it before she heard her friend's footsteps behind her.

They broke into matching grins when they caught sight of each other. Behind her smile, Georgia studied her friend closely. But there was nothing out of the ordinary about her. White tennis shoes. One scraped knee. Hair back in two French braids today.

"Are you ready?" she asked, bouncing on her toes with excitement.

"Ready," said Georgia.

"I could barely sleep last night," said Angela as they rowed. "I kept wondering if it was all real or not."

"Me, too," said Georgia. "I came back to ask you something yesterday, but you were already gone. And the lake was back to normal."

"What did you want to ask?"

"It wasn't important," Georgia said. "You must have been in a hurry to get home."

"Like you said, it was getting late. Do you know what you're going to wish for?" Angela asked.

Georgia nodded as the boat reached the island. She took a deep breath. It was time to concentrate on the reason they were here.

She studied the stones beneath her feet. She felt she needed to find the exact right one. Angela stayed beside her, though Georgia had hoped she might wander off a bit. She hadn't thought of how it would feel to speak her wish aloud with someone to hear it.

Finally, she spotted a white stone that caught her eye. It had glittering flecks of silver on one side. On the other side, it was covered in green algae and shot through with veins of black. Two different sides, just like her father.

One beautiful and one ruined.

Georgia held the stone in one hand while the other reached into her pocket to find the silver nickel she'd made sure to bring this morning. She squeezed them both as she closed her eyes tight.

"I wish . . . I wish my family would just—just go back to normal," she said.

And she let the stone go, opening her eyes to watch as it glided over the water, skipping nearly halfway back to shore.

This time, there was no moment of transformation. No clouds clearing or snow falling.

But that didn't mean there was no magic.

Georgia waited for Angela to say something, to ask Georgia what she meant. But she didn't. Instead, after a moment, she slipped her hand into Georgia's and said, "I hope it comes true."

"Thanks," Georgia murmured, surprised at how reassuring it was, feeling Angela's hand in her own. It seemed to be guiding her, though they weren't moving anywhere. "Me, too."

It wasn't the wish she'd meant to make. Not in those words, anyway. But what she wanted to wish—what she wanted to say about Daddy—she hadn't known how to say in front of Angela.

She knew the name people used for a man like her father. She didn't want Angela to think it, too.

That he was a *drunk*.

As if there was nothing more to him than what passed from his glass to his throat.

She knew that's what people said because of what she'd overheard on the last day of school. When they had put on a performance of *The Wizard of Oz* in the gym, with snacks and games on the field after to celebrate.

When Georgia's father hadn't shown up until after the play, arriving on the field with a sway to his walk.

When he had staggered into the table where Mrs. Poplar's untouched double Dutch chocolate cake sat sweating in the sun, along with half a dozen other homemade desserts, and sent everything tumbling to the ground. When Mama's face had gone red as the punch in her hand and she had swept over and said, "Oh, sweetheart, you're such a klutz—we really ought to get your vision checked!" before guiding him to the parking lot.

"A drunk," Mrs. Mackenzie—Georgia's favorite teacher— had whispered to another teacher just as Georgia slunk past them. "Such a shame."

Such a shame that Georgia *still* felt the shame of it. The shame and the terrible, piercing love.

She bent down and dipped her fingers in the water, as if she could wash them both—the shame and the love—from her hands. The water was magic, she reminded herself. The wishing lake would make her wish come true. It *had* to.

Chapter Seventeen

⌒

Georgia was helping set the table when she heard Mama's car coming down the dirt road a few hours later.

"Didn't expect her until after lunch," Aunt Marigold grumbled, planting her hands on her hips. "Good thing it's only ham sandwiches."

As the green car rolled to a stop, Georgia ran out the door.

"Mama!"

Georgia saw surprise cross Mama's face before she opened her arms for a hug. It was the kind of greeting Georgia usually reserved for Daddy, but today, she found that she couldn't wait to reach her mother. Her hug smelled like sunscreen and the detergent they always used. Georgia's eyes watered as she wrapped her arms around Mama's waist.

"Hello, sweetheart," Mama said. "Have you had fun?

Have you been good?"

Georgia hesitated, not sure how to answer the second question. She wasn't sure how Aunt Marigold would respond, and she didn't want to be accused of lying. "I like it here," she said instead. She looked up at her mother's face for a hint of whether her wish had worked, but her expression gave nothing away.

"Come on," Mama said. "Let's go in and say hello."

Aunt Marigold had laid an extra plate and was pouring iced tea when they came inside.

"Oh, thank goodness," Mama said. "I'm parched."

Aunt Marigold rustled up another ham sandwich and served them all leftover potato salad.

"I hope Georgia hasn't been any trouble," Mama said after a long drink of sweet tea.

Aunt Marigold glanced at Georgia. "No trouble at all," she said. "In fact, she's taken quite a shine to country life."

Georgia felt her shoulders slump with relief.

"Is that right?" Mama asked.

"I like it out here," Georgia said again. "There's lots to do."

When she was done with her lunch, she was sent upstairs once again to gather the things she'd need for the weekend while Mama and Aunt Marigold sat at the table, sipping and talking.

"—but then you understand what it's like, of course,"

Mama was murmuring when Georgia had finished packing and paused at the top of the stairs. "I don't know how you—"

But she must have heard Georgia's shoes coming down the hall, because she stopped talking abruptly.

"Understand what what's like?" Georgia asked as she reached the bottom step. Mama was looking down at her iced tea glass.

"Dealing with these summer weeds," Mama said. "They're always vicious, but this year they're trying to take over the garden at home. Speaking of which, we should head on out now."

Mama pushed back her chair, smoothing down her floral-print dress.

"We'll see you Sunday, then, Marigold," she said. "Thanks again for everything."

Aunt Marigold nodded. Her eyes landed on Georgia. "See you then."

"Bye, Aunt Marigold," said Georgia before following her mother out the door. Even though she couldn't wait to get home—to see Daddy and know if her wish had worked—she found it was hard to force herself through the doorway. She felt an ache in her chest as she walked to the car, kind of like the one she felt when Mama came to pick her up from Camp Pine Valley. Which was silly, because she would be back here in just two days.

Then Georgia thought of Aunt Marigold spending those days alone, and the ache grew worse. That was silly, too, though, wasn't it? Her aunt was used to being alone. She would probably be glad to have her house to herself again for a few days.

But when they reached the top of the driveway and Mama pulled out onto the road, Georgia looked back and saw her great-aunt standing on the porch, watching them go.

Mama was quiet on the drive back. She told Georgia her week had been fine, just fine, and that she thought her exam had gone well, but it was hard to tell with these things. Mostly, she asked Georgia about her week. Had she liked her aunt Marigold? Didn't she think it was so peaceful out there in the country?

When Mama spotted the Band-Aid on her knee, she asked what had happened, and Georgia told her truthfully that she'd tripped over a tree root.

Neither of them spoke about Daddy. Every time Georgia nearly got up the courage to ask about him, it slipped through her fingers again. But then, she reminded herself, she had only *just* made the wish. It would probably take some time to work.

He wasn't home yet when they got there, but that didn't mean anything. It was only two o'clock.

By the time Georgia heard the front door open at half

past five, she'd been sitting on her floor, trying to make an origami swan, for half an hour. She had been too nervous to wait for him outside. Her heart gave a painful shudder when she heard the door.

It clicked shut. No slam.

She dropped the half-formed swan from her palm as she ran from her room. Daddy stood in the doorway, hanging his hat and settling his briefcase on the little entry table.

Though it took all her willpower, she did not go to him. She waited for him to look up and see her. When he did, his face broke into his best smile, and he said, "There she is. My girl."

Still, Georgia stood, hovering, until her father opened his arms. "Don't you want to give your old dad a hug?"

It was *him*. It was really Daddy. She could tell by the way he spoke without slurring, stood without swaying.

She flew toward him and flung her arms around his waist. She must have hit him with more force than she meant to, because she heard him say, *"Oof."*

"Well, that's more like it," he added with a chuckle.

Georgia did not want to let go. He felt so solid in her arms, solid as one of the great oak trees that surrounded the wishing lake. She wanted to hold on to him forever, to tell him how much she needed him, to beg him never to leave her again.

But all she said was, "I missed you."

And then she let him go.

He looked down at her with his crinkling eyes—eyes that sparkled with light—and ruffled her hair. "Tell you what," he said. "Let's go out to the Chargrill for supper. A little welcome home treat, huh? What do you say?"

Georgia couldn't remember the last time they'd been to the Chargrill for burgers and milkshakes. All she knew was it had been before things had begun changing. Back when things were *normal*. A smile filled up her whole face as she nodded.

A door creaked open behind them, and Mama appeared from her bedroom.

"What's all this I hear?" she asked.

"Daddy's taking us to the Chargrill for dinner," Georgia said.

Her mother blinked at her father. "I bought a chicken."

"Can you put it in the freezer?" asked Daddy. "I'm famished anyhow, and I want to hear all about Georgia's week."

"You don't have plans?" asked Mama, knotting her arms across her chest. "A show?"

"Right now I have a dinner date to get to," he said, winking at Georgia. "So let's all get ready."

As Georgia skipped off to her room, she felt as though her feet barely touched the floorboards. *Normal.* Things were going back to normal. Mama couldn't see it, not yet, but Georgia didn't blame her. She didn't know about the wishing lake. About the magic stone Georgia had sent skipping across its enchanted waters.

Georgia was certain she would see soon.

And then they would be a normal family once more.

Chapter Eighteen

The smells of hamburgers and hot French fries hit Georgia as soon as they walked into the Chargrill, making her stomach rumble. Their waitress seated them at one of the big red booths. Mama and Daddy sat on opposite sides of the table, and Georgia slid in next to Daddy.

He put his arm around her shoulders, and she was glad she'd chosen to sit there.

They ordered three cheeseburgers and fries—no pickles for Mama—and a chocolate milkshake for Georgia.

The diner was full of other families and groups of teenagers laughing and sharing platters of fries. A couple of men sat on the swivel stools by the counter, watching the baseball game that was playing on the TV.

Daddy cleared his throat. "So, what's it been like out

there at the country house, chickadee? How do you like Aunt Marigold?"

"It's been fine, Daddy," Georgia said. "I mean, really good. And Aunt Marigold is nice. She makes me do lots of chores, but I don't mind much. I still have lots of time to read and explore and pet Ruby."

"That cow's still alive, huh? She was kind of mean, if memory serves."

"You just have to give her a peppermint," Georgia said knowledgeably. "Then she'll let you pet her. Hank taught me that."

"Who's Hank?" Mama asked.

"Used to work on the farm," Daddy said. "But that was a million years ago. I haven't heard that name since I was a boy. Last I knew he was in Alaska or somewhere like that. I can't believe he's back."

"He said home came calling," Georgia said.

"Is that right? Well, you tell him your daddy says hello."

The waiter came with Georgia's milkshake, and Cokes for Daddy and Mama. Georgia took a sip of the milkshake— smooth and thick—and glanced nervously across the table at her mother, who had barely said a word since they'd left the house.

Daddy reached for Georgia's milkshake and took a long, loud slurp, making Georgia laugh. She couldn't remember the last time she'd been this happy.

"Well, I'm glad your aunt Marigold has someone to keep her company for a while," said Mama, ignoring Daddy. "It can't be easy living out there alone like she does."

"She could move if she wanted to," said Daddy. "I think she likes it that way."

Mama narrowed her eyes. "I just meant—"

"She says city people don't know how to listen," Georgia said quickly. "And it's true. When I got there, it seemed so quiet. But now I notice all the cicadas and birds and crickets and stuff."

"Is she still making her plates and bowls and things?" Daddy asked.

Georgia shook her head. "She said not much anymore, but I think she's going to teach me."

She hoped so, at least.

"That's very kind of her," said Mama.

"She was always nice when I came to visit," Daddy said as their food arrived, steam rising off the plates.

"She said she used to read to you," said Georgia eagerly. "Just like you, um, used to read to me. She still has some of your books."

"So she did," Daddy said. "She always was good with kids."

"But she never had any of her own?" Georgia asked, sensing an opportunity.

Daddy shook his head. "No, she didn't. She was married

for a while, but it didn't last long."

"Why not?" asked Georgia, eating a French fry dripping with ketchup, so hot it nearly burned her tongue.

"It's not our business," Mama said sharply. "You know better than that, Georgia."

"She's just curious," Daddy said. "It's only natural. Marigold is a bit of an odd lady. Nice but odd."

Mama glared at him. Georgia felt her own shoulders go stiff. Her heart lurched.

"It's just that there's this place," blurted Georgia, desperate now to distract Mama and Daddy from each other. "A grave out in the woods. And I thought . . ."

She trailed off.

"I think you're scaring yourself, sweetheart," Daddy said, pausing to take a bite from his burger. "Someone probably buried their old dog out there. I don't remember any grave in the woods, and the only person who's died at that house is my grandfather—your great-grandfather. He's buried in the graveyard behind the Methodist church."

Georgia felt a frown tug at her mouth. She hadn't been sure at first whether the angel in the forest marked a grave or not, but then she'd discovered the locked bedroom at the country house. Who had that narrow bed belonged to if not the same person who was buried in the woods? Why would it be locked unless its owner was never coming back?

Georgia didn't think Daddy would lie to her. But maybe

he didn't know all of Aunt Marigold's secrets either. After all, he had only been a child himself when he had spent his summers there.

Suddenly Georgia remembered the flash of the boy she had imagined that day she'd scraped her knee, running beside her in the forest. Had it been the ghost of her father's boyhood self? An echo left over from when he himself had played in that forest? Perhaps there were other things Daddy could tell her.

"What about a lake?" she asked. "Do you remember that?"

She wasn't sure if this was breaking the rule she'd made with Angela not to tell anyone about the wishing lake, but she thought not. She just wanted to know if Daddy had been there, too. If he knew what she did.

She watched him closely for any sign that he had once discovered its magic, but he just thought for a few seconds, the lines between his eyes curling into parentheses. "I think there was an old pond where Hank took me to fish once or twice," he said. "But I spent most of my time there climbing trees, honestly."

"Oh."

As disappointment dropped through Georgia, the bell above the door chimed, and she turned to see a familiar-looking man walk through. She thought she might have seen him at one of her parents' parties. Back when her parents still *had* parties. He had a girl—a woman, Georgia supposed, though she didn't look much older than the counselors at Camp Pine Valley—on his arm.

"Is that Charlie Montgomery?" Mama asked. "Where's Lucy?"

Georgia recognized the name, too. Charlie Montgomery worked in Daddy's office, and Lucy was his wife. They'd gone over to the Montgomerys' for a barbeque once. That was why he looked familiar. Georgia had played with his son, Dylan, even though he was two years younger.

"They're—separated," said Daddy. He raised his hand to wave, and Mama made a noise like an angry cottonmouth snake.

"You mean he *left* them," she said.

Their eyes met across the table. "Well, sure, he could have picked someone a little older, but I'm not going to ignore the man," Daddy said. "He's got a right to be happy, doesn't he?"

Mama looked like she wished she *was* a cottonmouth just then.

"And what about Lucy?" she said. The edges of her words were sharp as blades. "And Dylan? What about their rights?"

"Look, that's not fair. I'm not saying he should be nominated for husband of the ye—"

"I'm finished," Mama said, folding her napkin into quarters and laying it on her plate. "Let's go."

From the corner of her eye, Georgia saw a muscle in Daddy's jaw tense. "I'm not," he said, "and neither is Georgia."

"I am, Daddy," said Georgia, hoping he would hear the plea in her voice. "I don't mind."

"Fine," he said, his voice suddenly wooden. His eyes no longer sparkled with light. They were two smoldering coals. "That's just fine. Y'all go wait in the car while I pay the check. Since you're in such a hurry to get out of here."

As she followed her mother from the diner, Georgia had to bite her lip to keep from crying. It still tasted of salt.

Almost as soon as they got home, Daddy disappeared into his study. Then he was heading for the door again.

"Good night, sweetheart," he said, dropping a kiss on Georgia's head. "I'll see you in the morning. Maybe we'll make waffles, huh?"

But it was a hurried kiss, and he didn't wait for her to answer before walking away.

Mama came to sit beside Georgia when the door shut behind Daddy. She scooted close and, after a minute, ran her fingers through Georgia's hair. But they felt stiff and caught at her tangles.

"How about a card game?" Mama asked. "Or a movie? I bet there's something on TV." Her voice was full of cheer, but it was all wrong.

Mama never had known how to comfort Georgia when

she was upset. Daddy had always been the one who had known how to lift her spirits.

"No thank you," she said. "I think I'll go to my room now."

Besides, why couldn't Mama just let the magic work? Why did she have to get so mad at Daddy over some people they barely knew?

"Georgia, wait." But her voice was tired, half-hearted. And Georgia did not want to turn around.

Still, maybe things would be all right. Daddy would come home from his show and he would be himself, and Mama would see that things were changing. Then she could start to forgive him.

Tomorrow would be better, Georgia told herself, as she shut the door firmly behind her.

Chapter Nineteen

When Georgia awoke again, it was morning.

There had been no slammed doors or hushed arguments in the night.

Along with the dread she was used to feeling in the morning, she felt a glimmer of hope.

She got up and crept to the kitchen. The door to her parents' room was closed, but it was still early. She went to the front room and looked through the windows. Daddy's car was parked outside. So he had come home, then. And there had been no fighting.

Maybe he'd come home early, and he and Mama had apologized to each other.

Georgia poured out a bowl of cornflakes—not a lot, because Daddy had said they would make waffles—and took it to the table.

Could the magic have worked after all? Maybe she had fixed everything. Mended her Humpty Dumpty family back together.

Through the window, she watched Mr. Molina from two doors down walking his dog down the sidewalk opposite their house. He stopped across from it, then crossed the street.

Inside, a door opened, and Georgia turned to see her mother, hair unbrushed, shuffle out from her bedroom. Her nightgown skimmed the floor.

"You're up early," Mama said.

"I get up early at Aunt Marigold's," said Georgia. "Is Daddy still asleep?"

Mama looked away. "I—I don't know," she said. "He didn't—come home."

"Yes he did," Georgia replied, confused. "His car is outside."

They both turned to look out the window. Georgia didn't understand what she was seeing. Mr. Molina had tied his dog to a tree and seemed to be reaching in through the driver's window of her father's car.

Then she saw him open the door and pull something out of the car and saw that the something was her father.

He hung limply from Mr. Molina's shoulder as the other man dragged him to his feet.

"Oh no," groaned Mama. "Oh no."

And then she was flying out the door in her slippers, flying down to meet Mr. Molina, to help him drag Daddy into the house, and for an awful moment, Georgia sat frozen in front of her wilting cornflakes, afraid that her father was dead.

Then she ran, too, down the front steps and onto the lawn, where Mama was apologizing to Mr. Molina and glancing around to see if anyone else was watching.

"It's okay," Mr. Molina said, straining under the effort of her father's weight. "I'm sure they're working him too hard at the office. Just the other day I was so tired I caught myself drifting off at a stoplight. These things happen."

"Georgia, go on back inside," Mama said sharply, catching sight of her standing there, gaping.

"Is he okay?" Georgia asked, voice small, words choked.

"Your father's going to be just fine," said Mr. Molina, with an uncomfortable smile, red-faced from his efforts. "He just—he needs some rest, that's all."

The lie made Georgia want to kick Mr. Molina in the shin. She could smell the drink seeping from the skin beneath her father's rumpled suit. He murmured something unintelligible. Or was he singing? She thought she could just hear Daddy slurring the opening bars of "Georgia on My Mind."

No, not Daddy. Daddy had disappeared again, the Shadow Man taking his place.

She turned on her heel and ran back into the house, into her bedroom, slamming the door behind her. She wished she could keep on running and running, run until her legs dropped out beneath her.

She had been wrong. Her family wasn't mended. They really were a Humpty Dumpty family. *All the king's horses and all the king's men . . .*

Not even magic could put them back together again.

She dug the silver nickel from her pocket and clutched it so tightly she knew it would leave marks across her palm.

I would do anything for you, sweetheart. Even give you the moon.

She squeezed her eyes shut, running her hands over and over the nickel and feeling the bloom of hope being swallowed up by the thorny darkness in her belly. The kind of dark you could get lost in if you weren't careful.

Chapter Twenty

~~~

Georgia didn't see her father for the rest of the day. He stayed in his study all morning and well into the afternoon, when Mama marched into Georgia's room and announced they were going to the movies and then for ice cream afterward.

The movie theater was too hot, the ice cream too cold, and when they arrived home, Daddy's car was gone again.

Mama didn't comment on any of this. When they got back, she headed straight to the sink for a wet paper towel to wipe away the chocolate ice cream smudges at the corners of Georgia's mouth, though Georgia protested she was plenty old enough to do it herself. Then Mama took the soggy ball to the trash can, where she hesitated, bent down, and picked out a bit of crumpled paper.

"What is it?" Georgia asked.

Mama looked up sharply, like she hadn't realized Georgia was still there.

"A bill," she said, shoving the paper into the pocket of her skirt. "Must have been thrown in by accident. Now, what do you want for dinner?"

But neither of them was hungry.

That night, while Mama was in the bathroom getting ready for bed, Georgia snuck into her room and found the checkered skirt she'd been wearing earlier, laid out across an armchair. The balled-up paper was still in the pocket.

It was a sheet of the stationery her father kept in his study for important letters.

A few untidy words had been scrawled across it.

To my girls,

I'm very sorry about this morning. I promise

But there was no promise. That was all that had been written.

Georgia heard the tap turn off in the bathroom and quickly stuffed the letter back into her mother's pocket before fleeing from the room.

She lay in bed a long time, thinking about the unfinished promise. What had Daddy been about to write? And why had he stopped himself?

The answer came to her before she realized she didn't want it.

He didn't want to make a promise he couldn't keep.

When Georgia awoke the next morning, the cicadas were already rattling in their branches, but they sounded different here than at the country house.

Lying in bed and listening to the tuneless wings, Georgia knew somehow that Daddy hadn't come home last night. Knew she would have woken to the sound of his clumsy footsteps. Still, she stumbled out to the kitchen, rubbing the sleep from her eyes ("stardust" Daddy had called it when she was little), and found Mama already there.

"Did Daddy come home?" she asked.

Mama shook her head—one quick turn of her chin in each direction.

It wasn't the first time he hadn't come home overnight. He always came back the next day. Still, Mama's face was as pale as the sugar cookie dough she was rolling out on the counter.

Without a word, Georgia took her place beside her mother and began to stamp out circles while Mama greased the cookie sheet. They worked in silence, Georgia occasionally brushing her arm against Mama's, hoping for a bit of comfort from her oven-warmed skin.

She found herself wishing that Angela were there next to them. Angela, who was never silent. Who had a way of making her feel like everything would be all right.

When the cookies were cool, they spread a glistening

layer of strawberry jam over half of them, then used the other half to make jam sandwiches. They sprinkled the tops with powdered sugar, each took one to eat, and still, Daddy didn't come home.

Georgia watched a minute tick by on the kitchen clock. Her heart felt strange. Heavy and useless in her chest, like a bumblebee with a torn wing.

"Go on and get your things while I pack these cookies up," Mama said finally. "Your aunt Marigold will be waiting for us."

It was only as they were pulling away from the house that Georgia looked in the rearview mirror and saw Daddy's car driving slowly down the street from the opposite direction. She breathed a sigh of relief even as the sight of it made a hardness rise in her throat.

Mama glanced back, too, but she didn't turn around. She kept right on driving.

They didn't talk for most of the way. Georgia put her hand out the window and felt the wind blow through it while she watched without much interest the familiar landmarks zipping by.

As they turned off the highway, it began to drizzle, and Mama rolled the windows up.

"Your daddy shouldn't have done that," she said suddenly. "He shouldn't do it, Georgia. I'm sorry that you—that you have to see it all. It's not right."

Georgia turned to look at her in surprise.

"Mama," she murmured. Because there was something different about Mama today, something that had made her speak instead of stay silent. "Why do you think he does it?"

She thought at first that Mama wouldn't answer. But then her brow crumpled like that crumpled-up note in the garbage can. The apology that Daddy couldn't give so Mama had to. "He says he can't play right without drinking," she said. "He says he needs it."

"But why, Mama?" Georgia asked. "Why can't he just stop?"

And whether she meant the drinking or the playing or the both of them together, she wasn't sure.

"I don't know, Georgia," Mama said. "It's just . . . something inside of him, I guess. Something that makes him need it."

"Well, I hate it," murmured Georgia.

Then they were turning down the driveway, and the sunflowers were bobbing on one side, like they were trying to shake off the rain. Ruby chewed a mouthful of grass as the car trundled past. It was almost as if Georgia had never left. As if the horrible weekend had never been.

Mama parked in front of the country house, but she didn't get out. Instead, she took Georgia's hand in hers. Georgia couldn't remember the last time she'd held hands with her mother.

"I'm going to fix it, Georgia," Mama said, turning her flinty eyes to her daughter. "I'll make it better, all right?"

Georgia recoiled. She pulled her hand away from her mother's. She'd thought Mama had been in a truth-telling mood, but what truth could there be in those words? If magic couldn't fix Daddy, what chance did Mama have?

"But you don't promise, do you?" she said quietly.

Mama hesitated. It was all the answer Georgia needed.

Then she was out of the car. Mama called to her, but the trees were so close, so safe.

As she fled into the forest, the country air felt like the warm embrace of home.

Chapter Twenty-one

The rainstorm had already come and gone, but its phantom lingered in the forest, making everything shimmer. Georgia stopped running when she was sure Mama hadn't followed. She breathed in the green air, filling her lungs with the newness of it.

She took off her shoes and carried them by the laces, letting her feet sink into the earth.

Just as she was about to jump over the dry ravine that lay on her path to the lake, she heard a noise. Footsteps, she thought, running over wet leaves.

She turned in the direction of the sound, thought she could just make out the shape of someone slipping through the trees.

"Angela?" she called.

The figure was moving toward where she had discovered

the grave—a part of the forest she had avoided ever since. After a second's hesitation, she followed. She darted through the trees and found herself in another grassy glade, where clumps of wildflowers shot up in the dappled sunlight.

It was a pretty little place, but while half of the clearing was splashed with sun, the other half was dipped in darkness. Creeping into the shade, she squinted past the glade. Shadow swallowed everything, so all she could make out were the shapes of the gnarled trees, which seemed to twist together in a giant ghostly web.

Something about it felt so familiar to Georgia, though she couldn't think what. Something in the murky depths seemed to call her closer.

She was about to take another step when her breath snagged in her chest. There, staring out at her from the shadows, was a face. She thought she could detect a dark head of hair and a flash of teeth, as if the face were grinning. But then it was gone again. Like a pale moon appearing for the merest moment from between dark clouds.

Georgia felt a shudder run through her. "Hello?" she called. "Is someone there? Angela?"

But it hadn't been Angela's face. That much she was sure of. Just as she was sure that whoever she had seen would not answer her call. Was *this* the presence she had felt sometimes, watching her in the forest?

She looked into the dimness for another moment but saw

nothing. She inched backward until she felt the first sunrays warm her arms. Then she turned and ran once more.

When she reached the nearest of the great oak trees, she could have kissed its ancient, furrowed bark. There were no shadows to hide behind here. Instead, she took a final backward glance that revealed nobody behind her before hopping over its roots.

The sound of gentle waves rolling in to meet the shore greeted her from the other side of the oak. She squelched the damp sand between her toes, squinting across the blue water to the little island with its white tree.

Not until her heart began to slow did she realize it had been throbbing in her chest.

Not broken after all, then. Not completely, at least.

"There you are!" called a familiar voice.

Georgia jumped, startled to see Angela waving at her from down the beach by the boat, their usual meeting spot.

Perhaps it was because she was still shaken from the encounter she'd just had, but for the first time, Georgia thought it odd—the way Angela was always waiting for her here or arriving at the same time. Like she knew when Georgia was coming.

Still, it was an enormous relief to see her friend, so Georgia turned the trespassing thought away.

As she came closer, Angela's bright face folded into a frown. "Are you okay?" she asked. "You're shaking."

Georgia looked down at her hands. Angela was right.

"Sit," she said.

Georgia sat obediently, and Angela plopped down beside her in the sand, studying her face. Georgia wished she wouldn't. But then again, would it be so terrible if she saw— if someone really *saw*—what was written there?

"It didn't come true, did it?" Angela asked gently.

Georgia was still thinking of the face in the shadows, and it took her a moment to realize what her friend was talking about. Her wish.

"No," she said. "It didn't. Maybe I did it wrong. Said the wrong thing."

Angela let out a heavy sigh, like she could feel the weight Georgia carried. Like it was her weight, too. A heavy trunk they carried between them, like girls did on the first day of camp, helping each other move into their cabins and banging their knees on the bunk bed posts.

"I'm sorry," she said. "Do you . . . do you want to talk about it?"

Georgia looked down at her toes, digging them into the sand. Nobody had ever asked her if she wanted to "talk about it" before. "It" was a thing best ignored.

But ignoring her half-broken heart wouldn't make it better. In fact, Georgia found suddenly that she *did* want to talk about it. That the words were right there, ready to spring out of her chest.

"My daddy drinks," she said. "A lot."

"Oh," said Angela. Georgia glanced at her face to see her reaction, but it was as flat and calm as the wishing lake. "But he didn't always? You, um, wished for things to go back to normal."

Georgia combed through her memories of Daddy. There had been a time before the Shadow Man, of course, but had there been a time before the drinking? She wasn't sure. Hadn't he held a drink in one hand the night he swept her from her bed and promised her the moon?

"Well, he didn't drink like he does now," she said. "Not as much. Now it's like all he ever does is work and drink. It—it makes him into someone different."

When *had* things changed? Again, Georgia searched her memory. Had it happened all at once—a sudden crescendo— or ever so slowly, like a piano falling out of tune? When had the parties stopped and the fighting started? Was it before or after the Shadow Man had arrived?

"I think it got worse when he started going out last year," said Georgia slowly, "to play piano sets around town."

"He's a piano player?"

"He's an accountant. But he loves the piano. And he's really good, too. It's what he wants to do. But Mama says he doesn't think he can play without drinking. She says that's why he does it."

A tiny frown flitted across Angela's face. "Do you think she's right?"

Georgia dug a line in the sand with her finger. "Maybe."

Except that Daddy *did* drink before he had started going out to play. Not as much, maybe. But still. And he hadn't been playing a show on the afternoon of the end-of-school party, when he'd shown up drunk. Besides, why should he need to drink to do the thing he was best at, the thing he loved to do more than anything else? It didn't make sense.

Then there was the way Daddy looked when he came home from work in the evenings. The way he couldn't quite muster his usual smile, as if it were a difficult word he couldn't remember how to pronounce.

She remembered their little game, from back when he used to play the piano at home every night.

"What do you think? Good enough for Nashville? Maybe even New York?"

"Yes, Daddy."

Daddy dreaming of something bigger. Something more. More than—

A vicious thought prickled deep within her, a newly grown thorn.

"I think," she said, "I think maybe he just drinks because he's unhappy."

She felt the truth of her words at once, and it shocked

her. How long had Daddy been unhappy? Had he felt that way when they'd gone sledding that Christmas Eve? When they'd read *Peter Pan* each night? When he'd promised her the moon in the sky?

But no. Georgia couldn't bear that thought. It had always been her and Daddy, hadn't it? An unbreakable team.

"What's it like?" Angela asked gently as a wave lapped at their toes. "When he drinks? I mean—does he ever, you know, hurt you?"

"It's not like that," Georgia said. "It's just that he becomes someone else. He still looks like Daddy, but he's so different. He can't talk straight or think straight. He and Mama yell at each other. That's if he comes home at all."

Angela didn't say anything for a moment. She twisted her ponytail around her fingers, thinking.

"Does he know how unhappy it makes you?" she asked finally. "Have you ever told him?"

Georgia shook her head. Wasn't it adults who were supposed to tell children when they had done something wrong? How could she tell Daddy what he was doing to her heart?

"I don't think I can," she murmured. "I wouldn't know how."

"Well, what about a letter, then?" asked Angela insistently.

Georgia turned to look at her sharply, thinking of the letter Mama had pulled from the trash can yesterday. But, of course, Angela knew nothing about that letter. Couldn't know.

"That way," Angela went on, "you can tell him how you feel without actually saying it to his face."

"A letter," repeated Georgia, as if she could tell by the way the word sat on her tongue if it would be a good idea or not.

Daddy had *started* to write her a letter. Maybe getting one from her would help him to finish it.

"I'll think about it," Georgia said. And then, "He's a good dad, you know. The *best* dad. He loves me."

Angela nodded. "Of course he does."

"We always used to read *Peter Pan* together." She needed Angela to know that she was telling the truth—that there was more to Daddy than his drinking. "There was this one year we all dressed up for Halloween, and he played Captain Hook. He found this big hook at the hardware store, and Mama made a patch to go over his eye. None of the other dads ever did anything like that."

Angela smiled at this. For the first time, Georgia realized she knew nothing about *Angela's* father. About any of her family.

All of a sudden, it felt strange, the way Angela knew so much about her and she knew almost nothing about Angela. Was it because she'd never bothered to ask or because there was something Angela didn't want her to know?

Her head felt fuzzy, full of questions she didn't have the

words to form exactly. The forest felt full of secrets.

Angela spoke before Georgia could find what she wanted to say. "About your wish," she said. "I was thinking about it this weekend, and I don't think it's your fault it didn't work." She glanced at Georgia apologetically. "I don't think it was ever going to work, actually."

Georgia sat up straighter, the mysteries of a moment ago temporarily forgotten. "What do you mean?"

"Well, remember the very first time we came?" Angela asked. "When you wished for the rain to stop?"

Georgia nodded.

"But as soon as we got past the oak trees, it started up again. Except I don't think it had just started. I think it never stopped. I think the lake's magic only works inside the tree ring."

Georgia remembered the sudden charge of rain that she'd run into that day. The way the forest had already softened to mud by the time she took her first step out into it.

"I think you're right," she said. "I guess I just—I thought I could use the magic to fix my family. But that was probably stupid."

Angela draped an arm around Georgia's shoulders and squeezed. "It wasn't stupid, Georgia," she said. "It wasn't stupid at all. I just think maybe some things are too big to only *wish* for. If you want them to change, you have to really do something, you know?"

"Like writing a letter."

Georgia was surprised to feel a strange sense of relief settling over her. This morning, she had been ready to give up on ever having a normal family again. Because if magic wasn't strong enough to mend what had broken between them, then nothing could be. But if Angela was right that the magic could never have worked anyway, then maybe they still stood a chance.

Maybe a letter wasn't such a bad idea after all.

Chapter Twenty-two

After Georgia and Angela hugged goodbye, Georgia got only a few paces into the woods before she turned back. She kept her footfalls light and quiet against the forest floor.

Her stomach squirmed with guilt as she thought of her friend—her summer sister—somewhere ahead, not knowing that Georgia was following her. After she had listened to Georgia talk about Daddy. Given her such good advice.

But she had to know. Couldn't shake the feeling that there were secrets in this forest—more than the magic of the wishing lake—and that Angela might be hiding one of them.

There was a suspicion in her mind that would surely fade like a fog if Georgia could just *see* where Angela lived. Just make sure of it for herself.

She knew the general direction of the Boatwright house from when she'd seen its rooftop from the branches of the wizard tree. But the forest was thicker on this side of the lake, and if there was a trail Angela took, Georgia hadn't found it.

Her ankles were scratched with briars by the time she suddenly saw a flash of blue up ahead. Blue paint. A few more steps and she could see the house. Run-down and sagging a bit to one side, like an old man with a bad hip. A For Sale sign still planted on the lawn, though no one would be able to see it so far back from the main road.

But there was also a car in the driveway. A station wagon.

Georgia took a step back behind a wild holly bush, making sure she couldn't be seen from the house. She spotted movement through one of the windows. A woman, hanging curtains. Behind her, the silhouette of a child—a tall girl, her hair pulled back in a ponytail—running nimbly up the stairs and out of sight.

Georgia felt a sigh of relief leave her chest. So this was Angela's home after all. She and her family *had* just moved in.

Her stomach squeezed with guilt again for not trusting her friend.

As she was about to turn away, she caught a glimpse of something else. For just a moment, she was sure she had seen another child darting past the upstairs window. A boy.

She must have imagined it, or perhaps the boy was a

135

visitor. Angela didn't have any siblings. It was the one thing she'd told Georgia about her family, on the very first day they met.

She watched the upstairs window for another moment before forcing herself to turn away.

When she was back on her side of the lake, Georgia changed course once more. Instead of taking her usual path back to the country house, she went the way she had gone once before.

This time, she didn't cross into the green glade. She just stood at its edge, staring for a long moment at the tangle of summer flowers and the gray-faced angel bowing solemnly over them.

The same heaviness came over her that she'd felt the first time she'd seen the grave. The certainty that, despite the lively flowers, sorrow had claimed this place as its own. But she had another feeling, too.

That somehow, this place and its secrets were connected to the wishing lake. And she was going to find out how.

By the time Georgia returned to the country house, it was late afternoon and Mama's car was gone from the driveway. Long gone, most likely. Only Ruby was there to notice when Georgia crept out into the overgrown grass. She gave a low moo, but Georgia shook her head.

"Sorry, girl. I don't have any peppermints right now."

She had no idea what kind of mood Aunt Marigold would be in. She held her breath as she opened the creaking screen door and pushed her way into the house.

It seemed empty at first. Aunt Marigold was not in the kitchen, and Georgia thought she was probably around back digging up vegetables for dinner.

Then, "In here," her great-aunt called. Her voice was followed by a loud *thump*, like something heavy hitting the floor.

The sounds were coming from the pottery studio.

Georgia stepped through the parlor into the little room, where Aunt Marigold was standing over a stone table in the corner, throwing a hunk of clay down onto its surface.

She looked up as Georgia entered. Her face was smudged with gray. "Come on," she said. "Your turn."

"My turn?" Georgia repeated, still hovering at the doorway.

"You said you wanted to learn," Aunt Marigold said, bringing one set of knuckles to her hip. "Or did you change your mind already?"

"No," Georgia replied quickly. "No, I want to learn."

Whatever she had expected from her aunt, it had not been *this*. A lecture on respecting your mother, maybe—delivered with a pointed finger—or sideways look of disappointment.

This was so much better.

"Well, then, get an apron and come and throw this clay."

She gestured toward the metal storage racks beside her, where a pile of identical beige aprons—all of them stained with clay and paint—hung from one side. Obediently, Georgia took one and pulled it over her head. Aunt Marigold made room for her to stand at the table.

"Now," she said, "take the clay in your hands and throw it down."

Georgia took the lump between her fingers. It was much wetter than she had expected, almost like mud. She grasped it in one hand and thrust it down onto the tabletop.

"No, no," tutted Aunt Marigold. "Throw it *hard*. Hard as you can."

Georgia picked up the clay, and this time she hurled it down onto the table, where it landed with a satisfying *smack!*

"Better," said her aunt. "Now keep doing that. Turn the clay so you hit each side."

Georgia did as she was told, throwing the clay ball again and again, until it wasn't so much a ball but a rough rectangle. It felt good, actually, heaving the clay down again and again until her right arm ached.

"Now you're going to wedge it," said Aunt Marigold. She put out her hands like she was going to show Georgia, but instead of touching the clay, she let them hover in space. She moved them like she was kneading an invisible loaf of dough.

"What's this for, anyway?" Georgia asked when the heels

of her hands ached with the effort of following her great-aunt's instructions.

"To get the air pockets out," said Aunt Marigold. "Which we've done. Now we'll throw it on the wheel."

She pointed to the contraption Georgia had noticed before. A large disc that sat inside what looked like a shallow bucket on top of a little table.

Aunt Marigold pulled a stool up beside the bucket and gestured for Georgia to sit. "This is how the clay gets shaped, see? We put it on the wheel, and the wheel spins while we mold it."

"What are we making?"

"I thought we could make a bowl. To replace the one that got broke."

Georgia nodded, and listened as Aunt Marigold showed her the foot pedal that made the disc in the bucket spin. This, she gathered, was the "wheel" her aunt was talking about. She showed Georgia how to sit with her knees on either side of it, and where to keep the sponges handy, and told her why they had to throw water on it before beginning.

"Now take your clay and press it down, hard on the wheel. Make sure it's centered."

She waited and watched as Georgia followed instructions. "Cup your hands around it. Firm but not too firm. Like you're holding a critter that's trying to escape, and you don't want to hurt it, but you don't want to let it go, see?"

"I think so," said Georgia, who had in fact once found a baby rabbit in her yard that had been hurt. She'd held the soft, silky thing in her hand for a single, trembled heartbeat before it slid out of her grasp and leaped off through the grass, one tiny paw held aloft.

Georgia imagined the small rabbit as she cupped her hands around the clay. It had been almost the same color as the hunk of clay in front of her, she thought as the wheel began to spin, and every bit as slippery.

Aunt Marigold's arms reached around Georgia, and Georgia breathed in her aunt's warm, grassy smell. Odd, the way it was already familiar, how it made her shoulders sink an inch lower to breathe it in.

Her hands hovering around Georgia's, Aunt Marigold showed her how to shape the clay into an even disc, then how to raise it up and hollow it out to make the shape of a bowl.

Georgia pressed in against the clay and felt it rise to meet her touch. She concentrated hard as she raised it higher, then pushed down in the middle.

But suddenly the neat cone of clay went lopsided, and the harder Georgia pressed against it, the more the clay seemed to want to find its way through the gaps in her fingers.

"No, no, no," said Aunt Marigold. "Not like that. You're pressing too hard, and you let the wheel get too fast. Try again."

But the same thing happened again. As soon as she tried to make a hollow, the whole thing went wonky, throwing the wheel off balance.

"I can't do it," she said after her third attempt.

"Yes you can," said Aunt Marigold. "You just can't force it, that's all. You're trying too hard."

"Then *you* show me," blurted Georgia. How could someone try *too* hard? She looked up at Aunt Marigold, half-afraid that she would end the lesson then and there.

Aunt Marigold just pursed her lips. "Get up," she said. She sat down, patted the clay back to the wheel using the heel of her palm, then used a sponge to rewet it.

"Clay has its own mind, see?" she said, making the wheel turn, slowly at first as she began to cup the clay with her fingers. She made an odd face, like she'd just remembered something unpleasant, then went on. "It's no use trying to control a thing that has a will of its own. It's like—like writing poetry. You can't just force a bunch of words into the shape of a poem. You have to let the words guide you as much as you guide the words. And it's just the same with clay."

Georgia felt the corners of her lips twitch. It was strange to hear her aunt—who had spoken of the murder of her chickens by a fox like it was an everyday occurrence—talking about a lump of clay as if it were a living thing with a precious soul.

"There, see?" Aunt Marigold said as she raised it up into a perfectly symmetrical cone. "And now—"

She pressed her thumbs into the top of the cone, and suddenly the cone had become a bowl. But as Aunt Marigold began to push against the inside of the bowl with her thumbs, she gave a gasp of pain and jerked her hands away from the clay as though it had been full of broken glass.

The bowl wobbled and sank.

"Are you okay?" Georgia asked.

Aunt Marigold was holding her right hand in her left, rubbing her thumb up and down her palm. Georgia looked closely at her great-aunt's hands for the first time. She noticed how the fingers were bent just slightly, like Daddy's hands when they were pressed against the piano keys. Except that Daddy's fingers straightened when he was done with his song.

"It's nothing," said Aunt Marigold hurriedly. "It's—"

"Is it your hands?"

Her aunt examined Georgia and sighed. "It's my arthritis," she said finally. "I've had it for years."

"Is that why you don't make any pottery anymore?" Georgia guessed.

Aunt Marigold cast a glance around the studio, and Georgia saw that same, sorry love in her aunt's eyes that she'd heard in her voice just a minute ago. "I only had a few years after I built this place until the pain started. Might as well put me in an O. Henry story."

Georgia felt a slow dawning of understanding. The biscuit sheet Aunt Marigold had dropped on the floor on Georgia's first morning. The way her aunt gave her the tasks that required harder work with her hands, like shucking the corn. Even the bowl smashed in the sink. Aunt Marigold hadn't meant to do that. She hadn't done it out of anger at Georgia.

Her hands were just failing her.

"But what are you going to do?" Georgia asked. "All by yourself, I mean? If it gets worse, will you be able to—"

"Now hold it right there." Aunt Marigold rose from her stool so she could look down at Georgia. "That's my own business, I'll thank you to remember. And while you're at it, you can recall that I got on perfectly fine before you showed up at my front door like a stray cat."

Georgia felt a flash of anger and wanted to argue, but this time she managed to stop herself in time. Aunt Marigold, she had started to see, was exactly like the clay she loved so much. Hard to argue with and impossible to control.

"Yes, ma'am."

"All right, then," said her aunt. "I think that's enough potting for one day. Go wash your hands good. You must have worked up an appetite from skipping lunch."

Georgia nodded. She had got as far as the doorway before she stopped and looked back at her aunt, who was stooped over the pottery wheel, scraping off the mess they'd made.

"Aunt Marigold?" she said. "I'm sorry, you know. For your—your troubles."

The sharp glint her aunt always had—the one that Georgia saw now was meant to camouflage the hurt beneath—softened for just a moment to a glow that almost looked like affection.

"And I'm sorry for yours, too, child," she said, before turning away again.

Georgia thought about Aunt Marigold's hands as she washed her own in the kitchen sink. Making this discovery about her arthritis was like finding a single page ripped out from a story. The story of what had made Aunt Marigold the way she was. What had led her to be an old woman living alone in a ramshackle house like this.

And finding one page only made her want to read the rest of the story all the more.

Perhaps she was just hungry with curiosity, or maybe it was that Georgia had the idea that if she just knew the whole story, maybe she could do something. Could help somehow. Could soothe the pain in Aunt Marigold's heart.

Perhaps it was not too late for some of Aunt Marigold's wounds to be mended, too.

Chapter Twenty-three

~~~

Hank returned the next morning. He was already sitting at the breakfast table, halfway through his grits, by the time Georgia appeared.

"Hope you're ready for some more painting today," he said, smiling through his scraggly beard.

"Hank was just telling me that the Boatwright place has been sold," Aunt Marigold said, putting a steaming bowl in front of Georgia. "I told him my sources had already informed me."

She gave Georgia a little conspiratorial smile.

"Bet they'll need some work done on that old woodpile of a house," said Hank. "I'll have to drop in soon."

Georgia remembered the way Angela's house had sagged, and thought there would be enough work at the Boatwright place to keep Hank busy for a year. But she kept quiet. If she said she'd been there, Aunt Marigold would ask questions. And besides, she was glad to see Hank. It was nice having him around. She didn't want him to be *too* busy.

When she had finished her breakfast, Hank handed her a few peppermints, and they walked out to see Ruby together. Hank rustled a plastic wrapper between his fingers, making Ruby's ears perk as her pace toward them quickened.

"How old is she?" Georgia asked as she reached her arm over the fence to give Ruby her candy.

"Fifteen years?" Hank guessed. "Twenty?"

"Did there used to be a lot of cows here?"

"Back when the farm was working?" Hank asked. "Oh, sure. That old barn out back is where we used to milk 'em. Your great-granddaddy kept hogs for a while, too. And horses."

"Horses?" Georgia asked.

"You like horses?"

"I rode them at camp," she said. Ruby's nose nudged against her shoulder, and Hank handed her another peppermint to give the cow.

"Ever seen a mustang?"

Hank laughed as Georgia's eyes widened. "Have *you*?" she asked.

"Out west. Wyoming. Montana."

Georgia had only ever read about them, maybe seen them

once on TV. "What are they like?"

"You've never seen anything so fast and wild and free in all your life," he said, a peaceful smile spreading across his face. "Makes you want to capture one just for a taste of that kind of freedom, but then you couldn't bear to lay a single hand on one, in case you tainted it. In case it's like stroking a butterfly's wings and taking its power to fly."

"I wish I could see one."

"Well, trust me, life is long," said Hank, pulling out a bandanna and wiping under the brim of his cap with it. "And the world is small."

As they turned back toward the house, another question bubbled up in Georgia's chest.

"Do you remember my daddy? He said to say hello."

"Sure I do. You tell him hello right back."

"What was he like?"

"Well, let's see," said Hank, picking up two buckets of paint and handing one to Georgia. "He was a little wild, as I remember. Mischievous. Never liked doin' chores. He was always running off somewhere, slipping through your fingers like butter."

"What else?"

Hank laughed. "If I had known I was gettin' interviewed this morning, I'd have worn my church suit."

But he seemed to think about the question some more as

he propped a ladder against the house. "He was always out in those woods. Usually up in a tree. And he always did like to sing or whistle. Marigold says he's some kind of musician now?"

"Piano," said Georgia.

Hank nodded, began to climb.

"Did he—" Georgia started. "I mean, did he like it here?"

Hank reached the top of the ladder and squinted down. "Well, I can't say I ever asked him, but I think he did. I think he liked the freedom."

She had other questions for Hank, too. But as she began to paint, Georgia fell quiet. Her mind was filled with the boy Daddy had once been. And she couldn't help but think it sounded like he had a lot in common with those mustangs out west.

That afternoon, it was a relief to pass from the long golden grasses into the shade of the trees.

The forest floor was an endless checkerboard of light and shadow, but Georgia's path through the ferns and rocks was well trodden by now. She darted along it, savoring the coolness of the air between the trees and eagerly awaiting her first glimpse of the lake.

Angela wasn't there yet when she stepped through the circle of oak trees, nor was she close behind Georgia, which was a first. Still, Georgia breathed a sigh of relief as she gazed out at the calm water. She stripped down to her swimsuit and shorts and went to sit at the lake's edge, submerging her feet in the silky water and letting the occasional wave bat at her knees, like a silver kitten pawing to play.

As she waited, Georgia's thoughts turned back to the conversation she'd had with Angela the day before and how last night, she'd sat down at the antique desk in her room and tried to start a letter to Daddy. But she couldn't seem to find the right words, and when she did, they came out in the wrong order.

Sometimes I feel so . . .

I'm very worried about . . .

I just want you to . . .

I can't lose you, Daddy.

Aunt Marigold had been right. Clay and words had a lot in common. Mostly, that they didn't like to cooperate.

She would have to try again tonight. Keep trying until she found what she wanted to say. Because Angela had been right too. She couldn't just keep *wishing* that Daddy would change. She had to make him see why he needed to. And somehow, Angela made her feel like she was brave enough to do it, just as Daddy had once made her feel brave enough to sled down a steep hill on her own.

Georgia heard footsteps walking through the leaves

beyond the oak trees, and after a few seconds, Angela appeared, wearing jean shorts over her swimsuit. Her face broke into a smile when she caught sight of Georgia.

Georgia smiled back, even as she felt another pang of guilt for following Angela the day before.

"Hi," she said.

"Hi," returned Angela. She cocked her head as she drew closer. "You have something on your face. Something white. Right there, above your nose."

"It's probably paint," said Georgia, feeling for the stray fleck and scratching it off.

"What were you painting?"

"Hank and I are painting Aunt Marigold's house."

"Who's Hank?" Angela asked.

"Her handyman."

"That sounds fun," Angela said, wrinkling her nose slightly. "Well, not really."

Georgia laughed. "It's not so bad. Hey, it's your turn to make a wish today."

"Are you sure?" Angela squinted and held a hand over her face as she looked out at the lake. "Yours didn't work last time, so it's okay if you want to go again."

"No," Georgia said firmly. "It's your turn. Do you know what you're going to wish for?" She gestured to the boat, and the two of them took hold of it at either end and flipped it gently. Then they slid it, seal-like, into the water.

"I had a few ideas," said Angela, "but I'm not sure yet. It's hard to choose when you can wish for anything. I mean . . . almost anything."

So they paddled out into the lake, but they didn't head straight for the island. Instead, they pulled their oars in and let the boat drift this way and that, both dangling their legs into the water.

Georgia liked how, even when it was silent between them, it was never a heavy silence like the way it was with Mama sometimes. It still felt like they were together, even though they weren't talking.

After a while, Angela sat up on her elbows.

"Do you stay here every summer?" she asked.

"No," said Georgia, moving her feet in slow circles through the water. "It's my first time. I didn't even really know my aunt before I came to stay, but I like her now. She's teaching me to make pottery."

"Ooh, that *actually* sounds fun," Angela said. "What can you make?"

"Well, I haven't actually made anything. I'm not good enough yet."

"You will be," said Angela confidently. "What do you usually do in the summers?"

"I used to go to camp."

At this, Angela lifted her feet from the water and turned around to face Georgia, her legs dripping water into the belly of the boat. "A real camp?" she asked. "Like with cabins and campfires and everything?"

"Sure," said Georgia. "It's up in the mountains. The camp is in a valley, and in the middle there's a lake like this one, only bigger."

"Do you miss it?"

Georgia thought of the first whiff of the wooden cabins on opening day, the taste of a toasted marshmallow dissolving on her tongue, the brief tickle of mountain breeze as it paused against her skin.

"Yeah," she said. "I do. It's the best place in the world."

Angela was quiet for a moment, studying the drops of lake water on her toes. Then she gasped, nearly startling Georgia out of the boat.

"What?" asked Georgia. "What's wrong?"

"Nothing," Angela said, laughing. "I just know what I'm going to wish for."

"What?" asked Georgia again.

"Camp Pine Valley!" exclaimed Angela. "What if we could bring it to us? If this lake can control the weather, why can't it become a camp? Why not *your* camp? At least for a few hours!"

Georgia drew her own legs out of the water, doubt and excitement coiling in her chest. "Do you really think it's possible?"

Angela shrugged. "There's only one way to find out."

Chapter Twenty-four

In a few minutes, they had rowed the boat ashore on the little island's pebbly beach. Angela scrambled out and bent down, examining the stones.

"Are you sure you don't want to wish for something else?" asked Georgia. "Something *you* want?"

Angela didn't look up. "But I've always wanted to go to camp," she said. "Wait, I've got one!"

She held up a flat gray stone that the water had smoothed into an almost perfect oval. Then she squeezed her eyes closed.

"I wish we could be at Camp Pine Valley," she said, lifting her voice so her words sailed out across the lake. Then she opened her eyes and cast the stone, watched it go skipping after the echo of her wish.

And then—nothing happened at all. The lake remained

still as glass. There was no whisper of wind through the trees.

"Maybe it was too big a wish," Georgia said, trying to hide her disappointment.

She didn't want to think about the other possibility—that the lake might have somehow run out of wishes to grant.

Angela's brows knit together. "I thought—" she started. Then she looked down and gave a little gasp.

Georgia followed her gaze to the surface of the lake. Her reflection stared back at her. Except behind it wasn't the pale outline of the wizard tree. Instead, shimmering turquoise mountains rose in the distance.

She spun around, squinting up into the sun, but nothing had changed behind her. The tree was still there, arching over the little island. Behind it were only more water and more trees.

But when she turned again to look at her reflection, there were mountains perched on either side of her shoulders. Georgia's heart skipped. She knew those smoky blue mountains. They rose in a giant ring around Camp Pine Valley.

"Do you see them, too?" she asked.

Angela nodded. "But how do we get there?"

Transfixed, Georgia leaned down. The mountains looked so solid she could almost touch them. Slowly, she reached out a hand and dipped it into the water. Next to her, she saw Angela bend down to do the same.

The moment her fingers touched the cool lake, it was as if an invisible hand was grabbing her, flipping her upside down. She let out a sharp cry and squeezed her eyes shut as she was swept off her feet. She felt a swooping sensation in her stomach, and a second later, something solid beneath her.

When Georgia opened her eyes, she was huddled against damp wooden planks.

As she rose to her feet, she became aware of many things all at once. First, she and Angela were crouched at the bottom of a lifeguard stand, just like the one that floated in the middle of Big Blue, the lake at Camp Pine Valley.

Almost as quickly, Georgia looked out across the windless water and saw that the ring of oak trees had disappeared. In their place, cabins were scattered across the lake's green banks, nestled in the shadow of the familiar mountains. The air was sunny and soft, and smelled of hemlock trees.

As the realization sank in that Angela's wish had worked—that they had somehow arrived at Camp Pine Valley—Georgia realized something else.

They were not alone here.

There was shouting coming from the crescent beach where the canoes were kept. A knot of girls was standing there, jumping up and down, yelling and pointing straight at her and Angela.

For a moment, Georgia thought the girls on the beach

must be screaming because they'd seen her and Angela appear out of thin air.

But then, scanning the water, Georgia saw pairs of girls in canoes, all turning their boats to face the tower and beginning to row toward them. Even from a distance, she could tell these girls' faces were not happy. Some of *them* were shouting, too, but angrily.

"Georgia," said Angela, "what's going on?"

"I'm not sure." Just as she spoke, she caught one of the words that the girls on the beach were yelling out.

Flag!

She suddenly saw that they were pointing not at her and Angela, as she had first thought, but at something above their heads. Georgia caught sight of a flag fluttering at the top of the tower. It was covered in signatures and painted handprints. In the middle, someone had painted the word "Falcons."

Georgia felt a smile pinch her cheeks.

Each cabin—named after a different bird—made a flag like this every year. The flags flew from poles outside the cabins all summer. Until it came time to play Capture the Flag.

She took the stairs to the top of the tower two at a time, breathing in the rush of the familiar game, letting it fill her chest with a sudden joy that felt as pure as the mountain air.

"What are you doing?" Angela cried from below.

"You'll see!" Georgia crowed, working as fast as she could to untie the flag, which had been fastened to the railing at the tower's top. Then she raced back down the stairs, nearly crashing into Angela, who was wearing a look of utter confusion.

"It's a tradition," Georgia said. "One day every summer, we try to capture each other's cabin flag. We have to get it back to our home base before the other cabin catches us."

Angela's eyes began to glitter. "And the other cabin—" she started.

"Is in those canoes, heading straight for us!"

The girls headed toward them were rowing so hard they might as well have been Vikings.

"Where's home base?" Angela asked.

"The beach, I think." Georgia pointed to where the other group of girls was now cheering and waving frantically. "I guess we have to swim."

"Guess again," Angela said, grinning now, the excitement of the game contagious. She gestured to a green canoe bobbing in the water next to the tower. "Quick! Get in."

They climbed into the boat. First Angela—nimble as always—then Georgia, who slipped on the wet bottom and set the canoe rocking dangerously. Angela shrieked happily. Georgia gripped the narrow sides to steady herself, then took up her paddle.

"Go!" she cried, plunging her oar into the water at the

same time as Angela. She glanced around. There were girls closing in on them.

They rowed with all their might toward the little sandy beach glittering in the distance. But Big Blue was wider than the wishing lake, and they had a long ways to row before they reached the safety of the warm sand.

"They're gaining on us!" Angela shouted over her shoulder.

"Paddle faster!" Georgia shouted back.

Following her own orders, Georgia sliced her oar fiercely through the water on the left, then the right. She didn't allow herself to look back until they had rowed over halfway to the beach.

When she did look, though, she saw that two of the canoes pursuing them had nearly caught up. The girls inside, their faces drawn tight with determination, could have reached out their oars and touched the side of Georgia and Angela's canoe. Another moment and the other boats would be nosing up on either side, trapping them.

Georgia peeked down into the water. She could see minnows flickering, and below, the murky bottom. Just a little farther, and they would be able to stand and touch the bottom.

"Angela," she said, "do you trust me?"

"Of course," Angela replied. "But why don't I like the sound of that?"

"Get them!" another voice called, close behind. "Grab the boat!"

Georgia gave one last enormous stroke of her paddle. "On the count of three, lean all your weight to the left!" she commanded. "One, two, three!"

At the same time, Angela and Georgia swayed to the left, and in the next instant, the canoe began to tip with them.

"We're capsizing!" Angela cried.

"I know," Georgia said. "After we flip, get under the boat!"

Then they were plunging into the cold water, Georgia gripping tightly to the flag. As soon as the boat had capsized, Georgia took a breath and ducked underneath it. She resurfaced inside the upturned boat, and a second later, Angela appeared, her hair streaming. The hollow of the boat's bottom created a narrow chamber that flashed with green light. There was just enough space for their heads to bob above the water without hitting the boat. Georgia reached for the ground with her toes and felt the muddy lake bottom squelch between her feet, just as she'd hoped.

"Now what?" Angela asked, panting and blinking the water from her eyes.

"Now we run!" Georgia replied, pushing the soles of her feet against the lake bed as hard as she could, urging the canoe on. Angela followed suit, and then they were speeding forward. They heard something banging against the sides of the boat, but with every step, the water became a bit shallower. They must be close.

A muted splash came behind them.

"Someone jumped in," Angela said, and when Georgia turned, she could just make out the shadow of a person swimming behind them.

"Let's swim for the beach," Georgia said. "Stay underwater as long as we can. Maybe they won't see us. They'll think we're still under here!"

Angela gave her a thumbs-up before taking a deep breath and diving out of sight. Georgia filled her chest with as much air as she could, then followed. She kept her eyes open as she swam, etching a path through the water with her arms.

Before she ran out of breath, the lake became too shallow to swim any farther, and she rose to the surface. Shouts shattered the air. As she stood, Georgia wiped the water from her eyes to see that she and Angela were standing mere feet from the beach.

"Come on!" the girls on the sand shouted, waving frantically.

"Quick!"

"Look out!"

"Behind you!"

Georgia rushed forward, sprinting through the shallow water the best she could until at last she felt the muddy lake bed give way to wet sand, and then she was running onto the beach, Angela at her heels.

Georgia only had time to glance back to see the canoes nosing ashore, a split second too late, before the girls on the beach engulfed her and Angela in a clamorous, many-armed embrace.

Chapter Twenty-five

~

When she and Angela finally found their way out of the knot of cheering girls, no one asked who they were or where they had come from. It was as if they had been there all along.

Georgia studied the girls. Each face, with its freckles or dimples or braces, felt familiar to her. But she couldn't quite place any of them. None of these girls had been in her cabin in summers past, but she felt she knew them all the same. Like she was meeting them in a dream.

There were other things that made this place feel dreamlike, too. The way the light hung in the air, softening all the colors. The way the sand beneath her feet felt comfortably warm instead of blazing hot. Georgia glanced up at the mountains and saw they were slightly blurry around the edges.

Of course, Georgia thought. It was like Angela said. The wishing lake's magic worked only within the boundary of the oak tree ring. Which meant that they had not really traveled to Camp Pine Valley. Instead, the lake must have somehow created its own looking-glass version of the camp for them.

She felt the first dip of disappointment that there would be no reunions with old friends or favorite counselors. But then Angela was there, throwing her arms around Georgia's neck, cheering, "We did it! We won!"

And Georgia suddenly realized that the person she wanted to share this with most *was* here. Angela. Her summer sister.

Georgia wrapped her arms around Angela's back and joined in the cheer. When Angela began to jump up and down, Georgia did, too. Her face broke into a smile, and a belly laugh bubbled up. Angela pulled loose and held up both hands for a double high five.

"That was awesome!" she said.

"Welcome to Camp Pine Valley," Georgia replied.

A whistle blew nearby. It was a counselor she hadn't noticed before, standing in a red bathing suit at the top of the beach.

"Back to your cabins, girls," she called.

That must mean it was three o'clock, Georgia thought. The time when campers returned to their cabins to shower and write letters or play cards.

Georgia, however, had other ideas. They had two hours left before Aunt Marigold would be expecting her home, and she didn't intend to waste a moment of it.

"Come on," she murmured, taking Angela's hand. As the counselor herded the rest of the girls in the direction of the cabins, Georgia and Angela slipped behind her and into a tin-roofed supply hut.

"Won't they notice we're gone?" Angela asked.

"I don't think so," Georgia said slowly. "I think it's more like we're in a dream. This isn't the *real* Camp Pine Valley. It's the lake's version of it."

But they were here together. And that was what counted.

Angela smiled. "Which means we can do whatever we want here."

Perhaps the wishing lake had not transported them hundreds of miles to the real Camp Pine Valley, but it had done a marvelous job of creating it from scratch.

From the amphitheater where campers sat for Evening Campfire—with its wooden benches carved through with generations of campers' names and initials—to the archery range—where the colors on the bull's-eye targets had long ago faded to shades of gray—every detail was as Georgia remembered it.

They ran barefoot through the field where she had spent afternoons playing soccer and flag football to the steep hill which, one day each summer, was covered with wet, soapy tarps for campers to slide down on their bellies. Georgia pointed out the cafeteria, which smelled more like garlic toast and pizza with every passing minute, and the sailing beach, where a little fleet of white sailboats lay upturned in the sand.

And in every direction, the blue mountains rose like tidal waves frozen at their crest.

Georgia saved the best for last. In the dappled shade where the meadows met the forest, there was a clumsy wooden stable. It was Georgia's favorite place in the whole camp.

As they approached the stable, she breathed in the smells of hay and leather and manure. Somehow, when they were mixed all together like that, they created a wonderful warm aroma. Of everything she loved to do at Camp Pine Valley, she loved riding the most.

They didn't have boots or jeans, and Georgia didn't know how to saddle and bridle the horses on her own, but it was enough to just be there in the stable, surrounded by the horses.

There were bays and dapples and paints. Some of them pawed against their stall doors when she and Angela came into sight, while others thrust their noses out curiously. Angela found a bucket of hay hanging from one of the doors, and they took handfuls to each of the horses, petting their manes and their soft, whiskery noses.

She and Angela didn't speak much as they tended to the horses. A calm had washed over Georgia, and after a while, she was half-lost in memories. Of other summer days at the stable, when her heart had been light and whole.

She thought of last July, when Mama and Daddy had come to drop her off. Had things still been normal then? Daddy had sung songs in the car, hadn't he? And Georgia and Mama had sung along some, too.

But there had been a false note to Daddy's songs. A tightness in Georgia's throat like she was holding her breath, the way she used to between bouts of thunder. Georgia couldn't remember where exactly the tightness had come from. Only that things had already started to change even then.

The uneasy feeling had gone away when they had driven through the camp gates. She left it in the car as she tore across the meadow to get her cabin assignment.

She had forgotten about it entirely by closing day.

But it had come back, as soon as Georgia spied Mama pulling up by herself to take Georgia home. Had snuffed out all the joy of summer, just like that.

When each of the horses had had their helpings of hay (and some of them seconds), Georgia and Angela left the stable behind and went to the lakeshore. Georgia led Angela to Pointer's Bluff, a big rock that jutted out over the water. They sat, letting their feet dangle off the edge, and looked out at the lake and the misty blue mountains beyond.

"It's beautiful," Angela breathed. The light reflecting on the water made her skin sparkle.

"I know," Georgia agreed.

"You really do miss it, huh?" said Angela. "You seem . . . different here, you know."

"Really?"

"Yeah. Like, happier."

"I guess I am," said Georgia.

Or I was.

The wishing lake might not have taken them to Camp Pine Valley, but it *had* taken them back in time. Back to the last time Georgia had felt truly happy. She thought of the joy that had rushed through her as she'd scrambled up the lifeguard tower toward the Falcons' flag. It had taken up every inch of space in her chest, leaving no room for dread or fear or sadness.

It was nice to realize that she could still feel that way.

And it was also terrible, realizing that she hadn't felt that kind of happiness for a whole year.

"But also, you seem, I don't know, *braver*?" Angela went on.

Georgia cocked her head. "Huh?"

"Like what you did with the canoe back there," Angela said. "Capsizing it like that, without even thinking twice. That was pretty daring."

"I guess so," Georgia said.

It was funny. She had always thought of Daddy as the one who made her brave. Thought she was strongest when he was by her side. But Angela was right. When she was at Camp Pine Valley, far away from home, she *did* feel all those things. Daring and brave and strong.

And she felt them when she was with Angela, too.

"It's probably almost five by now," Angela said quietly. "We should go back."

Georgia sighed. If they didn't go back, would it be so bad? To stay here, in this dream world, where she was strong and her heart felt nearly whole again?

But no. Aunt Marigold would be waiting. So Georgia stood and held a hand to help Angela up.

Together, they retraced their steps, back across the playing fields and the meadows, until they reached the canoeing beach. In the distance, Georgia could hear the voices of campers as they made their way toward the dining hall.

Then, from the corner of her eye, she spied something moving. She turned her head just in time to see a figure darting behind one of the cabins on the hill.

"What's wrong?" Angela asked, following Georgia's gaze.

"I just— I thought I saw a boy," Georgia said. "Up by the cabins."

"So?" Angela said. "Maybe he decided to play hooky from dinner."

"But there are no boys here," Georgia said, goose bumps

running up her arms. "It's a girls' camp."

Angela frowned. "Are you sure it was a boy?"

"No," Georgia admitted. "I guess it could have been a girl."

It was just—there was something about the way the figure had moved, darting out of sight, that reminded her of the one she'd seen hiding in the shadows of the forest the day before. The one who she thought might have been following her. Could he have followed her into Angela's wish?

"Come on," Angela said, placing a gentle hand on Georgia's back and casting a last look behind them. "Let's go. I'm getting the creeps."

"Yeah . . . okay." With one last glance, Georgia turned away and let Angela guide her back to the beach. "How do you think we get home?"

"The way we came in?" said Angela. "Let's go back to that tower and see if we can get home from there."

Unlike the rest of the canoes, which had been drawn all the way up the beach in a neat row, theirs was still waiting, half floating in the water. Wordlessly, they stepped in, took up their oars, and began to row.

Georgia's heart felt heavy as they paddled, but not in a bad way, exactly. It was a bit like when she got out of the water after swimming in the ocean for a long time, letting the waves lift her up in their embrace.

When they reached the tower, they climbed out of the

boat and sat on the edge of the dock, peering into the water. But all they could see was the reflection of the wooden structure and the mountains rising beyond.

"I thought we could get back through the reflection," said Angela.

"Maybe we have to ask?" Georgia suggested. "Maybe we have to tell the lake we're ready."

Angela cleared her throat. "We're ready now," she said loudly, chin tilted to the sky. "We're ready to go home."

They looked down at the water again. After a moment, its surface began to ripple, scattering their reflections.

When it went still again, the reflection had changed. The wizard tree was back, and the great oak trees, too. Georgia and Angela exchanged a look, then dipped their fingers into the water at the same time.

Georgia had the same sudden feeling of being flipped, her stomach somersaulting, and then a hard *thunk* as she landed. She was back on the little island in the middle of the wishing lake, sitting among the pebbles. Everything was exactly as they'd left it.

"Cool," Angela—who had landed next to her—breathed, grinning.

"Very cool," said Georgia, smiling back.

The sun was dipping in the sky, and the two of them made quick work of rowing the boat back to shore.

"Some wish, huh?" Angela said as they pulled the boat

up onto the sand, beneath the shade of the nearest oak tree.

"Some lake," said Georgia. "Thanks, Angela."

"For what?"

"Just . . . for making that wish. For everything."

Angela smiled. "Back at you, sister," she said, bumping her hip against Georgia's. "See you tomorrow?"

Georgia gave a little laugh. "Do you even have to ask?"

As she started back toward Aunt Marigold's, Georgia's lungs still felt full with mountain air. But with every step she took, the mountains felt farther away. And at the back of her thoughts, flitting in and out of the darkest corners, was the boy she'd seen. Or *thought* she'd seen.

It was only when she heard the loud *snap!* of a twig breaking in two behind her that she had the sinking feeling she had been right. Someone had been following her.

Someone still was.

Chapter Twenty-six

The boy stood a few paces behind her, between two pine trees.

His hair was tangled and in need of a trim. One of his pale cheeks was smudged with dirt. His eyes were dark—almost black—and wild, as though *he* were the one being stalked through the forest like prey. His mouth was parted in surprise, and Georgia thought her own expression must be a mirror of his.

"I can see you, you know," Georgia snapped at last. "So you might as well come out here."

She felt a sudden anger flash through her, quick and hot as lightning. Who was this boy who clung to the shadows, watching her? Who was trying to steal away the happiness of the afternoon, to curdle it into fear?

He had no right.

The boy didn't move at first, except to lift his chin a bit higher in defiance.

But then he took a step forward, and another. He didn't stop until they were standing face-to-face in the light of the glade.

She could see then that, though his eyes were dark, amber light flashed in them. He wore a striped T-shirt and jeans that had mud stains at the knees. He looked—no, *felt*—familiar. She didn't recognize his face, but she recognized *him*. Knew him. But how?

"Who are you?" she asked. She hoped her voice didn't sound scared, because, beneath her anger, she *was* a bit afraid.

The boy licked his lips and drummed his fingers in mid-air.

"Cole," he said. His voice, when it finally came, was softer than she'd expected.

Cole. It seemed to fit somehow. This boy with black eyes that flashed like fire.

"Why have you been following me?" Georgia asked, crossing her arms over her still-skittish heart.

Again, he hesitated. Then, "I've seen what you do," he said. "At that lake."

Georgia's stomach clenched. "What do you mean?"

"The magic."

So it had been him she'd seen by the cabins. There was

no point, then, in pretending. The only thing Georgia could do now was try to make sure their secret was still protected. As protected as it could be, anyway.

"Have you told anybody?"

He arched his eyebrows, then he shook his head.

"Are you *gonna* tell anybody?"

He stared at her a long moment, then shook it again. "I just want to know how it works," Cole said. "The magic."

So he didn't know about the skipping stones, then. Maybe he'd been too far to see them that closely.

Georgia wracked her brain for some way to say no. The wishing lake belonged to her and Angela. Perhaps the magic only worked for two people. If she brought Cole there, who was to say it wouldn't stop working altogether?

But he knew. He *knew*. And if she didn't do as he asked, he might decide to tell somebody after all.

"You can't make it do anything, you know," she said, a feeble attempt to put him off.

Cole shrugged. "I won't know until you teach me."

Georgia let her arms fall to her sides, defeated. "Fine," she said. "We'll teach you."

For the first time, Cole's face broke into a smile. It transformed his face completely, lighting up its dark edges. Georgia had to admit that it was a nice smile. Maybe this boy was just shy.

Maybe, she thought, things would be all right. Maybe

the lake wouldn't mind Cole coming along. After all, he had found it just like they had. Perhaps she was even *supposed* to bring him there, share its magic with him.

He looked as though he was about to turn to leave when he spoke again. "Don't you want to do more?"

"What do you mean?"

"The magic," he said. "Don't you want to use it for more than just, you know, *make-believe*?"

"I just told you," Georgia said. "There are rules."

"Some rules are meant to be broken, don't you think?"

Georgia decided it best not to answer this question. "How did you find it, anyway?" she asked instead. "Where did you come from?"

Cole's smile widened into a Cheshire cat grin.

"Ask Angela," he said with a wink. "See you, Georgia." And then, before she could ask how he knew her name, he had spun on his heels and was running again, back through the forest, pausing to swing from a low tree branch. Whistling a cheerful tune all the while.

Soon, he was nothing more than a shadow again.

Chapter Twenty-seven

When Georgia arrived back at Aunt Marigold's, Hank had finished painting the front of the house. The effect was dramatic. The country house looked younger, prouder. Not as weary as it had before.

"Have fun?" he called, startling her. She was still shaken from meeting Cole and hadn't noticed Hank standing to the side of the porch, washing his hands down with the hose.

"Yes," she said, stopping to steady her breath.

She couldn't get Cole's last words out of her head.

Ask Angela. See you, Georgia.

What had he meant? Did they know each other, or was it some kind of trick? But if it was a trick, then how did he know Georgia's name?

She realized Hank was staring at her. "Sure were in those woods a long time," he said. "What's a girl get up to out there for that long, anyhow?"

Georgia felt her shoulders rising to her ears, like a cat's hackles. She turned the motion into a shrug. "Just exploring."

Hank studied her another second. "Well, you're just in time for dinner."

Georgia caught a whiff of something salty and delicious.

"Pork chops," he said, closing his eyes and filling his lungs with the smell, too. "My favorite."

The screen door creaked open, and Aunt Marigold appeared. "Dinner's ready," she said. Eyes narrowing at Georgia: "You're late again today."

"I'm sorry," Georgia said, adding hopefully, "but at least it's not raining this time."

"Not yet," said her great-aunt, lifting her chin and scanning the horizon. "But with a sky like that, it's only a matter of time."

Over her shoulder, Georgia saw that the sky had taken on a dull yellow color, like the pages of an old book, the sun like a buttercup that had been pressed between its covers.

She gave the forest one last glimpse and, seeing no one there, followed Aunt Marigold inside. She only made it a step before her aunt pointed up the stairs. "You're filthy," she said. "Go change and wash up."

Georgia eyed the pork chops steaming on the table.

Aunt Marigold quirked an eyebrow at her hesitation.

"Unless you'd rather just have a bath?"

At which Georgia scampered upstairs without another word.

There were buttery mashed potatoes and fresh string beans to go with the pork chops. It was the best meal Georgia had eaten since she'd arrived at the country house. She imagined Aunt Marigold wincing each time she snapped the end from a bean and felt guilty that she hadn't come home in time to help cook.

When everyone was done, Georgia swept away the plates. At least she could wash those.

There was a cherry pie for dessert, and as they ate, Hank fanned out a stack of cards and offered one to Georgia. "Pick a card," he said.

She reached out and took one from the middle. The jack of diamonds. Once she had looked at it, she put it back in and watched him shuffle the stack. He cut it in half, offering her the bottom portion. "Take a look at the top card."

She flipped it up. The jack of diamonds.

"How did you do that?"

He shook his head. "A magician never reveals his secrets."

Aunt Marigold snorted, but Georgia was impressed. "Can you do more?"

Hank polished off the last bite of his cherry pie and smiled. Then he shuffled the deck once more, this time separating it into four stacks.

"Pick a card, any card."

Georgia watched his hands closely as he did trick after trick, guessing card after card, making them disappear and reappear again. But she couldn't see how he did them, and each time he performed a trick, she couldn't help but feel a little thrill of excitement. Even Aunt Marigold quirked an eyebrow in admiration when he reproduced the card Georgia had just finished ripping into pieces.

Finally, Aunt Marigold said it was time for Georgia to go to bed.

"But I'm not tired," Georgia protested. "Please?"

She didn't want to say good night to Hank just yet. She liked being around him. Liked his stories and his tricks, the sandpaper roughness of his voice, the way his laugh stampeded from his chest.

When she was around him, she could almost believe that everything was going to be all right.

"How about you and I sit on the porch," Hank said to Aunt Marigold, "while Georgia here catches us some fireflies." He turned to her. "If you can catch twenty, I might just teach you a trick."

Georgia grinned, then ran into the kitchen for a mason jar. As Hank and Aunt Marigold sat on the newly painted porch, rocking back and forth in their chairs, she ran through the grass, chasing after fireflies to cup in her hands and deposit into the jar. It was easy to see them. They were drops of golden ink on a deep blue canvas.

As she ran, Georgia's thoughts kept wandering back to Cole, and she had more questions. Where was he now? Had she done the right thing, agreeing to teach him the secrets of the lake? But then, she didn't *know* the secrets of the lake. Not really. She didn't know where the magic came from or how it worked.

She thought about Hank, too. About his "magic." She knew *that* magic wasn't real, of course. But then she thought about all the stories he'd told her, all the places he'd been. Was there really any telling what a man who had traveled so far and wide might have seen?

By the time she had plucked several dozen fireflies from the sky, Georgia was breathless, her mind spinning. She approached the porch just in time to hear Aunt Marigold laugh.

It was the first time she'd heard her great-aunt really laugh rather than just snort. If Hank's laughter stampeded, Aunt Marigold's was a strange teetering sound. Uncertain of itself, like a newly born animal.

"Ah, let's see what she's got for us," said Hank, leaning forward in his chair to accept Georgia's offering.

The fireflies shone and twinkled in the mason jar like stars in a tiny galaxy.

"I think she's got you there," said Aunt Marigold, eyeing

the jar. "You might even have to teach her *two* tricks."

"Now?" Georgia asked eagerly.

Aunt Marigold shook her head. "Later," she said. "Hank had better get going."

"Can I—can I walk him out?" Georgia asked suddenly, glancing at the rusty truck parked at the top of the drive.

"I suppose," Aunt Marigold said, sounding suspicious. "As long as you come right back."

So she and Hank set off, the firefly jar in his hand illuminating their shadowy path.

"Hank?" said Georgia. "Can I ask you something?"

"You can ask me anything," he said. "And I'll even do my best to answer."

"Well, I was wondering," Georgia started, "since you've seen so much and all . . ."

"Yes?"

"I guess what I want to know is—I mean—in all that time, all those places, did you ever see anything that you couldn't explain?"

He turned to look at her, and she was relieved to see that his smile was gone. He was taking her seriously. "Like supernatural, you mean?"

"More like magic," she blurted. "*Real* magic. Not like card tricks."

For a long moment, the only sounds were their footsteps on the dirt drive and the katydids humming overhead.

"Would this have anything to do with what you do out there in those woods all day?" he asked finally.

"I—I can't tell you."

"I see," said Hank. The lines on his forehead were etched deep with thought. "Well, I know this much. If you found a bit of magic in this world, you didn't come across it by chance. That magic came to *you*, and for some kinda reason."

They had reached the truck now. Hank turned to face her.

"And when it leaves you, that'll be for a reason, too," he said. "See, I think magic is a thing that only comes to you when you need it."

"But what if you don't know why it came to you?" Georgia asked, thinking of what Cole had said earlier. *Don't you want to use it for more than just* make-believe? "What if you don't know what you need it for?"

Hank reached out a hand and clapped her gently on the shoulder. "Ain't nobody who can tell you that but you," he said. "Good night, Georgia. Thanks for the light." He lifted the jar of fireflies in her direction.

"Good night," said Georgia. "And thanks, Hank."

Halfway back to the house, Georgia heard his truck coughing to life and turned to see the glow of fireflies being released into the night.

Chapter Twenty-eight

Aunt Marigold had been right about the rain after all. When Georgia drew back her curtains the next morning, the world was gray, as if the day had gone old before its time.

"You won't change the weather by staring at it," Aunt Marigold said over breakfast when it began to pour in earnest. "Come on. Let's go to the studio."

Georgia realized she *had* been staring, biting her lip as she wondered whether the rain would last all day. She needed to get to the lake, to ask Angela about Cole.

Then it dawned on her what her great-aunt had just said. *The studio.* "You mean we're having another lesson?"

Georgia hadn't been sure, after how the last lesson had ended, that her great-aunt would want to continue.

"Unless you don't want to," said Aunt Marigold curtly.

"No, I do."

She followed Aunt Marigold into the studio eagerly.

Georgia wedged the clay just as she'd done before, pushing and pulling at it until Aunt Marigold said it was ready for the wheel.

Again, when the wheel started spinning, the clay felt like it was trying to slip through her hands. But this time, instead of trying to squeeze it into shape, she pressed back against it gently. To her surprise, it cooperated. It rose into a cone, and when she pressed down to create the bowl's hollow, it didn't spin off to the side.

"That's it," said Aunt Marigold. "You're getting it now."

And Georgia, though she didn't dare risk looking away from the wheel, thought she heard the telltale crackle of a smile in her aunt's voice.

Georgia and Aunt Marigold stayed in the studio all morning while the rain thrashed down outside.

By lunchtime, Georgia had produced a line of wobbly, lopsided bowls. At the end of the line was a bowl that was not quite as lopsided as the rest, whose sides were almost perfectly smooth.

"It'll do," said Aunt Marigold, examining Georgia's last attempt with a look of satisfaction. "It'll do very nicely, I think. You're a quick learner, Georgia."

Georgia felt warm in the glow of this unexpected praise.

"What do we do next?"

"We fire it in the kiln," said Aunt Marigold, pulling the brown apron over her head and nodding toward an oven-like contraption in the corner. "Then we'll put the glaze on tomorrow."

"Oh," Georgia said, watching as her aunt fiddled with the kiln, a little disappointed that they wouldn't be able to finish that afternoon.

The rain showed no sign of letting up, and she knew her aunt would never let her go to the lake in such weather. Her reunion with Angela would have to wait until tomorrow.

Then a thought struck her. "Could we try something else after lunch?"

"Haven't you had enough for one day?"

Georgia shook her head. "I thought I could make something," she said, "for Daddy. Mama, too."

It would be nice to have something to give Daddy with his letter. Something she had made with her own two hands, to let him know that even though he had hurt her, had stolen the happiness from the past year, she still loved him. Still needed him. Needed to *believe* in him.

And Mama deserved something, too. Georgia felt bad about the way she'd run off on Sunday, when Mama had only been trying to help. Maybe she could make her something to apologize.

"I guess that'd be all right," Aunt Marigold said after a

moment. "But lunch first."

A little burst of joy lifted Georgia onto her tiptoes. If she couldn't be at the lake, she wanted to be here in the studio.

"Aunt Marigold?"

In the gray-misted light, her great-aunt looked softer. Strands of silver and copper hair had come loose from the thick braid that hung down her back, brushing against her cheeks. Her face was smooth and nearly peaceful.

"Mmm?"

"Why did you—do you—like it so much?" Georgia gestured around at the studio, at the row of shabby bowls. "To do all this?"

Aunt Marigold turned her head to the side. "Well, I don't know exactly," she said slowly. "I suppose it's just the making. The creating. It's nice to bring something beautiful into the world."

No longer looking at Georgia, she had taken her left hand in her right and begun to rub it.

"I think that's what I like about it, too," Georgia said softly. And she had the strongest urge to take Aunt Marigold's crooked hands into her own.

Chapter Twenty-nine

After a lunch of leftovers, Aunt Marigold and Georgia returned to the studio. Georgia had decided to make a vase for Mama to replace the one she'd broken years ago and a mug for Daddy to drink his coffee from.

Aunt Marigold sat behind her at the wheel, patiently coaching her, telling her to add more water, ease her grip, or speed up the spinning. In those hours, Georgia felt as if the whole world existed between the palms of her hands. Her hands felt stronger and surer with each attempt, never mind that she had to start over again and again.

Each time the wheel jumped into motion, her heart leaped with it.

She wondered if this was what it was like for Daddy when he played the piano. Would he be able to tell, when he looked at the mug, that it had been shaped with the kind of love that he used to put into the songs he played for her?

She thought of Angela, too, as she worked. She hoped Angela's parents had kept her inside today. That she wasn't waiting for Georgia at the lake.

More than anything, she wished Angela were there in the studio with her. She wanted to share with her friend how it felt to create something useful—something beautiful, even—from a shapeless lump of clay. The way she was learning to transform things, just like the wishing lake did, even if she wasn't exactly using magic.

By the time her stomach started growling that evening, she had made a mug with a curved handle and a jug-like vase with a rounded lip that was slightly thicker on one side than the other. Aunt Marigold had inspected both pieces and said they would be watertight.

"You should be real pleased with yourself," she'd said. "They're fine pieces of work."

Georgia had felt a spark of pride in her chest that warmed her from the inside out.

It was a shock when she opened the studio door to see the rest of the house waiting expectantly for their return, just as they'd left it. To hear the rain still drumming against the windows.

Georgia felt as though something had shifted while she'd been in the studio. But out here, everything was just the same. There was no imagining that something had shifted, though, between her and Aunt Marigold.

Georgia helped her great-aunt prepare dinner that night, volunteering to go out to the vegetable garden for the corn and tomatoes so Aunt Marigold wouldn't have to get wet. She shucked the ears of corn, careful to pull away the gossamer strings that caught between the kernels, then cut the kernels away and piled them in a bowl for the corn bread.

All the while, she watched Aunt Marigold from the corner of her eye, observing how she worked slowly, how she focused hard on what her hands were doing, how her fingers curled tight around the cutting knife like she was afraid it might slip away.

When Georgia saw her wince as she cut into an onion, she reached over for it.

"I can do it," she said softly. "Corn bread's ready for mixing."

Aunt Marigold hesitated. Pink patches like primroses appeared in her cheeks. But instead of arguing, she nodded. "All right, then," she said. And a moment later, "Thank you, Georgia."

At dinner that night, they talked about pottery. Together, they pored over pictures in a book called *History of Ceramics*, with Aunt Marigold pointing out different kinds of glazing and shaping techniques. She even suggested that next week they go to the library in town to see if they had any newer books on pottery.

Georgia marveled at how relaxed her aunt seemed. Almost happy. A different person from the one who had opened the door to her and Mama that first day and eyed Georgia with suspicion.

Why was this soft part of her aunt buried so deeply beneath such a hard exterior? Surely the softness had been there first. Once again, Georgia wondered what had happened to her aunt to make her hide away the best parts of herself.

She thought again of the grave in the woods, the narrow bed upstairs.

But she was too afraid to speak of them to Aunt Marigold. To ask what she wanted to ask. She was afraid that if she did, the hardness might return once more.

As she climbed the stairs to bed, Georgia ran her fingers along the wood of the locked door, as though she might be able to feel some answers in its grain.

Chapter Thirty

The rain had settled in for a good long stay, an uninvited guest.

It was there later that night, when Georgia sat at the desk in her room, writing draft after draft of the letter to Daddy, just as she'd spun mug after mug that morning. Never getting the words quite right.

And it was there the next morning, when Georgia woke up and came downstairs, bleary-eyed, to find Hank sopping wet in the kitchen, wringing water from his beard into the sink.

"Good morning," she said, causing him to startle.

"'Morning," he replied, grinning. "Didn't hear you coming."

"Where's Aunt Marigold?"

Hank shrugged. "Sleeping in, I suppose." He began to rummage in the pantry until he found a box of cocoa. "I ain't no chef," he said, holding up the box, "but I can make some hot chocolate. What d'ya say? I need some warming up this morning."

She watched him as he stirred the cocoa into the milk and steam began to rise from the pan.

"It's nice, you know," he said, looking over his shoulder at her, "seeing someone else in this house besides just Marigold for a change. This house is too big for her to be rattlin' around in on her own. She's gotten too used to her own company."

Georgia sat a little straighter in her seat. This might be her chance.

"Aunt Marigold is kind of different from most people, isn't she?" she asked carefully.

Hank snorted as he poured their cocoa into two mugs and brought them to the table. He sat down across from her. "Different is right," he said. "But that's what being alone for so long will do."

"Hank," she said, lowering her voice and leaning in. She didn't know where to start. Only that, even with Hank, she needed to tread lightly.

"I was just wondering . . . There's a door upstairs that won't open. I thought it might be broken. The lock or something. Maybe you could fix it?"

He shifted his weight, making the chair groan. For the first time since Georgia had met him, he looked uneasy.

She didn't know if he believed her story or not. At first, she thought he would brush her question away like a fly or make an excuse not to answer it. But then he took a long sip of cocoa and licked his lips.

"I don't expect the door is broken," he said. "I expect Marigold keeps it locked."

Georgia's heart thumped in her throat. "But why?"

"Bad memories," he grunted.

"What bad memories?" Georgia asked, her voice dropping almost to a whisper. "Who lived there, Hank?"

Hank hesitated, glancing at the staircase. "I don't like gossip," he said. "But I'll tell you what you want to know, Georgia, only because it might help you understand her a little more. And because she won't like it if you go bringing all this up with her. All right?"

"That's all I want," she said eagerly. "Just to understand."

He nodded. "That room," he said, "belonged to Marigold's father."

"Her *father*?" Georgia blurted. "But—"

But the little grave in the woods. And the narrow bed upstairs. She'd been so sure they had belonged to the same person. The same *child*.

"If it was just her father's room, why does she keep it locked?"

"Like I said, bad memories." Hank shook his head, but he couldn't shake the haze gathering in his eyes. "He was a fine boss to me, your great-grandfather. A good farmer. Always had a hand full of soil. That man knew the earth the way some people know the Lord. Knew it with his bones. But then he took a turn."

"A turn?"

"Well, first his wife—your great-grandmother—she died young. And then not long after, he got—sick, Georgia. And once the sickness took hold of him, it didn't let go. Or maybe he didn't have enough will to fight it, not after losing his wife. But it wasn't quick, and it wasn't easy. Marigold tried to keep the farm going as long as she could, but there was no one else to nurse him. And she couldn't do both. She spent most days up in that room with him, sittin' by his bedside."

So that explained the narrow bed. Narrow not because it was for a child, but because there needed to be room for someone to sit by the bed—to move around the room and tend to her patient. Not a mother nursing a child, but a child nursing her father.

Georgia thought of how Aunt Marigold had bandaged her knee the day she'd fallen in the forest. How tender her touch had been. She must have had years of practice.

"What was he sick with?" Georgia asked.

Hank let out a sigh that rattled deep in his chest. "Some people get sick with illnesses that got names, Georgia. Things you can see. Other people, they just . . . get sick. Your great-grandfather died in that room, with Marigold by his side. And that's why she keeps it locked, I suspect."

Georgia felt a frown tighten across her face. She thought of Aunt Marigold's hands. She'd told Georgia that she suffered from arthritis, but what if she'd been lying? What if she had the same, unnamed sickness her father had died from?

"Do you know about her hands?" Georgia asked.

Hank's eyebrows shot up. "Her arthritis, you mean? Sure. I got some comin' on in my knees."

So it *was* just arthritis, then. Georgia felt as if she were in a dark hallway, fumbling at door handles, trying to find the right one to open.

"What'll happen to her?" she asked. "If it keeps getting worse?"

Who would be there to nurse Aunt Marigold the way she'd nursed her father? Who would take care of her if she couldn't grow her vegetables or cook her supper or tend her house?

Hank looked down at his mug. "I don't know," he said. "You're asking questions I can't answer now."

When Aunt Marigold appeared a few moments later, flustered and apologizing and blaming "the damn rain" for causing her to sleep in, Hank and Georgia were sitting across from each other in somber silence.

"What's got into you two?" Aunt Marigold asked. "You look like someone's just died."

Chapter Thirty-one

Georgia was glad that Aunt Marigold could not actually read her mind, no matter how piercing her gaze. All day Georgia's thoughts kept flitting back to the conversation she'd had with Hank, like moths dancing around a flame. Knowing all the while the risk of singeing their paper-thin wings.

As her great-aunt gently pulled Georgia's clay pieces from the kiln, cradling them like infants, Georgia thought of Aunt Marigold's father, his own hands always full of earth.

As Aunt Marigold spoke about glazing and laid different brushes out on a clean cloth, Georgia wondered how her aunt would carve out a future with her broken hands.

Then her mind wandered back to the grave in the woods. Daddy had told her that her great-grandfather had been buried in a graveyard. And he had no reason to lie about such a thing.

But then, who had been buried there under the stone angel?

It was still spitting rain after lunch, and Georgia found her toes curling restlessly in her shoes, her gaze being pulled toward the forest.

It had been two whole days since she'd last visited the wishing lake. Two days since she'd seen Angela. She felt an ache of missing in her chest when she thought of her friend.

And she needed to ask her about Cole. Had he returned to the lake, looking for her? And just who *was* he?

Suddenly, the country house felt so crowded with secrets there was barely room to move without knocking into one.

That night, Georgia said she had a stomachache and went to bed early.

It was too hard, sitting across the table from Aunt Marigold when Georgia was still thinking about the past and how her great-aunt seemed to have lived through so much. Two different lives, even. The one that came before her father got sick and the one that came after.

How somewhere along the way, whether all at once or a bit at a time, her heart had been broken, and no one had ever come along to mend it.

She wondered if there had ever been a time—a moment, even—when everything had turned sour. If there was ever a way it all might have gone differently.

She heard Angela's voice in her head. *I just think maybe some things are too big to only wish for. If you want them to change, you have to really do something, you know?*

Finally, she sat down at the desk and pulled out the pile of unfinished letters she had hidden away in the top drawer.

Dear Daddy,

First of all, I want you to know . . .

No, that wasn't right.

There are some things I have to tell you. . . .

That wasn't it either.

Remember when we used to read together every night?

She looked at the picture she'd placed on the desk. The one of Mama and Daddy on the beach on Tybee Island, wind whipping their hair and sun reflected in their eyes. Mama's smile not tired, Daddy's smile not forced.

She felt for the nickel in her pocket, and thought of him, that same smile on his face, producing the coin from nowhere, like magic.

How could she put that smile—the hole it had left behind—into words?

A sharp *thwack* startled Georgia back to the moment. She looked around, slightly dazed, to see where the noise had come from. Nothing was amiss or out of place in the room. Downstairs, all was quiet. Aunt Marigold must have gone to bed while Georgia had been lost in her thoughts.

Thwack!

This time, Georgia's head snapped toward the window. She was almost sure something had struck it. Cautiously, she inched over to it and peered through.

But there was no one there.

Chapter Thirty-two

Georgia didn't dare to breathe as she snuck across the hall, downstairs, and pushed open a window to climb out of, since she knew the screen door would screech louder than a banshee. Now she stood outside staring into the shadows, feeling dizzy with her own daring. At least the rain had finally stopped.

"Hello?" she whispered.

Still, there was no one there.

But Georgia had been so sure of the sound of a stone hitting the window. She looked toward the trees. It was a moonless night. It would be even darker in the forest.

Yet something seemed to be tugging her toward the trees. The lake.

Taking a deep breath, she made her decision. She rifled through the tool bag Hank had left on the porch until she found what she was looking for. Then she ran swiftly through the field, the tall grasses seeming to whisper *hush, hush, hush* as her knobbly knees brushed against them.

When she reached the cover of the trees, she slowed her pace and turned on Hank's flashlight. Even with its light, she had to move carefully through the dark forest. High above, katydids crackled, making the air feel alive, and an owl let out a low mournful hoot. The sound sent a shiver down Georgia's spine.

To keep from feeling afraid, she hummed a tune under her breath. "Georgia on My Mind." The one Daddy used to sing to her.

Georgia—
A song of you
Comes as sweet and clear
As moonlight through the pines . . .

But even as she sang, she wondered if she'd made a mistake in coming. What if she lost her way in the dark? Walked right into a bear? Or perhaps there were ghosts that wandered these woods at night. . . .

She would have given anything for a bit of moonlight shining through the pines just then.

Finally, she saw the shape of a great oak tree up ahead and burst into a run. Soon she was standing by the dark pool of the wishing lake. It was so much different at night—even stiller than it usually was. Like a theater after the play is over and the audience has left for the evening.

"Hello?" she called again.

But there was no answer. Perhaps she had imagined the sound back at the house. Or it had been a bird flying into the window.

Feeling more silly now than scared, Georgia turned to go.

Then, "Georgia?" she heard a soft voice call.

She whirled around. "Angela?"

A second later, Angela's figure materialized from the shadows. She wore a shaky smile. "So it is you."

Georgia frowned. "Did you throw something at my window?"

Angela's eyebrows shot up, and she shook her head. "No," she said. "But I saw a flashlight headed toward the lake, and I thought it might be you. I came as fast as I could."

It took Georgia a moment to realize that Angela didn't seem like her usual self. She was breathless and wide-eyed. "We have to talk," she said.

"I wanted to talk to you, too," said Georgia. "About—"

"Cole," Angela finished. "I know."

"So you *do* know him."

Angela nodded.

Georgia felt a strange stab of jealousy, which she ignored.

Angela was allowed to know other people, after all. "Who is he?"

Angela let out a sigh and sank down into the sand, pulling her knees up to her chin. Georgia sat down facing her.

"He's, well, visiting," said Angela. "Staying for the summer. That's why I came when I saw your flashlight. I needed to find a way to get to you without him following me. So I could explain."

Georgia remembered the second child she'd seen in the window of Angela's house. The boy. It must have been Cole.

So all this time, Angela *had* been keeping a secret.

"Why didn't you mention him before?"

Angela's shoulders curled inward. "I didn't want to talk about him," she said quietly. "He's—he's *trouble*, Georgia. That's why he's here for the summer."

"You mean his family sent him here? And what do you mean, 'trouble'?"

Angela stared through the murky darkness at Georgia. "You couldn't tell when you met him?"

Georgia thought of the boy she'd met in the clearing. The dirt on his cheeks. The wild eyes. The way he'd been following her. There *was* something troubling about him.

Don't you want to use it for more than just make-believe?

"He knows about the lake," Georgia said. "He made me say I'd teach him about the magic."

203

"That's what I was afraid of," said Angela.

"What do you mean?"

"This magic," explained Angela, her eyes flicking toward the water, "it's powerful. We've seen that. Who knows what more it can do? In the wrong hands it could be—"

"Dangerous," Georgia finished, shivering.

She wished Angela would tell her more about Cole. Where he'd come from and what she meant by "trouble." He must be a cousin if he'd been sent to stay with Angela for the summer. Maybe he had something to do with why Angela never seemed to want to talk about her own family.

But she knew Angela was right about the magic. It was a responsibility. They were the wishing lake's guardians now. And if Angela didn't trust Cole, then neither did Georgia.

"That's why we'll have to be really careful around him," Angela said.

"You mean you're going to bring him here?"

Angela sighed. "What choice do I have? He knows about the lake now. I can't keep him away forever. At least if I bring him, we can keep an eye on him."

Georgia glanced around again. It had suddenly occurred to her that Cole could have been the one to throw the stone at her window. Could be here, watching them, right now.

As if reading her mind, Angela said, "Don't worry. I checked before I left to make sure he was asleep."

Georgia nodded, relieved. So she'd imagined the sound

after all. She reached across the sand for Angela's hand and squeezed it. "Don't worry," she said, trying to sound more confident than she felt. "We won't let him ruin it. It'll be two against one."

Angela squeezed right back, a small smile reappearing on her face. "Thanks, Georgia."

"We won't show him the magic. Not right away. You can bring him here, but we'll make him wait until we can trust him or—"

But what was the other choice? Never use the magic again?

The thought went through Georgia like an arrow, quickly followed by another. Would this be her and Angela's last time alone together at the lake? From now on, would Cole always be there, too, skulking in the shadows?

If this *was* the last time it would be just her and Angela, she didn't want it to be like this. The two of them huddled together in the dark, afraid.

She heard Daddy's voice in her head. *How about a little adventure?*

"Do you think the magic will work now?" she asked. "At night, I mean?"

Angela tilted her head in thought. "I don't know. Why? Do you have a wish you want to make?"

Georgia nodded. It had come to her, just then, staring out at the dark water. "We're already here, aren't we?"

"Then what are we waiting for?" said Angela. "Let's go."

"Race you," challenged Georgia, mustering a grin.

"You're on."

Their feet swept soundlessly across the sterling sand, and their palms slapped the shining wood of the boat at the exact same moment.

"Tie," they said together, laughing as they tilted the boat to one side. They pushed it easily into the water, leaving their troubles on the shore behind them.

As they rowed, Georgia told Angela what Hank had said about magic—how it finds you for a reason.

"I think he's right," she said. "Out of all the people in the world, *we* found this lake. There must be a reason. I just don't know what it is. Maybe there's a certain wish we're supposed to make?"

"May-be," Angela said slowly. "But maybe—"

"What?"

"It might be stupid, but—" Angela's voice was suddenly quiet again. Almost shy. "Maybe the lake wanted to bring us together. So we could be friends. This summer would be awful without you. Empty, you know?"

Georgia considered this. Could the answer be so simple? Did she *want* it to be?

"Yeah," she said. "But I would have been your friend even if there was no magic."

"Same here."

When the nose of the boat slid onto the pebbly island, Georgia wasted no time climbing out and finding a smooth pebble to cradle in her hands. It was round and silver, which felt right. She knew what she wanted to wish for, but she had no idea what was about to happen. "Ready?"

"Ready," Angela replied.

This time, Georgia didn't shut her eyes. She looked up instead. She thought of Daddy's face, silhouetted against the night sky all those years ago as he'd spun her in his arms.

"I wish for the moon," she whispered simply.

Then she flicked the pebble from her hands, watching as it winked through the air and across the water. She thought she heard Angela give a little gasp, but didn't turn around to see.

She looked up again, staring at the sky, willing something to happen.

But the dark sky was unmoved. She glanced down at the water, looking for a change in the reflection. It was so dark she could barely make out any reflection at all.

Then there was a small gurgling sound, and Angela gave another gasp. "Look!" she said, pointing a few feet out into the lake, where the water had started to bubble.

Suddenly, something appeared from the center of the bubbles. Then the water went still as the thing bobbed upon its surface. Georgia waded a few steps out and leaned down to examine it.

"It's a rope," she said.

"Grab it!"

Georgia took hold of it and began to pull. It wasn't a single rope, she saw, but a rope ladder, sturdy and oddly dry. Whatever was on the other end must not be very heavy, because it wasn't hard to pull. She tugged it back to shore with her and kept going, threading it through her palms.

"This must be the longest ladder in the world," she said.

Then she saw it. Wavering beneath the water. A glowing orb of light that rose a bit higher from the depths of the lake with every pull, like a pearl floating toward the surface.

"It's getting bigger," Angela whispered.

"And brighter," Georgia said, squinting as the orb began to shimmer a dazzling silver. It grew to the size of a dinner plate, then a tire, then a paddling pool. As it continued to grow, the whole lake seemed to sparkle.

When it was nearly to the surface, the orb became suddenly heavier. Angela came to help Georgia pull. Working together, they heaved the rope back until the orb of light broke free from the lake.

And then suddenly it was floating into the sky, the rope ladder uncoiling behind it like a giant kite string. Georgia realized what was about to happen just as her toes left the ground. Her heart leaped into her throat.

"Hold on to the ladder!" she cried to Angela as she was swept off the ground. "And climb!"

The ladder was surprisingly steady. She began to climb and, after a moment, felt Angela start up behind her.

Presently, she made out a shape above her, and saw that the ladder led up to an enormous silver basket that looked as though it had been woven from rays of silver light. Breathlessly, she lifted herself into the basket, then extended a hand to help Angela in, too.

The basket was hung from the orb above, connected by thin strands of silver, as if they were riding in a hot-air balloon.

But they weren't. They were suspended from the glowing full moon.

The girls gripped hands as they climbed to their feet and looked down over the edge of the basket. Below them, the wizard tree shrank to the size of a weed.

Georgia should have been afraid, and yet she wasn't.

"Angela," she said, lifting her chin, "look up."

Above them, the clouds had cleared to reveal stars like lanterns carried by invisible travelers. They winked and flared at one another in their own secret language of light.

"Wow," Angela breathed.

The basket bobbed up and down, as if the moon were chuckling at their amazement.

They moved in slow circles that spiraled higher and higher—but always stayed above the lake—until the air grew chilly and little bursts of clouds appeared around them. They ran their fingers through the clouds, trying to catch hold of them, but when they opened their palms, it was to find nothing there.

Georgia closed her eyes. She imagined Daddy standing beside her in the basket, reaching over to wrap his arm around her shoulders. *See*, he would say, *I told you I'd give you the moon.*

She felt a new delicate hope unfold inside her. She had known the lake was magic, of course, but *this*—this was a miracle, wasn't it? Daddy's promise coming true.

Maybe the lake hadn't been able to return Daddy to her, but that didn't mean he couldn't come back.

I'm not giving up on you, Daddy, she said without saying anything at all.

When she opened her eyes, he was gone, but the hope was still there. Exquisite and fine, like a single burning star plucked from the sky.

They had begun to descend again, back through the clouds toward earth. On the way down, the girls gazed out at the countryside that unfurled in every direction. Here and there, the land was dotted with light, but mostly it was miles of trees and fields painted silver by the very same moon that carried them.

The basket came to land just where the island's shore met the lake, and Georgia and Angela jumped onto the pebbly beach just in time to watch it drift over the water and disappear below the surface. In another moment, the moon followed, too, bowing to them as it sank peacefully into the lake.

The girls didn't move. They held hands and watched as it shrank in size, until it was no bigger than a pea.

Later—once she and Angela had rowed back to the shore and Georgia had stolen back in through the still-open window—Georgia sat at the desk once more. As though she had never left it.

Except now, it was bathed in the moonlight that had broken through the clouds as Georgia made her way back through the forest. And this time, she finally had the words to begin her letter.

Dear Daddy,
A long time ago, you promised you would do any-thing for me, even give me the moon. I don't need the moon anymore, Daddy.
But I do need you to keep your promise.

Chapter Thirty-three

~~~

When she woke up the next day, Georgia couldn't quite be sure the night before hadn't all been a dream. Yet all morning, while she and Hank began rebuilding Ruby's cowshed in the fiery sun, she could still feel the hope that shone like a star. That hope hadn't been there before last night. Of that, she *was* sure.

But it wasn't until she arrived at the lake that afternoon, breathless from running, to see two figures standing together on the banks of the lake, that she really believed it had all happened.

It was Angela and Cole. And if Cole was there, that meant the conversation she'd had with Angela about him must have happened, which meant the rest of it must have, too.

He looked up, seeing her before Angela did. Something

flashed briefly through his eyes, but it might have just been the reflection of the light dancing on the lake. Otherwise, his expression stayed blank.

Then Angela turned, too, and caught sight of her. She shot Georgia a meaningful look—*remember what I said last night*—and Georgia gave a small nod.

"Hi, Cole," she said as she approached, standing shoulder-to-shoulder with Angela.

"Hi," he replied, in a quiet voice that was almost bashful, as if maybe he regretted their encounter in the woods before.

"I already told him that we weren't ready to show him how the magic works," Angela said. "Right, Cole?"

"Yeah," he said flatly, sweeping his black hair from his eyes. "Okay."

Georgia felt her eyebrows arch up. Could it really be so easy? This boy seemed much different than the one she'd met in the woods. *Tamer.*

"So, what should we do?" Angela said, sounding relieved that Cole wasn't going to put up a fight.

Georgia squinted at the sun. Her skin glistened with sweat. "Let's swim."

For the first time, three of them packed into the boat. Cole didn't offer to help guide them into the lake or to help row. Not that Georgia minded. She'd rather do it herself. He sat on the prow, lying back in the sun with his eyes closed, like a lizard. As Georgia rowed, he hummed a tune, drumming his fingers through the air again like she'd seen him do before. As though he were bored.

When Georgia thought they'd rowed far enough, she pulled the dripping oars into the boat. "Ready?" she asked Angela.

Angela gave her a thumbs-up before shimmying out of her shorts. "Coming?" she asked Cole hesitantly.

"In a bit," he said, not opening his eyes.

She shrugged at Angela. Together, they jumped from the boat and into the cool water. It felt wonderfully clean against Georgia's sticky skin.

"Come on," Angela said when they surfaced, kicking away from the boat.

Georgia followed. When they had gotten far enough away that they could talk without Cole overhearing, they began to tread water.

"Was he mad when you told him no magic?" Georgia asked.

"I guess he seemed okay," Angela said, her head bobbing slightly as her legs kicked underwater. "But he doesn't like to talk a lot. So it was kind of hard to tell."

Georgia glanced back toward the boat, which was turning in slow circles while Cole stayed still as a wooden figure-head. "What kind of trouble did he get in, exactly? Did your parents tell you?"

Today, Angela's eyes were the same shade of blue as the

lake, like they were little wreaths of water. She shook her head. "I just know I have to be careful around him. *We* have to be careful."

Georgia knew there was something Angela still wasn't telling her.

"Speaking of parents," said Angela, kicking her toes up to float on her back, "did you decide to write a letter to your dad?"

Georgia nodded. Angela was changing the subject again, but Georgia wanted to tell her about the letter. "I wrote it last night," she said. "Part of it, at least. I finally think I know what I want to say."

Angela beamed. There was nothing hiding behind her smile. "That's great, Georgia," she said. "I bet it will make a difference."

"You really think so?"

"I think standing up for yourself always makes a difference," said Angela softly. "I really hope it works."

"Me, too."

A loud splash made them turn, just in time to see Cole's head disappearing into the water. From the size of the splash, Georgia guessed he had cannonballed off the boat. When he emerged, he was grinning.

"Anyone want to race?" he asked. "Around the pond and back to the boat?"

Georgia and Angela glanced at each other—both,

Georgia thought, annoyed that Cole had called the wishing lake a *pond*. But at least he wanted to do something. It was starting to creep Georgia out, the way he had lain so silent and still on the boat, leaving them no hints about what he might be thinking.

"Okay," Angela said. "Sure."

Cole counted to three, and then they each set off, their palms and feet slapping against the water. At first, it felt good and easy, the water smooth as air. Georgia was used to swimming like this—they swam races all the time at Camp Pine Valley.

But halfway around the lake, she felt a cramp bite in her side. She thought of the second helping of strawberry pie she'd had at lunch and wished that she'd skipped it. She wasn't sure she could make it all the way to the boat, but the island was only a few strokes away. Turning course, she made for the pebbly shore. She would stop and rest there until the cramp was gone.

"Are you okay?"

She turned to find Cole swimming beside her. Angela was still swimming up ahead.

"I'm fine. Just a cramp."

"I'll swim with you to the island," Cole said. "Angela can bring the boat over."

"Oh. Um, okay."

Together, they swam the last few strokes until they

could stand. Then they waded out of the water. Once he was standing on the rocks, Cole shook his whole scrawny body like a wet dog, sending droplets of lake water everywhere.

"Well, thanks," Georgia said, "for coming with me."

"Sure thing," Cole replied. They began to pick their way around the island. Cole peered up at the wizard tree, plucked one of its leaves and examined it.

"So, um, Angela says you're staying for the summer?" Georgia asked.

"I bet that's not all she said about me, is it?"

"She just said that your parents sent you—maybe you had gotten in some kind of trouble. That's all."

To her surprise, Cole's face broke into an easy smile. "Angela," he said, "doesn't know anything about *trouble*."

It felt wrong, talking to Cole about Angela when she wasn't here. But Georgia couldn't help herself. "What do you mean?"

"I heard her just now, giving you some kind of advice about your dad," he said. "But she doesn't know much about family either. At least, not *our* kind of family."

"*Our* kind?" Georgia asked.

"You know, the kind that teaches you about trouble."

Georgia didn't like the way this conversation was going. As if their families were one and the same. "You—don't get along with your family?" she asked.

217

Cole snorted. "Well, I'm here, aren't I? Not for long, though."

Before Georgia had the chance to ask him what he meant, she saw Angela had finally reached the boat and was looking around, confused.

"Over here!" Georgia called, waving her arms.

"What happened?" Angela called back.

"Just a cramp," Georgia said, waving a hand dismissively. "Row the boat over?"

Angela clambered up into the boat and began to cut through the water toward them.

"Why have you been following me?" Georgia asked suddenly. "I know the other day wasn't the first time. I've felt you there even when I couldn't see you. Why didn't you just come out and talk to me?"

Cole took a last look at the dove-white leaf in his hand before dropping it into the water. "I was curious about you," he said. "But I like sticking to the shadows. You see things differently from there, you know. You see people for who they really are."

Georgia suppressed a shiver. She couldn't bring herself to ask what Cole had seen when he'd looked at her.

"All I'm saying," Cole went on, his voice suddenly soft—kind, even—"is be careful who you trust, Georgia."

Then he began to whistle a tune, leaving Georgia to wonder who Cole was talking about—Daddy? Or Angela?

Chapter Thirty-four

W hen Georgia got home that afternoon, Aunt Marigold was on the phone with Mama. She wanted to know if Georgia would mind staying at Aunt Marigold's that weekend.

"It's just I've got an essay due on Monday," she said, "and I could really use some extra writing time."

Her voice was calm and easy. Georgia decided to believe her. She needed more time to finish her letter to Daddy, anyway. And to keep an eye on Cole with Angela. And to help Aunt Marigold with meals and chores. And besides all that . . . she *wanted* to stay. So she did.

Georgia did her best to tuck Cole's warning away in the days that followed, like a test she'd gotten a bad grade on and needed to hide from Mama.

And for the most part, she succeeded.

It seemed like Hank was coming around more and more, which meant that Georgia was kept busy in the mornings with painting and fixing and building things. She had even started to wonder if one day he might simply *stay*. Then she could come and listen to his stories and play cards with him whenever she wanted.

And, best of all, she wouldn't have to worry about Aunt Marigold. Hank would be there with his gentle hands to do what hers could not. He would be there to keep her from being lonely.

Most days, Aunt Marigold called Georgia in before lunch to teach her something new in the pottery studio. How to shape different objects on the wheel, to carve decorations into them, to fire and glaze.

Georgia had never before known such satisfaction from creating things. From standing back and admiring a humble cowshed or watching a mug be lifted from a kiln.

But then again, perhaps satisfaction wasn't the right word, for she couldn't get enough of the feeling. It was as if a flame had been lit inside her that kept her feeling warm and bright, but the fire was hungry. To keep it burning, she had to stoke it, had to keep going. Keep imagining new things to create.

At lunchtime, Georgia and Aunt Marigold hung up their aprons, washed the clay from under their nails, and went to the kitchen. Georgia had watched Aunt Marigold enough now to know when her hands were bothering her, knew how to take over the cutting or stirring or serving without making a fuss of things. Most times, Aunt Marigold would hand over the task without a word, unless it was to correct Georgia's technique.

And this, too, gave Georgia a quiet satisfaction.

After lunch, while Aunt Marigold and Hank sank into the rocking chairs on the front porch, Georgia disappeared into the forest. Her lungs filled with the wind she created as she ran, her eyes turning green in the mossy light.

Angela and Cole were always waiting there for her.

The three of them spent their afternoons rowing, swimming, and searching the banks for frogs. They made two fishing rods out of long sticks and twine and took turns with them—two of them fishing while the other searched for worms. They didn't catch much, except once a little trout, which they threw back right away.

"I think that was my favorite part," Angela confided to Georgia. "Sending it back home."

Even though they weren't making any wishes, Georgia never looked forward to her afternoons any less.

Cole didn't try to talk to Georgia on her own again that week. Didn't talk much at all, unless it was to challenge them to another race or a competition to see who could jump farthest from the side of the boat. Just when they were running out of things to do, he always seemed to have another idea. And usually, it was a fun one. Even Angela laughed when they tried to teach themselves underwater headstands, though she protested the idea of jumping into the water from the branches of the wizard tree.

Sometimes, Georgia found herself forgetting all about Angela's warnings, like when Cole helped string the bait for her or gave her a leg up into the oak tree he liked to climb. Or when he whistled a cheerful tune and she felt her foot tap instinctively against the ground. Or when—every once in a while—he would flash a smile if they found a particularly big frog. Then the air would seem to shimmer around him for an instant, and Georgia would find herself smiling back.

Those times, Georgia wondered if Angela had gotten it wrong somehow. If Cole was just misunderstood.

But other times, Cole would remain on the boat by himself, and Georgia would catch him glancing out toward the island or flexing his fingers, a brooding expression on his face. He never said a word about wanting them to show him the magic. Was he being patient or just biding his time? Did he want the magic for something in particular, or did he just want a piece of it for himself?

Georgia would start to think then about what he'd said when they had been alone together. *I'm here, aren't I? Not for long, though.* What had he meant by that?

Then Angela would call her name or splash water her way, always with the same warm smile, the delighted laugh, and Georgia's worries would break apart like a school of startled minnows.

On Thursday afternoon, when it was time to go back to Aunt Marigold's, Angela wrapped Georgia in a tight embrace.

"Good luck this weekend," she whispered in Georgia's ear. "Be strong. Whatever happens, I'll be here for you. Everything will be okay."

Cole raised his eyebrow at her over Angela's shoulder. Georgia didn't like the look on his face, like he knew something she didn't.

"Remember," he mouthed. "What I said."

Be careful who you trust.

Georgia looked quickly away. Of course she could trust Angela, Georgia thought. And if Angela said her letter would work, then it would.

Besides, she was ready.

She had her vase, her mug, and her finished letter lined up on her desk, ready to be packed into her little bag.

She had her silver nickel and her hope, twin treasures hidden safely away for the journey home.

Chapter Thirty-five

The next morning, Georgia was pulling carrots in the garden, up to her elbows in dirt, when she heard Mama's car coming down the drive. Her heart skipped in her chest as she ran in to wash up and get her things.

Aunt Marigold had packed up the vase and the mug for Georgia, wrapped them tightly in butcher's paper so they wouldn't break before she got them home. When it was time to go, she pressed them into Georgia's hands. Then, suddenly, she reached out and brushed her hand against Georgia's cheek.

"You take care now," she said. "I'll see you on Sunday."

Georgia wanted to ask if she would be okay all by herself for the weekend. But she didn't. Forced herself not to look back to see her aunt standing alone on the front porch as she and Mama drove off.

"How was your time with Aunt Marigold?" Mama asked over the sound of the wind whipping in through the windows as they picked up speed.

Georgia didn't know what to say. How could she fit those weeks into words? Anyone who had ever been to summer camp knew you could fit a whole life into two weeks, and that's how these last weeks had felt.

"It was good," she said, for there was no way to really explain it.

"I've missed you," Mama said. "A lot. I didn't want you to be away so long. It's just—"

"I know. Your essay."

Mama hesitated. "Yes," she said. "But also . . . I needed the time to talk things over with your father. Just like I told you I would. I told him it has to stop, Georgia."

Georgia turned away from the trees and fields flying by in flashes of amber and green and looked at Mama. "You did?"

"I did."

"What did he say?"

"He knows it's wrong. Acting the way—well, the way he's been acting. He knows. And he hasn't had a drink all week." She glanced at Georgia for a moment. "I think he means it this time."

Georgia should have been happy, she knew. Instead, she thought about the words *this time.* She traced them against her thigh with her finger.

This time meant it wasn't the first time Mama had talked to Daddy. Told him to stop drinking.

How many times had there been? How many of the arguments Georgia had heard from her bed late at night had been Mama asking, pleading, demanding for it to stop?

How long had Mama been fighting for Daddy to change while Georgia had just been wishing for it?

"Georgia? Did you hear what I said?"

"Yes, Mama."

"You'll see," said Mama, nodding to herself over the steering wheel. "Things are going to be all right now."

They sat in silence for a few minutes, and then Mama gestured to a new set of flash cards in her purse. "Want to quiz me?" she asked. "I have an exam for another class next Monday."

Georgia agreed. Like usual, she stumbled through the long words on the cards.

But unlike usual, Mama stumbled through the answers, too. She sighed and clicked her tongue at her own ignorance, mumbling things like, "I should know this one."

Georgia tried not to wince at the wrong answers. Mama's degree meant everything to her. That's why she usually knew almost all of the answers before she was ever quizzed on them. The thought that she might not come in at the top of her class, that she might not pass the program at all, had never occurred to Georgia. Not until now, at least.

"You know what?" Mama said when they'd gotten only halfway through the thick stack. "Let's stop there for now. I didn't get enough sleep last night, and I think my brain's still a little foggy. Turn on the radio, okay? Whatever station you want."

And so they spent the last half of the ride listening, neither of them talking. But every so often, Georgia stole a glance over at her mother. For the first time, she saw a woman instead of just Mama. A woman who was struggling to keep her life together, just like Georgia was.

Whose heart was breaking, too.

Like usual, Daddy was still at work when they arrived home.

Mama pushed the door open, and Georgia looked around at all the familiar things. The table lamps, the thread-bare rug, the painting on the wall that was always slightly crooked.

But Georgia couldn't help thinking that something felt wrong. Like when she came out of the movies and could tell right away there had been a storm while she was in the theater, just by the way the air hung heavy around her.

"You go unpack, and I'll make you a sandwich," Mama said. "You can eat in front of the TV. I clearly have some studying to do."

When Georgia was done with her sandwich and tired of TV, she went to her room and tried to read. But she couldn't concentrate. After a while, she closed her book and went outside to sit on the front steps.

The afternoon pavement was hot against her thighs. She could see a group of neighborhood kids gathering down the block, in the Molinas' yard, probably about to start a game of tag. She could have gone and joined in, but she didn't. She squinted up at the sky and wondered what Angela was doing at that very moment. She wished her friend could be there with her. She would know how to make Georgia feel brave, sitting here waiting for Daddy's car to pull up.

Which, presently, it did.

Chapter Thirty-six

Daddy didn't spot Georgia right away when he got out of the car. Unobserved, she watched the way he drew his briefcase from the front seat and closed the door wearily.

Only then did he see her. A dim smile flickered onto his face, like a flashlight nearly out of batteries.

"There she is," he said, setting his briefcase down and opening his arms. The desire to bury herself in his embrace was so powerful, it was all she could do to force herself to slowly close the distance between them.

He wrapped his arms around her but not as tight as usual. And he didn't hold her as long. He let her go and put his hands on her shoulders instead.

"Listen, sweetheart. I'm—I'm real sorry about last weekend." His own shoulders slumped; his eyes were dull. No moonlight sparkled from them. "I got a little carried away."

"It's okay, Daddy," Georgia said, even though it wasn't. Even though she was thinking of the words she'd written in the letter still stowed in her suitcase. *I know you haven't been happy, Daddy, but neither have I . . . not in a long time.*

He squeezed her shoulder. "That's my girl. Let's get inside. It's sweltering out here."

Inside, Mama was setting the table for dinner. "There you are," she said when the door opened. "I was wondering where you— Oh."

Her face pinched together when she spotted Daddy and then quickly rearranged itself. "Well, you're both just in time for dinner."

Dinner was the roast chicken they were supposed to eat two weeks before. They sat around the table, passing the salt and pepper, knives clinking against plates, just like old times.

Except that it wasn't. It wasn't anything like old times, when Daddy cracked jokes to make Georgia laugh and Mama slapped his hand but didn't really mean it. When he declared that Mama was the best cook in the world, especially on nights when she'd burned the food.

"Isn't that right, Georgia?" he asked with a wink. And Georgia always agreed.

Tonight, Mama and Daddy didn't speak to each other at all. Mama asked Georgia questions about her time in the country, and Georgia tried to answer them. But it was hard when she couldn't tell them about the lake or Angela, didn't want to spoil the surprises she'd brought them by telling them about her pottery lessons.

Sometimes Daddy would muster a smile at something Georgia said, or ask a question. But mostly, he didn't smile or say anything. And when he did smile, it wasn't *his* smile. His voice wasn't Daddy's voice.

It wasn't the Shadow Man's. But it wasn't Daddy's either.

When Georgia didn't think she could bear it any longer, she said she was tired and asked to be excused.

"Of course," said Mama. "Are you feeling all right?"

"I'm fine," Georgia said.

"Okay. Sleep tight, then."

"Good night, sweetheart," Daddy said, making one last attempt at a smile.

"Good night," Georgia said.

Back in her bedroom, she climbed into bed and pulled the covers around her chin. She tried to hold fast to the hope she had carried home with her, to not sink into the dark thicket of dread that was growing again in her belly.

For hours, she lay there, listening. Waiting. But there was only the occasional creaking of floorboards.

And silence. The kind of silence that rang through your ears and set your teeth on edge.

The kind that didn't belong in a house that had once been filled with laughter and music.

Chapter Thirty-seven

The next day, Georgia had a lot of time to think.

Mama went to the library in the morning to study and write a paper. Daddy said he had someone to meet in the morning, and then stayed in his study with the door closed all afternoon, talking on the phone in a low voice. Georgia wandered around the house, switching the TV on and off, opening and shutting books.

The other kids from her block were out playing again, riding their bikes up and down the sidewalks. But how could she face them after what Mr. Molina had seen earlier in the summer? And who knew who else might have looked out their window that morning to see Daddy being dragged from his car? The whole street probably knew by now.

Georgia couldn't face them, but she also didn't want to be alone. She didn't know how Aunt Marigold could bear it so much of the time. Her own thoughts kept running in circles.

Why did everything feel so wrong? It was a good thing, wasn't it, Daddy not drinking? It was what she'd been wishing for.

Except it wasn't. When Georgia had thrown her stone across the water earlier this summer, she had wished for things to go back to *normal*. Normal meant Daddy not drinking so much. But it didn't mean this.

All day, she kept folding and unfolding the letter she'd written. If he was really done drinking, was there any point in giving it to him? Would it only make him feel even worse?

She knew what Angela would say. Angela would tell her to give him the letter anyway. To tell him how she felt.

I think standing up for yourself always makes a difference, she had said.

Georgia folded the letter, tucked it into her drawer.

She was relieved when Mama came home with groceries for dinner, and there was finally something to do. Something to make.

Mama seemed surprised when Georgia asked to help her make the lasagna. Even more surprised when she watched Georgia cut up the onions and dice the garlic and sauté them in the pan the way Aunt Marigold had taught her to.

"When did you learn to cook?" she asked, hands on her hips.

"Aunt Marigold taught me," Georgia replied. "She needs help sometimes, because of her hands."

Mama wrapped an arm around Georgia's shoulders and dropped a kiss atop her head. "How thoughtful of you," she said. "And lucky for me."

Only when the lasagna was bubbled nearly to perfection and Georgia and Mama were putting the finishing touches on the salad and garlic bread did Daddy emerge from the study.

"Mmmm," he said, breathing in. "Something smells delicious."

Georgia's heart flooded with relief when she saw him smile. It was a real smile, the kind that lit her up with happiness inside. As he passed Georgia, he ruffled her hair. She couldn't remember the last time he'd done that.

"Did *you* make this?" he asked her.

"Me and Mama."

"My two girls," Daddy mused. "How lucky am I, hmm?"

Georgia grinned but not Mama. Mama didn't look relieved. She was watching Daddy like he was a bear that had blundered in through an open window.

Georgia didn't understand it. She couldn't smell anything on Daddy's breath. There was no sway in his step. He hadn't been drinking. So why was Mama looking at him that way?

"Mama," Georgia muttered. "The lasagna."

Mama seemed to come back to her senses and went to

the oven to take the lasagna out while Georgia laid the table. Daddy was already sitting down, drumming his fingers against the table and humming something under his breath.

When Georgia sat down across from him, she realized what it was.

Georgia on my mind . . .

"Did I ever tell you," he asked as Mama set the steaming lasagna down on the table, "about our honeymoon?"

"She's heard it a thousand times," Mama said flatly.

"I don't mind," Georgia said quickly. "I like to hear about it."

"How our picnic on the beach was interrupted by wild ponies, and we ended up feeding them our sandwiches, remember?" Daddy said, looking at Mama. "How every morning we got up at dawn to see the sunrise, and how the beach was covered in the most beautiful shells you ever saw?"

"And every night you'd fall asleep listening to the waves outside your window," Georgia added.

Mama was concentrating hard on slicing and serving the lasagna.

"That's right," said Daddy, nodding. "And on our very last morning there, we decided that island was about as close to heaven as a person could get. Until we met you, that is."

"And that's why you named me Georgia," Georgia finished. "Because I reminded you of that island."

"Because you were a little piece of heaven, too. Right, Amelia?"

"Right," said Mama, staring down at her plate.

Georgia's cheeks hurt from the span of her smile. She didn't understand why Mama didn't seem happy, too. This was not the hollowed-out Daddy from yesterday. This was *her* Daddy. Still here after all.

"Best lasagna I've ever tasted," he said after wolfing down an enormous bite. He glanced at something behind Georgia.

"Aunt Marigold's been teaching me to cook," Georgia said. "Succotash and corn bread and pies and biscuits. I can help with dinner from now on so Mama can study more."

"How did that happen, huh?" Daddy said after another huge bite. "You growing up so fast?" He glanced over Georgia's shoulder again. She looked back but didn't see anything out of the ordinary.

"We'll have to have Marigold come for dinner sometime," Daddy said. "Say thank you for having you there this summer."

After that, Daddy ate as though he'd been half-starved. When he was done, he let his fork drop to his plate with a loud clatter.

"Delicious," he said, once again glancing up behind Georgia. "Absolutely delicious. Ah, I just remembered—"

Mama looked up sharply. "Remembered what?"

"I've got a set tonight I shouldn't be late for," said Daddy, his eyes darting back and forth from the space beside Mama to the space beside Georgia. Not looking at either of them.

The kitchen clock behind Georgia ticked out the silent seconds. She realized with a blow that that's what Daddy must have been looking at over her shoulder.

Counting the minutes. The seconds. Until he could leave again.

Her stomach fell deeper with every tick.

When Mama spoke again, her voice had turned to steel. "You promised," she said. "You said you were taking a break."

"And I am," Daddy said, raising his palms innocently. "I am, Amelia. But it was too late to cancel tonight. It's just one little set, and then I'll be home. By ten. Ten thirty at the latest. All right?"

Mama threw her napkin on her plate and shook her head. "I knew it," she muttered.

"Please, sweetheart," Daddy said, pushing his chair back and standing. "Please understand. It's not like— I won't— I'll be on my best behavior."

Mama opened her mouth, but before she could say anything, Georgia heard herself speak. Mama wasn't the only one who could stand up for herself. "Do you promise?"

Daddy turned to look at her. "Promise?" he echoed.

She curled her fingers into fists to try to keep her voice from shaking. "Do you promise you'll be back by ten thirty? And you won't—you won't drink?"

It was the first time she had ever mentioned Daddy's drinking out loud to him. He went a shade paler before he answered.

"I promise, Georgia," he said. "Okay? I promise."

Chapter Thirty-eight

~

Georgia had thought that Mama would need to study more after dinner, but instead she asked Georgia if she wanted to watch a movie. So they sat together on the couch in the flickering television glow as twilight gave way to night.

Mama sat close to Georgia, her arm wrapped tightly around her the whole time. Now it was them watching the clock, counting the seconds. Ten o'clock came and went.

Ten thirty crept closer and closer.

The thorns in Georgia's belly grew sharper and sharper.

"Georgia," Mama said softly as the credits rolled. It was 10:28.

"He's going to come, Mama. He promised."

Ten thirty came and went, and there was no sign of Daddy.

Mama drew Georgia even closer. "I'm so sorry, sweetheart," she whispered, voice catching in her throat. "I thought it would be different this time."

Had Daddy just been putting on another show at dinner? Was that why Mama hadn't laughed or smiled at anything he said? Because she saw through the act?

Georgia refused to believe it. Not yet.

"He could still come," she said. "He could have gotten a flat tire."

So they waited, frozen together on the couch, as the minutes passed.

When the clock chimed eleven, Mama slowly unfolded herself from around Georgia. "That's enough now," she said. "Time for bed."

Georgia stayed in place for one more minute—*please, Daddy*—before nodding.

Mama tucked her in like she was a little girl again and even offered to read with her. Georgia shook her head. It was nice of Mama to offer, but reading before bed was something she and Daddy did together. It wouldn't be the same with anyone else.

As soon as Mama had closed her door, Georgia pulled back her covers and went to her bureau. She pulled out the letter, its creases deep from all the folding and unfolding she'd done earlier.

He had promised Mama he would stop.

He had promised Georgia to come home on time.

He had lied to both of them.

Georgia's face burned. She swallowed down the hot tears she could feel rushing to her eyes. She would not cry.

She would deliver her letter. She would tell Daddy how he was hurting her, and when he had her words in black and white in front of him, he would have to change.

Georgia sat at the foot of her bed, knees curled beneath her chin, for another half hour or so before creeping out of her room. There was no light shining from the crack under Mama's door.

First, she tiptoed to the mantel in the living room. She put the vase in the center, where Mama would see it in the morning. She wished she'd thought to pluck a flower or two from the garden to put inside.

Next, she crept to Daddy's study. He'd left the desk lamp on, and the room was cast in an orange glow. It smelled stale.

Georgia unfolded the letter and placed it at the center of the desk and set the mug gingerly beside the letter.

She was about to leave when she realized she had never signed the letter. She had left the space at the bottom of the page blank, in case she thought of something else she wanted to say.

It felt important to sign it. For Daddy to see her name at the end of these words she'd written. She opened his top desk drawer and pulled out a pen. Carefully, she wrote her name at the bottom of the letter.

Georgia Collins

Satisfied, she turned to drop the pen back in the drawer, and her eye caught on something. A small white card with an unfamiliar name printed across and more words underneath. In fact, there was an entire stack of the cards. She picked them up and flipped through them, each printed the exact same.

She couldn't understand what they were. No, she understood that. It was what they were doing *here* that she couldn't make sense of.

Beneath the stack of cards, there was a piece of paper, folded in half, with a list of addresses on it.

Alone, the addresses or the cards would have been simply strange. But together—there was only one explanation, wasn't there?

Suddenly, she heard footsteps in the hall. Quickly, she stuffed the paper with the addresses and the stack of cards back in the drawer. Then, just before closing it, she snatched the top card. She looked up just as she was stuffing the card in her pocket—just in time to see Daddy appear in the doorway.

Except it wasn't Daddy at all.

The Shadow Man staggered into the room.

Chapter Thirty-nine

"D addy," Georgia whispered.

His head whipped up. His eyes were bloodshot, unfocused.

"Georgia? Wh-what are you doing here?"

He spoke slowly, as though his mouth were half full of sand. He drew closer, and she realized that he was crying. Tear tracks stained his cheeks. His nose was red, his upper lip shining.

He took a few more clumsy steps toward the desk, then collapsed on the little sofa behind him.

"I'm s-s-sorry," he said, his eyes fluttering closed. "I'm sorry, Georgia."

Then his shoulders began to shake as sobs wracked through him. He mumbled something else Georgia couldn't understand.

She stood, frozen, behind the desk. She had never seen her father cry before and certainly not like this. She didn't know a grown man *could* cry this way, with his whole body, his face screwed up with despair. Like a helpless child.

She forced herself to go to him, to sit down beside him on the sofa. The smell was overwhelming. Stinging and sour. But she made herself stay.

"Daddy?" she murmured. "Daddy, what's wrong?"

He shook his head, unable to speak. She waited until the sobs had softened to sniffles.

"It was a mistake, Georgia," he muttered, bringing his forehead to the heels of his palms.

"What was?"

He shook his head. "All of it. All of it. I made so many mistakes."

What did he mean, *all of it*?

He looked up at her, and she recoiled from his horribly familiar face. It was contorted with anguish. He squinted at her, like he had just noticed she was there. His eyes had gone suddenly dark, and they burned into her. "What are you doing here?" he slurred. "Why aren't you asleep?"

"I just wanted—" Georgia began.

"You should go," Daddy said, standing up too quickly and then lurching to the desk for support. "You shouldn't be here. You shouldn't—see—"

His voice was rising with anger. He had his back to her

now, leaning both his hands against the desk.

"Daddy," she whispered.

It was a plea. One last plea for him to stop before he went too far. Before he ruined everything so completely it could never, ever be fixed again.

He turned, and his face was a red mask of rage. Any hint of Daddy had disappeared behind the Shadow Man once more.

She saw him reach out for something to grab. Saw his fingers find the mug, grip it in his hand. "I said, GET OUT!" he roared.

Then he pulled his arm back like he was about to pitch a baseball. The mug soared across the room and hit the far wall.

And in that instant, Georgia realized she had been wrong about heartbreak. It didn't always happen little by little, so slow you almost didn't notice it.

Sometimes it happened all at once. Sometimes, it was as easy as shattering a mug against a wall.

Chapter Forty

~

Georgia and Mama set out for Aunt Marigold's almost as soon as the sun came up. Georgia had barely slept at all, and when she finally gave up and went out to the kitchen before dawn, Mama was already there, red-eyed, nursing a mug of tea. Neither of them was hungry, and there was no point sitting around and waiting.

Neither of them wanted to see Daddy.

They stared at the dusty road ahead of them, each lost in her own thoughts.

Over and over, Georgia saw Daddy pitch the mug toward the wall. Over and over, she heard it shatter. Then, seconds later, the pounding of feet, Mama flying through the door. Daddy yelling, Georgia crying, Mama whisking her away. *What happened, what happened?* But Georgia couldn't answer. Couldn't explain the feeling of her heart cracking apart like a pot left too long in a kiln.

Could never bear to tell anyone about the expression on the Shadow Man's face when he'd looked at her. The way his dark eyes had burned.

Mama sat with Georgia in her room for a while, holding her and whispering comforts that Georgia didn't really hear. Eventually, she left again, and there was more yelling, more creaking of floorboards.

Just like old times.

Now, watching the wilting summer countryside whip past, Georgia felt bone tired.

There were no assurances from Mama today. No hopeful words about how she could fix things. There were lots of things packed into the car that morning, but hope was not one of them this time.

The Shadow Man had taken that, too.

When they pulled up at the country house after what felt like hours and hours, Mama turned to Georgia.

"Georgia, I—"

Georgia could see her searching for something—anything—to say. "I'm so sorry about your mug," she said finally. "You must have worked so hard on it. And my vase is beautiful. I love it."

Then she pulled Georgia close and kissed her.

And even though Georgia knew there was nothing Mama *could* say to fix things—any more than words could fix the broken mug—and even though she didn't want any false words of comfort, she felt a little wave of anger roll over her.

Daddy had always known how to comfort her, make her feel better. Until he had stopped trying. Now Mama was the one trying, but she just didn't know how.

Aunt Marigold was waiting for them on the porch. "Wasn't expecting you so early," she said.

Wordlessly, Georgia slid into the house and up the stairs before anyone could stop her. She heard Mama and Aunt Marigold talking as she put away her things, thought she might even have heard Mama crying.

When everything else had been unpacked, Georgia took the little card that she'd stolen from Daddy's desk out of her pocket. She felt its weight in her hands, traced the letters with her fingers, tapped her finger against its sharp corners.

Then she heard a knock at the door and shoved it back in her pocket just as Mama appeared.

"I came to say goodbye."

"'Bye, Mama," Georgia said stiffly.

"You'll be okay here this week? With Aunt Marigold?"

"Yes, Mama."

Her mother hesitated, like this wasn't quite the answer she was looking for. Then she gave a little nod. "All right, then. We'll—we'll talk next week, okay? I'll figure something out by then."

Maybe Mama was just fumbling again for the right thing

to say. Or maybe she thought the drinking was all of it. Maybe she didn't know what Georgia did. Hadn't seen the cards Daddy kept in his desk, with the sheet of addresses underneath.

"Bye, Mama," said Georgia again.

Then Mama closed the door, and Georgia was alone. She flopped down onto the bed and pulled out the card once more.

A business card.

On it was written the name Tony Darling. A stranger's name.

Below that, it said, "Jazz Pianist and Performer."

And then there was a phone number she didn't know.

Georgia hadn't understood what the stack of cards meant at first. Maybe Daddy had been given the wrong order of business cards. But then why would he keep them in his desk drawer instead of returning them?

Then there was the last name. *Darling.* Georgia had ever met only one family with that name—in *Peter Pan.* Daddy's favorite book.

So not quite a stranger's name after all.

And there had been the addresses. The list of bars and clubs and hotels. All of them in Nashville. Nashville, where musicians went to get discovered.

Why would Daddy have those addresses written down unless he was planning on going? And why would he give himself a new name? A new identity? Unless he was tired of his old one. Tired of his old life.

Whatever Mama had said about Daddy drinking so he could play better, Georgia had always known, even before she'd said it out loud, that Daddy drank because he was unhappy. She just hadn't known *why*. She'd told herself that it was his job and the fact that he couldn't play music full-time.

Georgia forced herself to remember what Daddy had said last night. *It was a mistake, Georgia. . . . All of it. All of it. I made so many mistakes.*

He hadn't meant the drinking or the late nights spent in clubs.

He had meant Georgia. And Mama. The life they shared together.

She remembered that night in the diner when they'd seen Mr. Montgomery walk in with his new girlfriend.

The man deserves to be happy, Daddy had said.

Georgia had a sudden vision of her father in the car, heading west on the highway, suitcases piled high in the back seat. Daddy singing as he drove away.

Daddy. Because it hadn't been the Shadow Man who had made those business cards, written down those addresses. All along, they had been one and the same. It wasn't just the Shadow Man who had broken Georgia's heart. It was Daddy, too.

Daddy, hoping to see his name up in lights one day.

But it wouldn't be *his* name. It would be Tony Darling. Pianist and *performer*.

Daddy had put on a performance, all right. Making Georgia believe he loved her enough to do anything for her. When he couldn't even stop drinking for her.

When he couldn't even stay.

Georgia began to rip up the business card. She tore it into quarters, then tore the quarters into tiny scraps, destroying first the words, then the letters. Then she gathered the pieces up in her palm and went to the window. Hoisting it open with one arm, she flung the bits of paper out the window, watched them scatter across the grass like ash.

Next, she pulled the silver nickel out of her pocket. It was shiny as always, winking at her as if they shared some secret joke.

She hurled it out the window as hard as she could.

Chapter Forty-one

~~~

After that, Georgia thought about going to the lake, but in the end she decided she couldn't bear to face Angela yet. Couldn't bear to see her face full of hope when she asked Georgia how Daddy had reacted to her letter. Or Cole's indifferent shrug—his knowing eyes.

Instead, she crawled into bed and drifted in and out of a troubled sleep. When she awoke, it was to find Aunt Marigold peeking her head through the open door.

"Sorry," she said. "I didn't mean to wake you."

But she didn't leave. Instead, she took a few steps into the room. "Are you feeling all right? Your mama told me you— well, that you had a hard weekend."

Georgia didn't reply. She could see that Aunt Marigold wanted to comfort her. Just like Mama had wanted to. But there was nothing her great-aunt could do. Couldn't she see that? The one person who had the power to make everything better had decided not to.

Aunt Marigold cleared her throat. "I just wanted to say, that is, I know I haven't always been very—forthcoming— Georgia. But if you wanted to talk about—"

"No," said Georgia. The word echoed through the room. Like the shattering of the mug against the wall last night. Final.

From the corner of her eye, she saw Aunt Marigold stiffen.

"Well, then, maybe you'd just like to listen," her great-aunt said. "Because I think I might understand some of the things you're going through."

At this, Georgia's chin whipped up. Her eyes narrowed. "Understand?" she asked, her voice not quite her own. "How could you understand? Your daddy didn't leave you. He stayed right here in this house with you until the day he died. It's not the same."

Aunt Marigold's face blanched, then colored. Her lips pressed into pale slivers. Georgia felt guilty and defiant all at the same time. She didn't know why it felt good to speak this way, but it did.

She waited for Aunt Marigold to demand to know how she knew this. For her to hiss that her past was none of Georgia's business.

She could take the anger. *Wanted* it, even.

But after a moment, Aunt Marigold's face returned to its

usual color. When she spoke, her voice was even. "Georgia," she said, "your daddy isn't leaving you either. It's much more complicated than that."

Georgia sneered. "Complicated is just a word grown-ups use when they don't want to tell the truth," she said. "And they *never* tell the truth."

"Never?" Aunt Marigold asked. "When have I ever lied to you?"

Georgia could feel the blood racing in her veins.

"You didn't tell me about your daddy being sick," she said. "Hank did. And you didn't tell me about your hands until I saw for myself. And I bet you won't tell me who's buried out in the woods underneath that angel statue."

At this, Aunt Marigold's whole body jerked up. "Georgia, I—" she started. Then she stopped. "I guess you're right," she said, her voice cold and quiet as falling snow. "I guess I am a liar."

Chapter Forty-two

When Georgia crept out of the house to the lake, late-afternoon clouds bloomed in deep colors overhead. Aunt Marigold was nowhere to be seen. Georgia already felt a persistent throb of regret when she thought of how she'd spoken to her, and yet she couldn't quite bring herself to want to take it back either.

She found a stick on the forest floor and whacked at the undergrowth on either side of the narrow trail she'd made for herself. She let her feet stomp against the ground. Maybe it was a childish thing to do, but then she *was* a child, and each whack and stomp felt good.

She kept her eyes on her feet, which is why, when she crested the little ridge between the two oak trees, she almost ran into the person who suddenly dropped from its lowest branch.

She cried out as she nearly tripped over herself to avoid a collision.

When she had regained her balance, she looked up and found herself staring into a familiar ruddy face.

"Cole!"

He flashed her a smile. "Sorry. Didn't mean to scare you."

"What were you doing?" Georgia asked, returning his smile with a scowl. "You almost knocked me over."

"I was climbing," Cole said with a shrug. "And you should watch where you're going. Hey, you, um, don't look so good."

Ignoring this, Georgia cast her gaze over the beach, but Angela was nowhere to be seen.

"Where's Angela?" she asked.

"Went home," Cole said. "Said you probably weren't coming today."

"Oh." She let herself sink onto the sand. Cole sat down next to her.

"I did tell you, you know."

"Told me what?"

"That she didn't know what she was talking about. Not when it comes to family."

"But you do?" Georgia turned, expecting to see him smirking back. But he was just looking at her expectantly.

"Sure," he said.

"So what do you know about it?"

Cole picked a leaf off a low-hanging branch and began to tear it up as he spoke. "I know what it's like not to be good enough. To realize they aren't who you thought they were. I know what it's like when you realize you're alone."

"I'm not alone," Georgia said quickly.

Cole looked at her, raised his eyebrows. "Aren't you?" he asked.

Georgia was about to tell Cole that he didn't know everything, that she had Mama and Aunt Marigold and Angela, when suddenly she realized—she *did* feel alone.

"My daddy drinks," she blurted out. "And now I think he might leave us. My mama said we'd 'figure it out.' And my aunt Marigold said she could help. But I know they're just lying."

Cole was staring at her now. He nodded. "Most everyone's a liar," he replied softly. "That's why I like to stick to the shadows, like I told you before. You see people for who they are before they can make you believe they're somebody else."

Georgia stared at him, shocked. She'd expected him to say something comforting. To try to make her feel better like all the others.

But hadn't she been thinking the same thing? Hadn't she accused Aunt Marigold of being a liar hours before? Slowly, she nodded.

"It's not such a bad thing, you know," he said. "Being on

your own. There's no rules when it's just you. Nobody to hold you back. Nobody to care."

He said this last bit as if it was a good thing, too. Georgia frowned.

"What did your family do?" she asked. "Why did they send you away?"

"It doesn't matter," said Cole. "I'm not going back."

"You're not?"

"Nope. I'm gonna run away."

Georgia felt her eyebrows shoot up. "To where?"

Cole stared out at the lake like he was looking into the future. "Everywhere. I don't ever want to settle down. I just want to travel around. Be free."

Cole's words made Georgia think of the wild mustangs Hank had told her about. She wondered what it would be like to give your heart to the wind instead of having to carry it around in your chest.

"I have this feeling," she said, "like anger but bigger." She pictured the dark thicket inside her, climbing and snarling its way higher and higher. "I don't know how to make it stop."

Cole nodded and was about to speak when—

"Georgia?"

Georgia snapped her head up to see Angela walking toward them, a worried frown darkening her face. Georgia stood up too quickly, like she'd been caught red-handed. "Hi."

Angela's eyes flitted from Georgia to Cole. "I thought I heard voices," she said. "What happened? This weekend, I mean? Did it—"

"I don't want to talk about it," said Georgia.

She realized uneasily that she was disappointed to see her friend. All weekend, she had longed to be with Angela again. But suddenly, it was Cole she wanted to talk to. Cole who seemed to understand that Daddy had been the moon, and that without his light, Georgia was lost. He wasn't trying to make her feel better, like Angela would. That was impossible. He just made her feel a little less alone in the darkness.

She wondered why she had been so quick to believe Angela about him. After all, what trouble had he caused them? And even if he was trouble, maybe he had his reasons. Maybe no one had ever bothered to take the time to learn what they were.

Maybe trouble had found him and not the other way around.

Besides, Cole had trusted her, hadn't he? Enough to tell her his plan. In fact, Georgia realized, he'd told her more about himself in the last five minutes than Angela ever had about herself.

Pink blossoms appeared on Angela's cheeks. "Oh. Um, okay," she murmured. "Well, what should we do, then? Do you want to swim? Or fish?"

Georgia shook her head.

"We could go to the island," said Cole softly.

Angela gave him a sharp look. "We told you, no magic yet."

"No," said Georgia suddenly. "No, Cole's right. We should go to the island."

She needed a distraction. Something more than swimming or fishing. She needed to know that the magic hadn't deserted her, too.

Angela slowly turned her gaze to Georgia and stared at her, wide-eyed. "Are you sure?"

"He deserves a chance, doesn't he?" asked Georgia, shooting Cole a glance.

"Come on," Cole said. "She needs something to take her mind off things."

Angela kept her gaze fixed on Georgia. Her expression was hurt, uncertain. It reminded her too much of Mama's.

"It'll be fine, Angela," she said. "We can trust him."

"Well, okay," Angela replied finally. "Whatever you think."

Georgia looked at Cole and nodded toward the boat. "Come on," she said.

Before she turned away, she saw his face break into a winning smile.

Chapter Forty-three

There was a tense silence in the boat as they rowed to the island. Once again, Georgia sat in the back with the oars, Angela in the middle, and Cole in the front, leaning back on the prow and lifting his pale face to the sunshine. The wind kept blowing in from the side, sending the girls' hair blowing with it.

Angela sat facing Georgia, but Georgia was careful to avoid her gaze. She knew it would be full of questions.

Cole turned to look at the island. "How does it work, anyway?" he asked. "You know, the magic."

Georgia finally glanced at Angela, who gave a defeated shrug. They'd never said they would keep the magic from him forever. And he had been patient, hadn't he?

"There are skipping stones on the island," Georgia explained. "You make a wish and skip your stone at the same time."

"But it can't be any wish," said Angela quickly. "It has to be something the lake can actually do."

"What's that mean?"

"The wishes only work inside the oak trees," Georgia said. "So you can't wish that your house was made of gold or something."

"But I could wish for gold," Cole said, sitting up, "and take it with me."

Angela sighed impatiently. "No, you can't. Whatever you wish for, it disappears as soon as you leave. The magic isn't to help any of us get rich or famous or anything like that."

"Well, we can still use it to have some *real* fun."

"What's that supposed to mean?" Angela asked.

"Hold on," Georgia said as the prow of the boat slid up onto the pebbly beach.

Cole was the first out of the boat. He stepped onto the island and walked in a slow circle around it, studying the pebbles at his feet. Angela watched him closely, arms crossed and elbows jutting out, only taking her eyes off him to glance at Georgia now and then.

"Are we really going to let him make a wish?" she hissed when Cole was on the other side of the wizard tree.

"Whatever he wishes for, it can't be *that* bad, can it?" Georgia asked. What was Angela so afraid of? "It's like you said. There are rules. The lake won't let him do anything crazy."

Angela had been right, of course. The magic couldn't

make them rich or famous. Couldn't mend families or hearts. So, what, Georgia wondered again, was it all for? Just to entertain them over a long summer? To provide her with a temporary escape from thinking about Daddy? But what point was there in escaping if you always ended up back in the place you were trying to run from?

No. Cole had been right the first time they'd met. There had to be *more*. And maybe he could figure out how to get it.

"Fine," said Angela, a hint of anger in her voice now. "But I don't understand. What did he say to you? Why do you trust him all of the sudden?"

"Nothing," Georgia lied. "I just—think he's waited long enough."

Cole bent down next to the boat to pick up a handful of stones. He dropped them one by one onto the beach, looking deep in thought, until he was holding only one.

"I've got my wish," he said.

Before either of them could ask what it was, he was already muttering something under his breath. Georgia thought she could make out the word "ocean." Then the stone was skipping across the lake.

No sooner had it sunk below the surface than the lake began to ripple, little waves appearing everywhere. Georgia leaned over the water to see what it held in its reflection. It was hard to make anything out because, unlike the other times, the lake wasn't still. But she thought she could make out some kind of white surface—snow, maybe.

"Come on," Cole said. "Let's go."

Georgia turned to Angela. "Are you coming?"

Angela bit her lip, then nodded. Together, the three of them dipped their fingers into the water. As everything began to shift, Georgia glanced at Cole.

For a brief second, a look of fear crossed his face. Then his eyes flashed with something else. Something that made them glitter in a way that made Georgia want to turn her gaze.

Something that looked like hunger.

Georgia felt herself being flipped just like she had the day the lake had become Camp Pine Valley. There was a whooshing sound, a ringing in her ears, and then—

The sound of waves crashing against the shore.

Georgia felt herself land on something soft. She looked around. They were still on an island. It was bigger now, though not by much. And covered with brilliant white sand. Every few feet, black rocks peeked through the sand like scabs on a pale knee, and scrubby little plants grew here and there, no higher than Georgia's ankles. Other than that, the island was deserted.

She shaded her eyes and looked toward the water.

It stretched on as far as the eye could see, turning from green to blue to gray. The waves that came rushing in were white and foamy.

Cole had landed them in the middle of the ocean.

Chapter Forty-four

~

"Where are we?" Angela asked. Then, rounding on Cole, "What did you do?"

"I wished we could have our own deserted island," he said. "Cool, huh?"

Angela was staring out at the endless sea; whether mesmerized or horrified, it was impossible to tell. Georgia felt her own chest thrum anxiously. The lake turning into a summer camp was one thing but a whole ocean? They were all alone out here. What if something happened?

But she didn't want Cole to think she was weak or scared. So she nodded. "Cool."

"How will we get back?" Angela asked in a small voice.

"Like we did before," Georgia said, trying to sound confident. "From Camp Pine Valley. When we're ready to go, the water will take us."

Surely that was right. The lake would take them back home when they were ready.

And if it didn't?

Georgia thought of how Daddy would react if Aunt Marigold called to say that Georgia was missing. How he would feel if *she* was the one who disappeared this time. Would he blame himself?

She allowed herself a single moment of pleasure at the thought. It felt wicked and right.

"Let's swim," said Cole, ambling toward the water.

"But the waves," Angela said. "They're too high."

Georgia had been thinking the same thing. But Cole pointed to a little dinghy Georgia hadn't noticed, pulled up atop a layer of black rock. "We'll take this out," he said, "to where the water's calmer."

Georgia looped her arm through Angela's. She could see from her friend's face that Angela was frightened. She didn't think she'd ever seen her friend scared like this before, and Georgia didn't like it. She knew she had pressured Angela into inviting Cole to the island, and now she felt like she needed to make it up to her. Reassure her. "Want to go?" she asked gently. "It'll be fun. We'll stick together, okay? Promise."

Angela smiled weakly. "Okay," she said. "Not long, though, otherwise we'll be late getting home."

"Deal," Georgia said. "Race you?"

Then they were flying together through the sand toward the boat, just like they did back at the wishing lake.

This time, Cole and Georgia shared rowing duties. The little boat sailed easily over the whitecaps. Angela and Georgia laughed when the ocean spray hit their faces.

On the other side of the waves, the water was calm except for the occasional burst of wind rippling over it. Angela pointed down.

"Look!" she said. "You can see all the way to the bottom. And there's fish!"

Cole dropped the boat's little anchor. He was the first to dive in. The water, when Georgia and Angela jumped in, was warm and soothing.

Cole emerged next to them, his hair sopping around his face. He wore a gleeful expression. "Follow me," he said. Then he dived back under and began to swim. Georgia and Angela exchanged a glance, then each took a deep breath.

Georgia opened her eyes underwater, blinking until they didn't sting anymore. Light rippled like tiger stripes over the sandy bottom. There was no sound except a muted crackling noise, and the gentle *swish* of her arms carving through the water.

It was an entirely different world beneath the surface. Peaceful.

Just when she wasn't sure she could hold her breath any longer, she saw Cole pointing to something up ahead. There were barnacled rocks half-sunken in the sand, some of them covered with coral or algae that swayed with the current. Here and there among the rocks, little colorful fish darted and swam.

Georgia let herself float to the surface, where she took a breath, then dived back down. The fish were the kind you saw in aquariums. Their colors were so bright they looked as though they must have been painted on—blue scales that flashed with neon pink, turquoise fish with tails as yellow as daffodils. They didn't seem to notice the swimmers floating above them.

Angela gripped her wrist and pointed to a rock where a purple starfish had attached itself. It was double the size of Georgia's palm. Together, they surfaced again, gasping for breath.

"Not so bad, is it?" Cole asked, before diving down once more.

Angela rolled her eyes, but Georgia could see that she was already eager to be back underwater. "Again?" Georgia asked.

"Again," Angela agreed.

They swam and swam, each taking turns pointing out things they saw below. A hermit crab crawling along the sandy floor, the flash of an eel flicking its tail into its dark lair, and even—for a few wonderful moments—a small sea turtle that glided through the rocks like a bird in flight. Its round, caramel eyes examined them before it turned away and disappeared into the shadowy depths.

Georgia liked how the water made her nearly weightless. How it made her forget everything else. How it held her and rocked her, making her feel like nothing could touch her. She thought she could be happy swimming there forever.

But then something *did* touch her. Angela, tugging at her shoulder.

Georgia followed Angela to the surface. "We need to go," Angela said breathlessly. "Now."

Angela stared out at the horizon. The wind, Georgia saw, was blowing more fiercely now, and there were angry, sooty clouds in the sky. They seemed to have swept in upon the island from all sides while the swimmers were underwater, like an army surrounding its enemy.

This time, Georgia didn't argue. When Cole surfaced a moment later, she pointed in the direction of the clouds. He nodded but didn't look concerned.

"I was getting tired anyway," he said.

When they were back in the boat, Angela shut her eyes tightly and said, "We're ready to go home now."

But nothing happened. No reflection appeared in the choppy water below.

The swells were getting larger by the minute, the boat swaying more and more with each one that passed beneath it.

"Maybe we have to go back to the island," Georgia said.

"Back to where we started. Like when we were at Camp Pine Valley and we went back to the lifeguard tower."

Angela nodded. Her face was ashen.

They set off toward the island, but it wasn't as easy getting back as it had been getting out. The waves came more quickly now. They had to time their approach carefully and, even then, managed to get soaked when a wave rose out of nowhere and crashed down upon them.

Each time a wave drove them closer to the island, the current seemed to suck them back out again.

"The tide must be going out," Georgia shouted over the clamoring waves. "We need to row harder!"

But after each wave they crested, another one rose behind them. Every time a wave crashed into them, Georgia felt a little thrill of danger go through her chest. Water had begun to pool at their feet.

A crack of thunder announced the rain, and a bolt of lightning lit up the water around them.

Georgia looked at Cole, but he was staring straight ahead, determination set in every line of his face. Angela let out a whimper.

"Are we getting any closer?" she asked.

Georgia didn't answer. The biggest swell yet loomed behind them, a roaring gray monster, fifteen feet high at least. A sudden rush of fear made Georgia go cold.

"Faster!" she yelled to Cole, plunging her paddle into the

water. Her arms were burning. The swell would capsize their boat, and what chance would they have swimming in this storm?

But before Georgia could even find her voice to warn Angela, the wave was breaking over them. She lifted her hands as though they might actually protect her. Her eyes squeezed shut just as the water stampeded into her chest, knocking her over. She felt her head hit something hard and then she was tumbling through the water, being dragged this direction and then that. She tried to swim toward the surface, but she was being pulled in two.

Georgia shot out a hand, hoping to catch hold of Angela or Cole but found no one there.

She felt the outgoing tide sucking her backward. If only she could get to the surface—above the undertow—maybe she could ride a wave in to shore.

She forced her body to relax. To rise. To float.

Just as she felt her lungs beginning to catch fire, her face broke through the water. She had only a second to suck in a breath of air before she felt the curl of a wave against her back.

Then she was underwater again, tumbling over and over in the wave's grip. But it was pushing her in the right direction now.

Suddenly, the wave seemed to release her, and her belly skimmed against rough sand until she felt air enter her lungs again. A hacking cough exploded from her chest, sending water sputtering out with it.

She opened her eyes. The storm was gone. The sky above her was brilliant and blue, and she was lying on the pebbly beach of the wishing lake.

Alone.

Chapter Forty-five

~~~

Still gasping for air, Georgia looked around the beach. The lake stretched out in front of her, calm as ever, as if nothing had happened at all. But there was no sign of Angela or Cole.

A sickening dread washed over her. One final wave.

"Angela!" she called. "Cole!"

Frantically, she looked around until she heard a splashing sound. A second later, a head popped up just a few feet from shore. Cole emerged, his eyes wild.

"Where's Angela?" Georgia called.

He shook his head.

If something had happened to Angela—if it was Georgia's fault—how would she ever forgive herself?

But then a second head surfaced, and Angela appeared, coughing madly as she struggled to stand.

"Angela!" Georgia shouted, running to help. "Are you okay?"

Still unable to speak, Angela nodded. When they were both standing on dry sand, Georgia wrapped her arms around her friend, who embraced her back. Cole collapsed on the sand next to them, laying his hands on his belly and panting.

Then he began to laugh.

Georgia frowned. Her heart was still racing.

But then Cole caught her eye, arched his eyebrows at her as if inviting her into the joke, and she felt a smile sneaking up her own face. As she and Angela broke apart, Georgia felt a shaking in her belly she realized was a giggle. She, too, began to laugh. She couldn't *stop* laughing, in fact. It was from the relief, she told herself, that Angela was all right. That they had survived.

Angela stared at her, mouth slightly agape. "It's not funny," she said, her voice hoarse. "That wasn't safe. We could have gotten really hurt."

"But we're fine," said Cole, sitting up on his elbows. "We just had a little fun is all."

"*Fun?*" Angela echoed. "That's your idea of *fun?*"

Georgia had finally managed to swallow down her laughter, but she still felt strange and giddy. She knew Angela was right. It *had* been dangerous.

Yet she had gotten herself home safely, and what's more,

she'd done it all on her own. She hadn't needed anyone.

"Well, we're all okay now, aren't we?" she said.

Angela blinked, and Georgia felt a sudden jolt when she realized Angela's eyes were filling with tears. "You're taking his side?" Angela asked. "What happened to you this weekend? It's like you're a different person."

"Angela, I—"

But before Georgia could try to explain, Angela had turned away and was disappearing through the oak trees.

"Don't let her spoil it," Cole said, shaking his wet hair from his eyes. "I wanted you to see what it feels like."

"What *what* feels like?"

"Being on your own. Being free. It's pretty great, huh?"

Free. That's what Georgia had felt when they'd been swimming beneath the water, before the storm came.

Georgia looked away. "Angela was right," she said. She couldn't bring herself to agree with him. Not after she'd already hurt Angela. It was too much of a betrayal. "We almost died."

"But we didn't. And you didn't need anybody to save you. You did it all on your own."

Georgia's eyes flicked up to Cole's face. He was smiling at her almost proudly. She felt a chill go through her. She had been thinking the same thing.

It *had* felt good. Saving herself from the waves. It made her feel strangely powerful.

"I have to go," she said, not waiting for Cole's answer before slipping away.

Aunt Marigold was waiting in one of the rocking chairs on the porch when Georgia returned.

"You're late," she said matter-of-factly.

"Sorry," Georgia mumbled.

Her great-aunt narrowed her eyes when she saw that Georgia was wet from head to toe.

"Where have you been?" she asked. "What have you been doing out there?"

Georgia shrugged. "Just playing."

"In the creek?" Aunt Marigold asked.

"I'll go get changed," Georgia said, making for the door.

In a flash, her aunt had sprung out of her rocking chair and blocked the doorway, hands planted on her hips.

"I'm supposed to take care of you," she said.

"So?"

"*So* suppose somethin' happened to you out in those woods. Suppose you slipped and hit your head on a rock in the creek."

"My friend Angela would be there," Georgia said, warmth spreading into her cheeks as she spoke the word. *Were* they still friends?

"I've never even met this Angela. And how would she know what to do in an emergency? I don't know if I want you playing out there anymore. I don't know if it's safe."

There was that word again, the same one Angela had used. Why was everyone so concerned with keeping her "safe" all of a sudden? What was that supposed to mean anyway? How could someone keep you safe when the most important part of you was already broken?

It's too late! she wanted to yell. *You missed your chance.*

"I said I'm fine," she muttered instead, through gritted teeth.

Aunt Marigold held her gaze with sad, searching eyes. "Well, I guess I'm not the only liar here, am I?"

Then she stepped aside to let Georgia pass.

Georgia couldn't sleep that night.

She and Aunt Marigold had barely spoken over dinner. Georgia couldn't meet her eyes. There was a feeling she'd gotten when Aunt Marigold had stared at her earlier, called *her* a liar. Almost like shame. Like when you think you're alone and suddenly you realize someone's been watching you, and you sit up straight and wonder what they saw.

And what about the way she'd treated Angela? Angela, who had done nothing but be a good friend to her all summer. Georgia had bullied her into letting Cole make his wish and then brushed her off after they'd all nearly drowned. Every time she thought of it, she felt guilt gnawing at her.

But then there was the dizzy laughter that had risen in

her chest after they'd washed up on the beach. She could still feel it fluttering there, like a frantic, trapped bird.

It didn't make any sense. To be tumbling under the water one minute—sure she would never see the surface again—and smiling and laughing the next. Laughing because she felt like she'd won. Because somehow, she had felt for the first time in a long time, like she was in control.

No matter what she'd told Aunt Marigold, it didn't feel like they were playing at the lake today. It finally felt like something more important. Like the lake was teaching her something.

Maybe Cole was right. Maybe the lesson was that nobody was going to be there to save her anymore. But that was okay because she didn't *need* saving.

From now on, she would be just fine on her own.

Chapter Forty-six

The next morning, Georgia was awoken suddenly by a strange sound. For a second, she thought it might be an alarm clock. But there was no alarm clock in this room, and anyway, the sound hadn't been that close. A bird squawking outside, maybe.

She closed her eyes, wanting to go back to sleep, but then she heard a voice murmuring.

She threw back her covers and opened the door. There was something about how quiet the voice was that made Georgia's eyes narrow. Someone was talking like they didn't want anyone to hear.

Georgia crept the rest of the way down the hall, careful not to make the floorboards creak, and stopped at the top of the stairs. But the voice had stopped, too.

When she got to the bottom of the staircase, it was just

Aunt Marigold sitting at the table on her own.

"Who were you talking to?" Georgia asked, glancing around the kitchen and the living room as though someone might be hiding in the corner.

Aunt Marigold looked up blankly. "No one," she said. "Just myself."

Had Georgia heard another voice, she wondered, or could it have just been Aunt Marigold? But since when did her great-aunt talk to herself?

Hank didn't come that morning, which left Georgia and Aunt Marigold on their own. The silence was louder between them than when she'd first come. And heavier, too. Georgia hated it.

With every moment that passed, she wanted to apologize for how she had been acting. But every moment, her mouth wrapped tighter around the words, refusing to let them out.

Aunt Marigold seemed not to notice. When Georgia stole glances at her, it was to find her staring out into the distance, or her eyes narrowed on something Georgia couldn't see, her right hand cradling her left. Once or twice, she took a deep breath as if to speak, but instead she only sighed.

Georgia was grateful for her great-aunt's distraction. It made the silence less painful.

Finally, after lunch, Georgia made her way toward the door while Aunt Marigold was washing the dishes. But she hadn't quite reached it when Aunt Marigold called her back.

"Where are you going?" she asked, her words clipped.

"To the woods."

"To do what?"

"Just . . . to see Angela."

If she couldn't make things right with her aunt, she needed to at least try with her friend.

Aunt Marigold shook her head. "I don't think it's a good idea, Georgia."

Georgia glanced at the door, then back at Aunt Marigold. They both knew there was nothing her aunt could do to stop her if she made a run for it. Instead, she looked back at her aunt. "Please," she said. "I need this."

Aunt Marigold closed her eyes and took in a long breath. When she opened them, they were softer. "One hour," she said. "No swimming, no climbing trees. Just—be careful, Georgia. Promise?"

Georgia nodded. "Promise."

And then she was free once more.

Georgia held her breath as she climbed through the gap in the oak trees. What if Angela had decided not to come back to the lake after yesterday?

But when she arrived at the beach, her friend was sitting by herself on the sand, her knees curled up under her chin.

She glanced at Georgia as she approached, then went back to staring out at the lake.

"Hey," Georgia said.

"Hi," said Angela, not lifting her head.

Georgia flopped down beside her. "Where's Cole?"

"How should I know? Why does it matter, anyway?"

"It doesn't," Georgia said, trying to ignore the flicker of disappointment she felt. "I only came to see you. Look, about yesterday . . . I'm really sorry. Honestly."

Somehow it was easier to apologize to Angela than to Aunt Marigold. Maybe because she had seen the hurt in her friend's eyes. Could see it even now.

Angela was still as a statue for a moment before she gave a little nod. "You scared me," she said. Then, finally, she turned her head to look at Georgia. "Did something happen this weekend? Is that why you were acting so strange?"

Georgia felt the air leave her body like a balloon deflating. She didn't want to talk about it. Not ever. Talking about Daddy meant thinking about him. Thinking about him meant thinking about all the things he had chosen over her.

But she owed Angela an explanation.

"I don't know," she said flatly. "He came home when I was leaving the letter in his office. He was—he was really bad. He yelled at me and smashed the mug I made. And I think, well, I think he might be leaving us."

"*Leaving* you?" Angela asked, eyes rounding, reflecting

Georgia's own fear back at her. "Why do you think that?"

"I just know," said Georgia. She was too weary to explain about the business cards. The addresses. Tony Darling. The wistful look Daddy always got in his eyes when he talked about bright lights in big cities.

"I'm so sorry, Georgia," Angela said. "But it's not your fault, you know."

Now it was Georgia's turn to stare out at the lake. "Maybe not," she murmured. "But I'm not enough for him to stay either."

"If he leaves, it's because he's a coward," Angela said. "Not because of you."

Georgia shrugged. It was easy to think that when it was someone else's father you were talking about.

"I guess I understand why you were acting that way yesterday," Angela said. "But . . . it won't make you feel better, you know."

Georgia's heart skipped a beat. "What won't?"

"Acting like him."

"Like my dad?"

"Like Cole."

Georgia felt hot under the collar of her shirt. She wasn't trying to act like anyone. "I don't know what you're talking about."

"I just mean—" Angela paused, searching for the right words. Then she reached over, interlaced her fingers with

Georgia's, and took a deep breath. "I know you're upset. But you can't just use the magic to hide from what your daddy did. You can't run away. You have to, you know, face it."

Georgia felt herself bristle and remembered what Cole had said about Angela. *Angela doesn't know anything about trouble.*

"And you won't protect yourself from getting hurt again by hurting yourself," Angela went on. "Or by shutting people out. You've still got your mom, and your aunt. And *me*. None of us would ever leave you."

Now Georgia stiffened. She thought of the strained silence that waited for her back at the country house. She pulled her hand away from Angela. Cole had been right. Angela didn't know anything.

Daddy's love had once been as sure as the moon in the sky. If it could change, anything could. Any*one* could.

"I have to go," she said.

Angela's brows furrowed in confusion. "Did I say something wrong?"

"Aunt Marigold only gave me an hour," Georgia said. "I'll see you later, Angela."

And for once, it was Georgia disappearing into the trees without a trace.

Chapter Forty-seven

Aunt Marigold looked relieved when Georgia returned that afternoon. Still, they hardly spoke to each other as they prepared supper and sat down to eat. By bedtime, the silence was deep enough to sink into.

It wasn't until Georgia had nearly fallen asleep that she thought she heard the sound of footsteps pausing outside her door. She waited for a knock, but it never came.

The next morning, she wasn't sure whether she had simply dreamed the sound.

Either way, it was a relief at breakfast when Aunt Marigold finally broke the silence between them.

"Good morning," she said as Georgia sat down to a plate of blueberry muffins.

There was something different about her great-aunt. Her shoulders were slumped inward, and the lines in her face seemed to have deepened overnight. For the first time since Georgia had met Aunt Marigold, she looked old. *Weary*.

"Good morning," Georgia replied in what she hoped was a polite voice.

Aunt Marigold pulled out the chair across from Georgia and sat.

"I thought I could show you slab pots this afternoon," she said.

Georgia heard the rest of the unfinished sentence. *Instead of your going into the forest.* But she didn't bother to argue. She wasn't sure if she wanted to see Cole *or* Angela today.

"Okay," she said. Neither of them had touched the muffins.

Aunt Marigold let out a sigh. "But there are some things we need to talk about this morning," she said. "Things I need to tell you."

"I don't—" Georgia started to protest.

"Yes, yes, you don't want to talk about it," Aunt Marigold interrupted impatiently. "I know. But I want to tell you the truth about that room upstairs you were so curious about. And about—about what you found in the forest. I expect you'll want to hear what I have to say."

Georgia sat up straighter in her chair. Was Aunt Marigold going to tell her about the grave? "You mean the—"

But the rest of her sentence was lost underneath a shrieking sound that made them both jump. It was the loudest noise Georgia had ever heard in the country house, and it wasn't until it came again that Georgia realized what it was.

The phone was ringing.

She also realized that this had been the sound that had awoken her the previous morning. She couldn't identify it then because she'd never heard the phone ring here. Because the sound was so out of place.

For a second, Aunt Marigold didn't move.

"Aren't you going to get that?" Georgia asked.

Wordlessly, Aunt Marigold swept into the living room. Just before she picked up the old-fashioned phone from a little table in the living room, Georgia had the sudden urge to tell her not to. The ringing felt like an alarm, warning them of something to come.

She picked up the phone. "Hello? Yes, hello, Amelia."

Mama.

Aunt Marigold glanced back at Georgia, then down again. Listening.

"No," she said finally. "No, I'm afraid we haven't. I'll call if we do, all right? And you call if—yes. Yes. All right. Goodbye, then."

Then she hung up the phone and—her back to Georgia— seemed to smooth out the creases in her overalls before turning around again.

"What did Mama say?"

"Georgia."

"She called yesterday morning, too, didn't she?" Georgia pressed. That was who her great-aunt had been talking to.

Aunt Marigold's shoulders sunk lower. She turned and walked slowly across the room, like a soldier about to surrender.

"She wanted to know if we'd seen your daddy," she said. "Apparently he never came home night before last. She hasn't heard from him since then."

So, there it was.

Daddy had done it. He was leaving them.

Had *left* them.

Suddenly, leaving was all Georgia wanted to do, too.

"Your Mama didn't want to worry you, Georgia. I'm sure everything—"

But Georgia wasn't listening any longer. So, they had all been lying to her. Mama. Aunt Marigold. Angela.

Cole's words rang through her head. *You can't trust anyone.*

She dodged around Aunt Marigold and bolted for the door. Heard her great-aunt calling her back but burst through it anyway. Then her legs were pumping fast, faster than ever, as she fled through the forest.

Was this, she wondered, how Daddy had felt when he packed up the car and left?

GET OUT! he'd roared at her that night in the study.

That's what she was trying to do. To run from the dark

thing growing inside her, threatening to swallow her whole.

She had known this was coming, hadn't she? She shouldn't be surprised.

But she was. Shocked, even, at the way her heart could keep breaking, even after she had thought it had already been smashed to smithereens. Would it just keep breaking again and again? Would it never, ever stop?

When she arrived between the oak trees, she leaned against one of them for a minute to catch her breath, which was coming in ragged, shallow bursts.

She was surprised to look up and find Cole and Angela both on the beach, even though it wasn't afternoon. They seemed to be arguing about something. Angela, spotting Georgia, waved her over.

Slowly, Georgia forced her legs to start moving again, but they felt strange and wobbly as she walked onto the little beach.

"There you are," Angela said, coming to meet her halfway. She stopped short when she saw Georgia's face. "What's— what's wrong?"

Georgia shook her head. She couldn't find the words.

"It's him, isn't it?" Cole said, standing behind Angela, his face grim. "Your dad?"

"Yes," Georgia whispered.

"He left," said Cole. It wasn't a question.

Angela gasped, her hand flying to her mouth. Then she

was reaching her arms around Georgia, slowly lowering her down to sit in the sand. "Are you sure?" she asked. "There must be something we can do."

"We tried already," Georgia said numbly. "Remember? The magic can't help me."

"Not a wish," Angela replied. "Something else. You'll write him another letter."

A letter. Like a single piece of flimsy paper could fix anything.

She kicked her foot into the sand. "Don't you get it?" she cried. "It's over. He's already gone."

"She *can't* get it," Cole said. "But I do. Didn't I tell you that you can't trust people?"

"That's not true," Angela said, desperation climbing in her voice. "You can trust *me*, Georgia."

"Maybe," said Cole. "Maybe till the end of summer. Then Georgia will leave and you'll probably forget all about her before next summer."

"That's not true!" Angela cried again. "Why are you saying these things? Don't listen to him, Georgia. We're friends, remember? *Sisters.*"

But that wasn't exactly what Angela had said at the beginning of summer, was it? She'd wanted to be *summer* sisters.

Maybe Cole was right. Maybe Angela had only ever wanted her until the end of the summer. Then she, too, would turn her back on Georgia. She wouldn't mean to—not like Daddy. But slowly she would forget to write, forget to call, until they were strangers to each other.

It hurt to breathe. Hurt to think.

"But maybe there is something you can do," said Cole. "Something you can wish for."

"The lake can't bring him back," Georgia whispered.

"No," said Cole. His eyes were flashing again, and his voice had gone quiet. "But maybe it can take *us* away."

"What are you talking about?" Angela spat.

"You can make the biggest wish yet," he said. The light in his gaze was like light bouncing off the silver blade of a knife. Georgia couldn't look away. "Wish that we could just fly away from here. We can go together. See the world. Leave all this behind so we never have to think about it again. We'll be a pair of feathers floating on the wind."

Feathers.

Once, she had felt weightless as a sack of feathers in Daddy's arms.

Racing with the wind at Camp Pine Valley, fingers tangled in the mane of her horse.

But now she had never felt so heavy in her whole life. The vines of anger and sorrow inside her were threatening to burst out of her, to wind around and around her, trapping her in their darkness forever.

Could she really fly away and leave them behind? Did she want to?

She wanted to feel the way she'd felt swimming in the bejeweled underwater world Cole had conjured. She wanted to be like one of Hank's mustangs. Wild and free, never letting anyone close enough to touch her, to steal her freedom.

"Come on, Georgia," Cole said. "How about a little adventure?"

"Georgia, don't listen to him," Angela was begging. "*Please* don't listen. The magic won't work like that. It only works within the tree line. What happens if you try to cross over it? You could fall and get seriously hurt."

"How do you know?" Cole asked coolly. "You've never tried anything like this."

It was all beginning to make sense. *This*, at last, was what the magic had been meant for.

Not to mend Georgia's life but to help her escape it. To lift her on the wind and carry her to faraway places.

Perhaps she couldn't have the moon after all.

But maybe she could have the sky.

She looked up through the branches of Cole's favorite climbing tree at the blue stretch above.

If her wish worked, she would not end up like Aunt Marigold, weighed down by whatever secrets she had waited just too long to share. Georgia would drift from place to place as she pleased, just as Hank had done. Never staying long enough to lay down roots. Never long enough to let anyone else break her heart.

And she wouldn't be alone. She and Cole would go together. Fellow travelers on the same road. Perhaps there was even more magic out there, just waiting for them to find it.

She didn't have to sit around waiting for Mama to arrive and tell her that Daddy had left them. Tell her more lies about how everything was going to be fine, just fine. She could leave him, too. She could leave it all.

Aunt Marigold would probably be relieved to see her go, after the way Georgia had treated her this past week.

And as for Mama, Georgia would write to let her know she was okay. Mama would finish school, start a new job. In time, she would forget all about Georgia.

You can't run away. Angela's voice echoed distantly in her head.

Ignoring the voice, the twinge of doubt it sent vibrating through her chest, she turned to face Angela. "You don't have to come," she said quietly. "You *shouldn't* come. You should stay here."

Cole reached down a hand to help her up.

After the slightest pause, Georgia took it.

"Georgia, no!" Angela said, grabbing Georgia's other hand. But Georgia shook her off as gently as she could.

"You're right," she said, her heart beginning to pound. "You have been a good friend, Angela."

Angela stood, too. "I won't let you do it!" she cried,

scrambling toward the rowboat. "I won't let you in."

But just then, Georgia looked down at her feet and saw a tiny gray pebble, just like the ones on the island, tumbling in on a little wave. It was like a sign. She reached for it with one hand. Cole still held the other.

Angela saw what Georgia was doing. "No!" she cried.

"Do it," said Cole's voice in her ear. "Do it now."

Georgia closed her eyes. "I wish—" she started. "I wish—I wish we could fly. Far away from here."

She threw the stone across the lake, and in the same moment she let it go, she felt Angela's fingers slip into hers. Whether she had meant to stop Georgia from throwing the stone or to grasp her hand, Georgia didn't know.

But the next moment, she opened her eyes and saw three pairs of feet lifting off the ground.

Chapter Forty-eight

"It's working," Cole said, breaking into a grin. "You did it."

As she floated into the air, Georgia thought of Peter Pan leading the Darling children out through the nursery window. How she used to close her eyes and imagine what it would be like to fly with them over London at night, spinning around church spires and off into the stars.

The Darlings began to forget their family the moment their toes left the ground. Their worries of a moment before became distant memories.

Would the same thing happen for her?

On her other side, Angela grabbed Georgia's hand more tightly.

"You didn't have to come," Georgia said.

"Yes I did," Angela said. "Wherever you go, I go, too. I'm

not like your dad, Georgia. I'm not going to leave you all alone."

"I'm not alone," said Georgia, glancing over at Cole. But Cole had already let go of her hand. He had his arms over his head, trying to swim through the air.

Georgia stroked the sky with her own free hand, trying to follow. She frowned. She felt more like a balloon than a bird. The air felt thicker than she had imagined, harder to find her way through.

They were only six feet or so off the ground when the first gust of wind caught them, sweeping them up, up, up.

Angela drew in a quick breath, and Georgia felt her own heart shudder. This didn't feel like it had when they swam in the calm sea together, carefree and peaceful. It felt more like when their boat had been snatched up by the stormy swells, just before it had been capsized.

"This feels wrong," Angela said.

"It's not—how I thought it would be," Georgia whispered. She tried once again to sweep her arm through the air. Nothing happened except that she rose a few inches higher.

They had floated above the waters of the lake now. Georgia looked down, watched the island shrinking to the size of Aunt Marigold's potting wheel. Cole was floating along on his back just out of reach. He, at least, looked unconcerned. He had gotten what he wanted, Georgia realized. Hadn't he told her from the beginning that he wasn't intending to stay in this place?

All along, he had wanted to use the magic to run away. And he had convinced Georgia to come with him. For her sake? Or for his?

She felt the first fluttering of real fear, as though she'd awakened from a trance. What had she done?

Fear. She could still feel fear.

And if she could still feel fear—

Before she could stop herself, she thought of Daddy throwing her mug against the wall. Imagined him crumpling up the letter she'd left. Packing his suitcase to leave.

She gasped in pain as tears prickled in her eyes. It was all still there. The sadness. The anger. The thorns that scratched and gnawed. She had not escaped them or forgotten them.

Angela had been right. She couldn't run away from them. She would carry her sorrows with her wherever she went.

"Maybe we can get back down," Georgia said. "Try to flap your arms up."

Neither girl was willing to let go of the other's hand, and so they tried to push up through the air with their other arms. But nothing happened.

Another gust of wind pushed them away from the island.

"We're heading for the tree line now!" Angela cried.

They were too high. If the wish broke and they fell—

Georgia thought of Aunt Marigold. How she would never

forgive herself for not keeping Georgia safe.

She thought of Mama. Mama, who hated the quiet, living in a house all alone.

How could Georgia have thought of leaving them like Daddy had left her? How could she have put Angela in danger like this?

They had to get down.

"I wish we could get down now," Georgia called out. "I wish we could go back to the ground."

"It's too late," said Cole, who had interlaced his hands behind his head, as if he were lying on the beach instead of the sky. "You wished the lake would take us far away. You can't take it back now."

He was right. They merely floated closer to the oak trees. Another minute and—

Suddenly, Georgia caught a whiff of something in the air.

"Do you smell that?" she asked Angela.

Angela nodded. "It smells like—"

Smoke.

When Georgia turned her head toward the country house, she saw it. A column of dirty gray smoke rising from the house.

Too dark to be a wood fire from the chimney, and besides, why would Aunt Marigold have lit the hearth in the middle of summer?

"It's a fire," Angela murmured.

Georgia's insides gave a violent twist. What if her aunt was trapped inside?

For the briefest moment, she thought about giving up and letting the wind fly her away. Because what if it was already too late? How could she bear losing Aunt Marigold, too?

But she cast the fantasy away as quickly as it came to her. This was *real*. She had to get down. Had to get back to the country house to make sure her great-aunt was all right.

"Aunt Marigold!" she shouted.

Suddenly, the world around her sharpened into focus. Georgia looked down and saw that her feet were skimming the highest oak tree branches. She needed to grab hold of one.

But they were just out of reach. And now she and Angela were floating higher, and any second, they would cross over the oak trees, beyond the lake's borders.

Angela made a wild jerking motion. Georgia didn't realize what she was doing at first but then she saw. Angela had managed to hook the top of her foot under a branch that was sticking up from the oak tree below them. Now she was forcing her foot against the bottom of the branch to pull them down. And it was working.

But something strange was happening to Angela. While the rest of the world seemed sharper, she had grown fainter somehow. Foggier. Like at any moment you might be able to see straight through her. Georgia shook her head. It was probably an illusion caused by the bright sunlight against her skin.

"Keep going!" Georgia shouted.

Angela had just gotten them low enough so that she could hold the branch with one hand instead of a foot when Georgia felt something tugging at her other arm.

Cole.

"Come on," he said. "This was your wish. Don't be afraid."

Georgia *was* afraid. Afraid of what she had done. Afraid of what she would find if she ever made it back to the country house.

But more afraid of what would happen if she didn't.

"Let go!" she demanded.

"No," said Cole fiercely, grabbing her hand more tightly. "You can't get rid of me that easy."

But he, too, looked as though he were starting to fade around the edges.

Then Georgia felt herself being jerked sharply downward. Angela was pulling her with all her might, pulling her until Georgia could almost touch the treetop.

Angela let go of her hand, and Georgia's arm shot out to reach the branch hanging below her.

In the same instant, Georgia saw Angela swing herself off the tree branch. She used her momentum to do a kind of somersault in the air so that her feet were higher than her head, and then she aimed a two-footed kick directly at Cole's chest.

Cole's eyes burned. Georgia broke free of his grip. Now she was holding on to the branch with two hands, but Angela wasn't holding on at all.

"Angela!" Georgia cried. She thrust out one arm. Angela could've reached it, but she made no move to take it. She shook her head.

She seemed to shimmer in the sunlight. A prism of light suspended in air.

"Go, Georgia," she said. "Go help your aunt. Don't you understand? It's not just you who needs people. People are counting on you. You belong down there."

"Angela!" Georgia cried again. This time, her voice breaking with anguish. "Come back!"

Her friend smiled at her. She didn't seem afraid anymore. It was like all along she'd only been scared for Georgia's sake. And now that Georgia was safe, Angela didn't mind what happened to her.

"Don't let me go," Angela said simply.

But the words made no sense, because now she was out of reach. There would be no pulling her back. Another gust of wind and she was flying up, up, like a glass kite, following behind Cole, who was still staring at Georgia with dark, hungry eyes.

Another moment and they had both disappeared like wisps of cloud fading into the sky.

Chapter Forty-nine

Georgia found herself alone at the top of the oak tree, blinking at the empty sky. She perched, frozen for a moment, before scrambling down as fast as she could, expertly mapping her path through the branches. Her breath was still coming in sharp gasps, and tears stung at her eyes.

What had just happened?

Her heart throbbed as she thought of Angela slowly fading. Letting go of the branch so she could get to Cole. So she could keep Georgia safe.

Don't let me go.

But Angela hadn't taken Georgia's hand when she had the chance. And then she'd simply . . . disappeared.

Georgia couldn't think about it now. She had to get to Aunt Marigold before it was too late for her, too.

When she reached the ground, she flung herself through

the forest, running so fast that the trees blurred together into a knotted tapestry of brown and green. Twice she tripped, but each time she picked herself up and kept running.

Once, she swore she felt Angela running beside her. Whispering in her ear. *Go, Georgia!*

But when she looked over her shoulder, she was alone.

The smell of smoke grew stronger as she neared the house.

"Aunt Marigold!" Georgia shouted as she broke through the tree line. The fire, she could see now, was coming from the kitchen. Flames were licking against the windows just above the sink. A curtain of smoke was slowly billowing toward her.

Frantically, Georgia's eyes darted around, trying to spot her aunt. But there was only Ruby, pacing back and forth in her pasture and mooing, her eyes huge with fear.

A figure suddenly emerged from the front door. Georgia cried out with relief before she saw that it was Hank. He half collapsed on the porch, coughing and spluttering into his arms.

"Hank!" Georgia shouted. "Where's Aunt Marigold?"

"In-side," Hank panted. "I couldn't—my lungs—"

He exploded into another fit of coughing. Georgia ran past him as he called out to her, but she was already barreling through the open door.

Hot, stinging air filled her lungs, and she, too, began to cough. She pulled her shirt up over her nose, searching through the smoke for her great-aunt.

There! She could make out a figure splayed on the ground in the kitchen, nearly hidden on the other side of the table. Georgia felt a swooping sensation in her chest.

"No," she whispered.

Then she took a deep breath through her shirt and sprang across the room. The far wall was enveloped in flame now. Aunt Marigold lay on the floor, arms stretched out on either side, eyes closed. Georgia couldn't tell if she was breathing or not.

The air was hot. Too hot. Every breath burned her lungs.

Georgia bent down and gripped her great-aunt under her shoulders, hooking her arms through and pulling her torso up. Aunt Marigold's head lolled like a rag doll's. Georgia let out a choked sob as she pulled her across the room. But the air was so thick with smoke, and Aunt Marigold was so heavy. Impossibly heavy for someone so small.

Just a few steps from the door, Georgia felt her legs start to give out. If she could just find the strength—

Then there was someone beside her, someone helping to pull.

Together, she and Hank tugged Aunt Marigold the final few feet. Then at last, they were out on the porch, and Georgia was gasping. Sucking in breath after breath of air that wasn't quite fresh but that didn't hurt her lungs to breathe either. Hank laid Aunt Marigold down in the grass, then collapsed again and began to cough.

There was a sound in the air. Ruby mooing. And beyond that, a screaming sound. What was it? The phone ringing again? Georgia couldn't think straight.

She scrambled to her aunt's side, watching the lined face for signs of life. She took hold of one of her great-aunt's hands—unnaturally warm in her own. She held it gently.

"Please," she said. Her vision blurred with tears. "Please don't die, Aunt Marigold. Don't leave me."

As if in response, Aunt Marigold's chest rose feebly.

The screaming drew louder and louder until Georgia looked up to see a fire truck speeding down the driveway. An ambulance was right behind it.

Suddenly there were people everywhere, swarming the house with hoses and prying Georgia away from Aunt Marigold, who had still not moved. They were asking her questions, questions she couldn't hear, and lifting her arms and her legs one by one to check for burns while they loaded Aunt Marigold onto a stretcher.

"Is she okay?" Georgia asked the man who was walking with his arm around her.

"We don't know, honey," he said. "We're gonna get her to the hospital and do everything we can."

"I have to go, too," she managed to reply.

"Don't you worry. We're gonna make sure you're okay."

They were taking Aunt Marigold's stretcher now,

hurrying toward the ambulance. Hank was being checked over by another paramedic.

"I want to go with her," Georgia said. "I can't leave her."

The man squeezed Georgia's shoulder. She still had not looked up to see his face. "They need all the room they can get to help her, okay? But we've got someone coming for you right now. I'm gonna wait right here with you until they get here. I'm sure you'll see her in no time."

"But you can't promise," said Georgia quietly.

"No," the man said after a moment. "No, I can't do that."

Georgia watched as her great-aunt disappeared into the back of the ambulance. The doors shut behind her, and the ambulance started back down the drive.

Screams filled the air once more.

Chapter Fifty

~~~

Hank and Georgia were carted off in separate ambulances a few minutes after Aunt Marigold's disappeared.

Georgia was not allowed to see her great-aunt when she got to the hospital. Instead, she was taken to be examined herself while someone called Mama. After the doctor had decided she hadn't suffered any damage from smoke inhalation, she was left to wait in a little bed behind a curtain until Mama arrived. A nurse came by every few minutes to check on her and, once, to bring her cookies.

"They couldn't get hold of your mom or dad," the nurse had informed her. "But we'll keep trying. Don't you worry."

"And my aunt Marigold? And Hank?" Georgia asked, sitting up straight in her seat.

The nurse just shook her head. "They're with the doctors.

I'll let you know when there's any news."

So, Georgia lay numbly in the bed, staring at a pile of *Highlights* magazines. She tried not to think because, when she thought at all, she thought of Angela.

And then it felt as though Angela had been pulled straight out of her chest instead of from the air.

She couldn't stop seeing the pair of them—Angela and Cole—slowly fading away. Like a pair of mirages that disappeared when you got too close. What did it mean?

Just when she felt she might explode with the effort of not thinking, the curtain was pulled back again, and Hank appeared, wearing a hospital robe.

"Hank!" Georgia shouted. She flew from her bed and into his arms. He wrapped them around her. He still smelled like smoke. Burned things.

"Well, hey there, little lady," he wheezed. "You been checked out?"

Georgia nodded, still not ready to let go of him. "Are you okay?"

"Take more than a little fire like that to finish me off," he said. "But my lungs hurt like hell."

Finally, Georgia pulled away and looked up at him. He had a long scratch along one of his cheeks. "Have you heard anything about Aunt Marigold?" she asked.

He shook his head. "Naw, Georgia," he said. "Not yet."

"You were there," Georgia murmured. "You were there and I wasn't."

"But you came, Georgia," Hank said. "You came just in time. I didn't see her downstairs. Thought she was upstairs. Searched the whole house. And by then my lungs— I needed fresh air."

"She was in the kitchen," Georgia said. "On the other side of the table."

"I figured as much when I came back in and saw you with her. Stupid mistake. Lucky for me—for Marigold—that you were there to find her."

They sat together for a while, Hank barely squeezing onto the bed beside her. They didn't speak, but Hank took one of Georgia's hands in his own, and every once in a while, patted it with his other.

Finally, the nurse reappeared. She frowned at Hank. "You aren't supposed to be here," she said. "You should be in your room."

Hank shot Georgia a wink, but she could see the worry in his eyes. "Oops," he said, lumbering to his feet. "Musta gotten lost."

"The doctors are done with her," said the nurse, looking at Georgia. "You can see her now. Come on with me."

Georgia's heartbeat quickened as she shot up. "Aren't you coming?" she said to Hank. He shook his head.

"Back to my room," he said. "Nurse's orders."

The nurse nodded. "She really shouldn't have more than one visitor right now, anyway."

Georgia followed her alone down a long bright hallway that smelled funny and was full of beeping noises. Georgia wished they would walk faster.

Finally, they came to an open door, and the nurse ushered her inside. "You two take your time. I'll just go try your mama again," she said in a quiet voice, giving Georgia's shoulder a squeeze.

Alone now, Georgia tiptoed into the room, her eyes glued to the slight figure in the bed. Her great-aunt looked gray and wrinkled, like the fire had shriveled her all up. Her eyes were closed, and she wasn't moving. She looked—

Georgia was frozen in place, too afraid to come any nearer, when she saw Aunt Marigold's eyes crack open.

"Well, don't just stand there," she croaked. "Pour me some water, child."

The relief that flooded Georgia's chest was like a gust of cold wind. So sudden and strong it brought tears to her eyes.

She poured a glass of water from a pitcher and handed it to Aunt Marigold.

"Your hands are shaking," said her great-aunt. There was a rasp in her voice that hadn't been there before.

"I thought—" Georgia started. "I thought you might be—that I was going to lose you, too."

She felt her knees give way as she dropped down onto the bed and began to cry in earnest. Aunt Marigold put a hand on her back.

"There, now," she soothed. "There's no need for all this. You should be proud, Georgia. You ran into a burning building to save me. Not many folks could say the same."

Proud was the last thing Georgia felt.

"So, you're going to be okay?"

"Well, I'm not gonna say that my pride hasn't been badly bruised," Aunt Marigold replied. "But everything else will heal."

She handed Georgia a tissue to blow her nose with and one to dry her eyes on.

"What happened?" Georgia asked when the tissues were balled up in her hand. "The fire, I mean. How did it start?"

Aunt Marigold sighed, and again, Georgia noticed the rasp that echoed in her throat. "My damn hands," she said. "I was making lunch, and I dropped a glass of water. When I went to clear it up, one of the dish towels got caught on the stove burner. I smelled it burning and tried to get up to pull it off, but I slipped on the water. Must have hit my head on one of the cabinets. Next thing I know, I'm waking up here and they tell me my niece and my handyman dragged me out of the house in the nick of time."

She reached out to smooth her long hair, which was hanging in loose waves around her shoulders. "You really should be proud, you know," she said, taking one of Georgia's hands in her own. "I suppose you're something of a hero now."

At this, another sob rose in Georgia's throat. Would Aunt Marigold say that if she knew what had happened at the lake earlier that day? That Georgia had nearly turned her back on Aunt Marigold and Mama?

She was no hero. She had been a coward.

Aunt Marigold didn't try to stop her crying this time. She just brushed her fingertips back and forth across Georgia's back, now and again murmuring, "There, there," and "It's all right, child."

When finally Georgia's sobs subsided, Aunt Marigold folded her hands in her lap. "Georgia," she said hoarsely, "what did you mean when you said you thought I was leaving you, *too*?"

There was no point in trying to avoid the question. Aunt Marigold would find out soon enough anyhow.

"Daddy," she said quietly. "He's not just missing. He left. He left *us*. For good."

Aunt Marigold's brow furrowed. "Georgia, I don't think your daddy—"

But then she began to cough, a deep hacking noise that made Georgia cringe. The little monitor next to her began beeping faster. "Are you okay?" Georgia asked, alarmed.

Aunt Marigold nodded. "From—the—smoke," she panted.

When her coughing had quieted and the beeping had slowed again, Georgia began to explain. Better for Aunt

Marigold to save her breath. She told her everything that had happened. About the letter she'd written, about the business cards and addresses she'd found, about Daddy coming into the office and finding her there and the mug smashing to pieces against the wall.

She didn't look at her great-aunt while she was speaking, and when she was done, she was surprised to glance up to see that Aunt Marigold wore an expression of calm composure.

"Your mama told me about all that," she said. "Well, all except the bit about what you found in the desk. And I'm real sorry you had to see your daddy like that, Georgia. But I don't think he has any plans to leave you."

"But he already *did* leave," Georgia protested. "Mama said so when she called earlier."

"She called again just a few minutes after you ran off," replied Aunt Marigold. "He was picked up by the police last night, passed out in his car. He spent last night in jail, and she was just about to go get him when she called."

Georgia felt a little chill of shock. Could what Aunt Marigold was saying be true? She couldn't imagine Daddy in *jail*. But then she thought of the morning she'd woken up to see his car parked outside. Mr. Molina dragging his limp form out from the driver's seat. And then she believed it. And she also knew jail wasn't the worst that could have happened to him.

"He's really not leaving? What about the business cards, then?"

313

"Have you ever heard of a stage name?" Aunt Marigold asked. "Lots of performers use them."

"But Daddy's been playing all over town for a year," Georgia said. "Why would he need a stage name *now*? And what about all those clubs and things in Nashville?"

Aunt Marigold gave a weary shrug of her shoulders. "You'll have to ask your mama about that," she said.

Georgia waited to feel relieved. She had been wrong. Daddy hadn't left them. Maybe didn't even have plans to.

But all she could feel was anger. Sadness. Shame. And a growing flutter of fear.

Because if Daddy had left them, at least there would have been an end to it. Maybe she and Mama would have found a way to go on with their lives together. But now what? Would they limp along this way forever, all of them trapped in the shadow of Daddy's drinking?

"What is it, Georgia?" came Aunt Marigold's voice.

"I thought I'd be relieved," said Georgia quietly. "But I'm not. It's like—it's like either way, he's already left us. Maybe he didn't choose another life, but he chose the drinking, didn't he? He chose drinking over us a long time ago."

"Oh, Georgia." Aunt Marigold sighed. And then, "You don't look very comfortable there. Take the chair, why don't you? I'm going to tell you a story."

Chapter Fifty-one

When Georgia was settled in the armchair next to the hospital bed, her knees tucked under her chin, Aunt Marigold took a deep breath.

"I've lived a good life," she said, "no matter what it may look like from the outside. I had a happy childhood with parents who loved me. I've had a roof over my head and nature at my door for all my years. I have lots of things to be thankful for, Georgia, and I don't forget that. But life gives with one hand and it takes with the other."

She cradled her own hands together. Her eyes had taken on a misty look, like a lace curtain had been drawn over them.

"The first I learned about that was when my mama died—had a stroke right in the middle of church. I was twenty-two. It was the hardest thing I could imagine, to lose my mother. I thought the grieving would never end. But it did, or at least it got better. Not for my father, though. He couldn't get over her passing. And that's when it started for him."

"What started?"

Aunt Marigold's eyes flickered back to Georgia. "The drinking," she said. "It started and it never stopped."

Georgia felt her mouth drop into a little o. "Your daddy drank, too?"

"And drank and drank and drank," said Aunt Marigold, nodding in time with her own words. "He drank until he couldn't run the farm anymore. Then he sold most of our land and fired all our farmhands so he could keep on drinking. He drank until he was so sick he couldn't leave the house, then until he couldn't leave the bed."

The narrow bed. The rocking chair.

"You stayed with him," Georgia said. "You took care of him."

"Not at first," said Aunt Marigold. "I was young. I had other dreams. Being an artist. Having a family of my own. I moved away and got married. But it didn't last. I couldn't leave my father by himself. My husband didn't much care for playing second fiddle. Not that I blame him."

Georgia remembered what Daddy had said, about Aunt Marigold being married once but it not lasting long.

"So he—he left you?" she asked.

Aunt Marigold nodded.

"Couldn't you have tried again?" Georgia said gently. "Tried to meet somebody new?"

"It took my father over a decade to die," replied Aunt Marigold. "I was afraid if I left, he would get worse. I hoped if I stayed, I could make him better. And while he died, life—well, it just passed me by. He got worse and worse, needed me more and more. And by the time he had died, my world had shrunk down to the size of a house. Then there was my pottery, and that kept me content for a while. But—"

"Your hands," Georgia finished.

Aunt Marigold's lips twitched. "All those years wringing out washcloths and changing bedsheets," she said. "They took their toll, I guess."

Georgia's chest burned as though a tiny bit of fire smoldered on inside her. How could a man be so selfish? "Don't you—I mean, aren't you angry at him?"

Now Aunt Marigold turned to look at Georgia with her sharp eyes, the flecks of gold in them standing out against her ashen skin. "I was very angry," she said. "For a very long time. But not anymore. At least, not at him, Georgia."

"But why not?" Georgia burst out. "He took everything from you. I'd—I'd *hate* him for what he did."

"Because I remember who my daddy was before his life went sideways, and I know he wasn't what people said he was. He wasn't a drunk or a lush or a tippler. He wasn't a bad or weak man. He was just sick. He was an alcoholic, Georgia. He had a disease. Just like your daddy does."

Georgia felt her brows furrow. She shook her head in confusion. *Sick? Diseased?* Her daddy was neither of those things.

"My daddy isn't sick," she said. "Mama says he drinks because he needs it to help him play. And he wants that more than he wants us."

"I thought it was a choice, too, at first," said Aunt Marigold. "I blamed him for it, just like you're blaming your daddy. But the longer I stayed, the more I saw how much the drinking took from him. In his last days, when we both knew he was dying and he still begged me to get him one last drink—that's when I realized he had no choice. The alcohol had taken over him. Because nobody would choose a life like that, Georgia. Or a death."

She reached out one of her hands and wrapped it around Georgia's. "It's not a choice for your daddy either," she said. "At least, not the way you're thinking. Your daddy wishes he could stop. I know he does. But right now, he's not in control. That's what alcohol does to some people—controls them. It's a darkness that just takes over."

Georgia felt a cold chill as she remembered how she had felt by the lake earlier that day. Like the thorny blackness in her belly might keep growing and growing until it had trapped her in a cage of shadow. She had thought she was trying to escape it, but what if it was that dark power that had taken her over, tricked her into making that terrible wish? What if she and Daddy were more alike than she realized?

"Georgia?" said Aunt Marigold. "You understand what I'm saying? That man who threw your mug at the wall—that's not your daddy. That's the drink."

The Shadow Man. Had Georgia been right all along? That it wasn't Daddy doing all the yelling, the fighting, the drinking, the lying? That it was another man hiding inside him?

She thought of the crumpled note she'd found in Mama's pocket. *I'm very sorry about this morning. I promise*

He couldn't find the strength to promise. But he *had* said he was sorry.

She thought of the way his face had been contorted in misery when he'd found her in his study. If the drinking and the playing made him happy, why would he have broken down in tears?

Maybe Aunt Marigold was right. Maybe he did want to stop. Maybe he just couldn't find the strength.

And if drinking wasn't a choice, that meant that Daddy hadn't chosen it over her. Not exactly. He'd left her—again and again, he'd left her—but he hadn't *wanted* to. It wasn't because she wasn't good enough. Not because he didn't love her.

But then she heard his voice—*GET OUT!*—and saw him slam her mug into the wall. Remembered the way her heart felt like it had shattered, too. Her hand clenched under Aunt Marigold's. Wanting to stop wasn't enough. She *needed* Daddy to be stronger than the Shadow Man.

"I'm not saying you can't be angry," her great-aunt said, as though she were reading Georgia's mind. "Fighting mad, even. You have every right to be. You've been hurt. Betrayed. But don't let the anger make you forget the love. You still love your daddy, don't you?"

Georgia thought about this for a split second, then nodded. If the shame was always there, so was the love. The other side of the coin.

"Good. You keep that love in your heart where it belongs. And you keep the love your daddy has for you there, too. He still loves you, Georgia. That person you know is still there. It's just— Well, I suppose it's like you said. It's like he's left. Like on a trip. But that doesn't mean he won't come back."

"But how?" Georgia said. She could hear the desperation in her own voice. "How do I get him to come back?"

Aunt Marigold squeezed Georgia's hand. "You don't, child. *You* don't. You don't waste your precious life waiting for him to change or trying to make it so. Running into one burning building was more than enough. There's no use losing yourself tryin' to save somebody else, hear?"

Georgia felt tears welling once more in her eyes. "There

must be something," she said. "Something I can do."

"It must have taken a lot of courage for you to write that letter," Aunt Marigold replied. "Did you tell him that his drinking was hurting you?"

Georgia nodded.

"And that you wanted him to stop?"

Another nod.

"And that you loved him?"

"Yes."

"Then you've done all you can for now. Just keep remembering the man you know. Keep loving him as best you can. And don't stop hoping for him to get better. But you have to remember that it's not your responsibility to *make* him better."

"But will he—" Georgia asked, her voice small as a distant echo. "*Will* he get better? Or will he be like your daddy?"

Aunt Marigold didn't answer for a long moment. Down the hall, Georgia could hear murmured voices moving closer.

"Things were different for my daddy," Aunt Marigold replied. "We didn't know as much back then. And besides, he had two demons to fight. The grief and the drink. It wasn't a fair fight."

Aunt Marigold's voice broke on this last word, and she squeezed her eyes shut for a long moment. When she opened them, they were shining. She cleared her throat.

"There are treatments now. So many ways he can find

help. But he has to find the strength to ask for it. Change doesn't happen by wishing, you know. The only person who can change your daddy back is your daddy."

Aunt Marigold sounded so like Angela that for a moment, Georgia couldn't find her breath. Before she could gather her thoughts to respond, the door creaked open, and the nurse from earlier appeared.

"Look who I found," she said with a smile, stepping aside to reveal Mama, her face pale and hair untidy.

"Georgia," she breathed. "Oh, Georgia!"

"Mama!" cried Georgia. She had never been so happy to see her mother in her life.

Then she and Mama were both hurrying toward each other, meeting in an embrace.

"Georgia," Mama said again. She said it over and over into Georgia's hair before pulling away, taking Georgia by the shoulders and looking her up and down. "They said you were all right. Is that true? Are you really okay?"

"I'm fine," Georgia replied. "Honest, Mama."

Breathing a sigh of relief, Mama hugged her daughter into her chest once more. "And you, Marigold?" she said. "How are you?"

"Just a bump on the head and some smoke in my lungs," Aunt Marigold rasped. Her voice had grown thin while she'd been talking to Georgia. "Nothing to worry yourself about."

"Even so," said the nurse, who was still hovering in the

doorway, "you need to be getting some rest now. Visiting hours are almost over."

Mama nodded. "Of course," she said. "We'll leave you to it."

One arm still draped over Georgia's shoulders, Mama led her from the room. At the doorway, Georgia stopped and looked back at her great-aunt. She was staring at Georgia.

"Bye, Aunt Marigold," said Georgia. "Feel better."

She had so much more to ask. So much more to say. But it would do for now.

"Goodbye, Georgia," said Aunt Marigold, before settling her arms overtop her blankets and closing her eyes.

Chapter Fifty-two

⁓

From the hospital, they drove straight back to the country house.

"I suppose we should go and see what the damage is," Mama said. "And you'll need to get your things."

It hadn't occurred to Georgia to wonder about the state of house. She only wanted to get back so she could return to the lake.

"So," Mama said as they pulled away from the hospital, "will you tell me what happened?"

Like most of the questions between them, it was easier asked than answered.

The way Angela and Cole had faded away, almost like she had been watching a magic trick . . .

That magic came to you, *and for some kinda reason,* Georgia heard Hank's voice say. *And when it leaves you, that'll be for a reason, too.*

"Georgia?"

"Sorry, Mama. I was just . . . thinking."

Georgia started her story with being at the top of the oak tree and seeing the smoke rising from the house. Mama's hand covered her mouth as Georgia explained how she'd run in and, with Hank's help, pulled her great-aunt out to safety.

"That was a very brave thing to do," said Mama, her hands trembling on the steering wheel. "But when I think what might have happened—you running into a house on fire like that . . ."

"Aunt Marigold said Daddy was in jail," Georgia said quietly, staring out the window at the passing fields. The late-afternoon light had turned them golden.

She heard Mama let out a long sigh. "He's back at home now. He wanted to come, but I—I said maybe it was better if he didn't."

Mama paused, like she was waiting for Georgia to say something. When she didn't, Mama went on. "There's no excuse, Georgia, for what he did the other night. But you should know that he feels terribly about how he acted. How he's been acting. He knew things have been hard on you, but reading your letter, well—I think it hit home."

"But he kept drinking anyway," Georgia said.

"Yes," replied Mama stiffly. "He did. I think he was

trying to escape his feelings about what he'd done."

So he *had* been trying to escape, in his own way.

"Do you know about Tony Darling?" Georgia asked, finally turning to look at Mama, whose eyes widened slightly.

"I do," she said. "How do you?"

Georgia answered the question with one of her own. "Why did Daddy make up a fake identity? Is it because he was going to leave us?"

Mama shook her head. "No, sweetheart. He was having trouble getting bookings. I guess he's been showing up late and drinking too much to finish his sets. He thought if he could get the bookings under another name, by the time he showed up and they realized it was him, it would be too late to get anyone else and he would have a second chance to prove he could do the job. But that idea, it hasn't been working too well."

So, the drinking had never been helping Daddy to play. It had taken that from him, too.

The thought of Daddy losing his music made Georgia ache, but in a way it was a relief. Music was Daddy's passion. He would never choose to give it up. Which meant Aunt Marigold was right about drinking not being a choice.

"I found a list of clubs and things," Georgia said. "In Nashville. I thought—"

Mama sighed. "He had an idea that if things didn't turn

around here, he might start staying up there to play. On the weekends. Make a name for himself. That maybe we could all move there and start over."

Daddy had wanted a new life, after all. But he had wanted it for *all* of them.

Georgia knew what she needed to ask next, though she wasn't sure she wanted to. "Daddy's not happy, is he?"

"No," said Mama, wincing slightly, like a mosquito had just bitten her. Georgia could see how hard it was for her mother to say these things after keeping them to herself for so long. "No, I don't think he is."

"Aunt Marigold's daddy drank because he was unhappy, too. But that's because his wife died."

Mama nodded. "That's true," she said, speaking slowly. Thoughtfully. "But for some people, unhappiness is more complicated. It creeps up on you, and there's not always a simple reason why. And the drinking—well, I think it was a solution until it became a problem. It helped him forget he was unhappy, until it started making him even more unhappy, which made him drink even more." She paused, then squeezed Georgia's hand. "But Georgia, your daddy loves you more than anything else in the world. He wanted me to tell you."

She wanted to believe Mama. So badly it hurt.

"Is he going to get help?" she asked. "Aunt Marigold said there are lots of treatments now, but Daddy has to decide he wants help before he can get better."

Now it was Mama's turn to stare out the window. When she looked back at Georgia, there were tears in her eyes. "I don't know," she admitted. "He says— Well, I hope he'll be ready for help, soon, sweetheart."

When would soon be? Next week? Next year? Or was soon like the horizon—just an illusion? Something they would never reach?

Chapter Fifty-three

~~

The car rumbled onto Aunt Marigold's driveway, and Mama gasped. The kitchen wall was blackened to a crisp. There were deep ruts in the yard from where the ambulances and fire trucks had been. One pickup truck remained parked in front of the house, with a man inside who was writing something on a notepad. He looked up as Mama parked their car.

"That must be the fire marshal," she said. "I should go speak to him."

While Mama went to talk to the fire marshal, Georgia walked over to check on Ruby, who was peering anxiously out from her new cowshed. Georgia wished she had some peppermints. Even without them, Ruby let her scratch beneath her ears. "Don't worry, girl," Georgia whispered.

"Everything's going to be okay now."

She glanced toward the forest, and her heartbeat quickened.

"Mama," she called. "I need to go look for something." She gestured toward the trees. "I lost it earlier, before the fire."

That much was true, wasn't it?

Mama frowned. "Well, all right," she said. "But don't be long."

"I won't," Georgia promised.

When she crossed into the familiar shadow of the trees, the forest was full of hushed noises.

Chirrup, swish, whisper.

At every sound, Georgia glanced around, waiting for a figure to appear. But none did. As she climbed between the two oak trees, she held her breath like a secret.

Standing on the banks of the lake, she blinked several times, trying to make sense of what she was seeing.

The water had transformed from its usual brilliant blue to a murky brown. There were oak trees scattered here and there around its banks, but the giant fairy ring Georgia remembered was no longer there. The island in the middle of the lake still was, but the tree growing atop it was just a normal redbud tree. It looked nothing like an old, gnarled wizard.

The boat, too, had been changed. Its gleaming wood had

hardened into dull plastic with chipped paint.

The lake had transformed itself one last time. The magic had been swept away, and all that was left was a muddy little pond.

"Angela?" Georgia called. Her voice was small, and there was no answer. She tried again, louder this time. "Angela? Are you there?"

For the first time, when Georgia needed her, her friend did not appear.

There was still one place Georgia needed to check. One thing she needed to find out for certain. And she would have to be quick about it, or Mama would worry.

Turning her back on the pond, she headed into the forest once more. Not the way she'd come but the way she had gone the time she had followed Angela back to the Boatwright house.

Running where she could, she picked a path through the unfamiliar woods as the afternoon light grew purple around the edges. After ten minutes or so, the forest became less dense. Then she saw it. The farmhouse.

The station wagon was parked in the driveway, just like last time. The For Sale sign had been taken down. Two bicycles were leaned against the side of the house.

Both of them just the right size for a child.

Georgia held her breath as she scanned the windows. But she couldn't see anyone at all. Then, just when she thought she couldn't bear the uncertainty any longer, the front door opened. A tall woman walked out first, followed by a man with red hair.

"Let's go," the woman called. "Before we miss all the previews!"

A second later, two children tumbled out the door. A boy and a girl.

"I want popcorn!" the boy cried.

"And Twizzlers!" added the girl.

They both had red hair, like their father, and freckles that dappled their arms. The girl looked to be about Georgia's age, the boy slightly younger.

Georgia shrank back into the shadows, not wanting this family to catch her spying on them. These strangers.

Angela didn't live here. Neither did Cole. They never had.

Georgia felt a strange mixture of sorrow and relief as she turned away from the happy family packing into their car. But she didn't feel surprised, exactly.

For some part of her had realized, when she'd seen Angela and Cole fading away, that they hadn't just stumbled upon the magic of the lake, as Georgia had.

They had been part of it.

Chapter Fifty-four

That night, Georgia and Mama stayed at a motel by the hospital. Aunt Marigold was released the next morning. Hank had already been allowed to go home.

"We can get Marigold settled in," Mama said as they drove to the hospital, "and see that she has everything she needs before we head home. Or I suppose she could stay in a motel if she'd rather. I'd offer to have her come stay with us, but, well . . ."

Mama trailed off. Georgia was still stuck on the word "home." Was home still the same place? She pictured their tidy house on its tidy street. Thought of their garden with the seashells strewn among the flowers. Remembered upside-down snowmen in the yard and snuggling up next to Daddy to read before bedtime. And then:

Ice tinkling against a glass. A stifled sob. A door slamming.

No. That house didn't feel like home any longer. Hadn't felt that way in a long time. Did she still belong there simply because that's where Daddy was?

She remembered what Aunt Marigold had said earlier. *There's no use losing yourself tryin' to save somebody else.*

Then, painfully, it was Angela's voice she heard. *I think standing up for yourself always makes a difference.*

"Mama?"

She knew the words were right even though just thinking them felt wrong.

"I don't want to go home," she forced herself to say. "Not until Daddy's ready to change. *Really* ready. I want to stay with Aunt Marigold. And I think you should, too."

Aunt Marigold had said she should keep remembering the Daddy she loved. But Georgia knew that every day she shared a house with the Shadow Man would make it harder to remember the real Daddy. His smile. His voice. His love.

How could she love the man who had put cracks in her heart? Who had made her want to turn her back on the world to protect it from getting hurt again?

She thought of picking vegetables from the garden and helping Aunt Marigold with dinner. Feeding Ruby peppermints. The smell of clay between her hands. The peace it gave her to focus on the making of things, not the breaking.

If her heart was ever going to heal, she needed that

feeling. Needed to know that Aunt Marigold wasn't alone any longer.

Her gaze met Mama's. There was surprise in her round eyes. "We'll have to see about the house," Mama said. "When it will be ready to—and how Marigold's recovery—but if that's really what you want . . ."

She trailed off.

"It's what I need, Mama," said Georgia.

Slowly Mama nodded. "Well, then," she said, "I suppose that's that."

A different nurse from the day before insisted on rolling Aunt Marigold outside in a wheelchair. As a result, Aunt Marigold wore a thunderous expression as she stood up when they reached the car, shaking off the nurse's attempt to help her into the front seat.

Once they were safely away from the hospital and on the highway, Mama turned to Aunt Marigold. "The fire marshal said it would be all right to go back to the house today," she said. "But they've blocked off the kitchen area until we can get it cleaned and the wall repaired. I'm afraid there was quite a lot of damage there."

Aunt Marigold didn't say anything. She just pursed her lips tighter.

"And one more thing," Mama went on. "Georgia and I thought we would stay with you for a little while. Until you're back on your feet, that is."

"If you like," said Aunt Marigold, as though it didn't matter to her either way. But from the back seat, Georgia could see some of the worry fall away from her narrow shoulders. She still looked frail, but her complexion had changed back from ashen almost to its usual peachy color.

"If it's all right," Mama went on, "Georgia would like to stay at least to the end of the summer. Then we can—reevaluate."

"Well, I reckon that would be fine," said Aunt Marigold, flicking her green eyes up to meet Georgia's in the rearview mirror.

Georgia mustered a little smile of thanks but then turned her attention back to Mama. Did that mean that *she* wasn't staying? That she was going back to Daddy, once Aunt Marigold was "back on her feet"?

But Mama said no more. Her eyes were set firmly on the road ahead, just as they always were.

Chapter Fifty-five

~~~~

When they arrived back at the country house, Aunt Marigold wrung her hands as she cast aside the tarp that had been hung like a curtain between the kitchen and the rest of the house. "What a fool I am," she muttered to herself, shaking her head as she assessed the damage.

"Don't be silly," Mama replied. "It could happen to anyone."

Though, Georgia knew, this wasn't quite true. The fire had started because of Aunt Marigold's hands. And what if Georgia hadn't been here, hadn't made it back in time?

Aunt Marigold needed someone here with her. Not just to keep her company but to keep her safe.

Georgia realized she was staring, and the concern must have been obvious on her face, because her great-aunt shot her a glare hot enough to curdle milk.

"Why don't you go upstairs and lie down for a while?" Mama said.

"Fine," Aunt Marigold replied. "But I need a word with Georgia."

Mama looked surprised but gestured for Georgia to follow Aunt Marigold as she made her way up the stairs, passing her a pitcher of water and a glass to take up.

Georgia hovered awkwardly in the doorway as her great-aunt threw back her sheets and climbed into the bed, huffing as she did. Only when she was settled under them did Georgia creep forward and sit down in the chair in the corner of the room.

"I only wanted to say," said Aunt Marigold, her voice stern, "that you're welcome here as long as you like, Georgia. But not if it's because you have some grand ideas about becoming my nurse and spending your days taking care of me. I don't need any of that."

"But you do," Georgia said, trying to make her voice as firm as her great-aunt's. "You do need help. You might have another accide—"

"I won't," said Aunt Marigold, sticking her chin out defiantly. "And even if I did need help, I wouldn't take it from a child. Your job is to play. Go to school. Dream. Not spend your time worrying about an old lady."

Georgia bit the corner of her lip, thinking. "What if I got something out of it, too?"

Aunt Marigold frowned. "What do you mean?"

"What if I keep helping out—not all the time but just with the things you need—in exchange for my pottery lessons?"

"Your pottery lessons?" Aunt Marigold repeated blankly.

"I want to keep learning, and you're the best teacher I could ask for," Georgia said. "But it wouldn't be right for you to give them for free. So it wouldn't be like charity, me helping out. It would be a swap."

Her great-aunt contemplated this for a moment. "Hmph," she said finally with a little shrug of her shoulders.

Georgia felt her mouth lift in a little smile. "I'll take that as a yes," she said.

She turned to go but stopped suddenly in the doorway. "Aunt Marigold?"

"Mmm?" Her great-aunt was already picking up a book from her bedside table.

"There's something you never told me. Something I've been wanting to know. About the grave?"

Georgia had lain awake most of the night, thinking about Angela, Cole, the lake—all of it. Trying to untangle it all in her mind.

But she had awoken that morning thinking of the angel in the forest.

"Ah yes," said Aunt Marigold, sounding reluctant as she set the book aside. "I did say I would tell you about it, didn't I?"

She began to cough, and Georgia passed her a glass of water.

"Well, first of all," croaked Aunt Marigold when the coughing fit had passed. "It's not a grave. Although I see why you might have been confused."

Georgia's brow furrowed. She had been so sure. That feeling of coldness and sorrow that seemed to surround the little glade . . .

"What is it, then?"

Her great-aunt sighed. "A garden of sorts, I suppose," she said. "A garden of wishes."

Georgia went very still. "*Wishes?*" she echoed.

"I used to go there to bury them," said Aunt Marigold, gazing out the window, where a soft rain had begun to fall. "Each time I had a wish—a dream—that I knew would never come true. I would go there and I would plant a seed. That way, at least something beautiful would grow out of all those dreams that weren't to be. A little part of them would get to live."

Georgia thought of the flowers painstakingly painted onto the plates and bowls her aunt had made, and hoped that some of the dishes had survived the fire.

She thought of the sunflower Aunt Marigold had left in a vase in her room after she'd fallen and scraped her knee.

She looked at her great-aunt, whose green eyes were sparkling, and felt as though Aunt Marigold had suddenly dropped a veil she had been wearing all this time. Or perhaps an armor.

"I wished for my father to get better," Aunt Marigold said softly. "For the talent to become a famous artist. For my marriage to work. I wished that someday I would have a little girl whose wishes would all come true, unlike mine."

Goose bumps erupted on Georgia's arms.

"And the angel?" she said, her voice trembling.

"I stopped going to church after Mama had her stroke there," her great-aunt replied. "Too difficult. I suppose that garden was the closest thing I had to a church. Besides, it was nice to think of an angel out there, watching over those wishes, making sure they rested peacefully."

"I'm sorry," Georgia said. "I'm sorry they didn't come true."

Aunt Marigold shook her head. "What did I say yesterday? I don't need anyone being sorry for me. And besides . . . maybe we don't always get what we wish for, but sometimes life gives us other gifts instead. Things we didn't know to ask for."

Georgia nodded, a lump rising in her throat. She wanted to reply, but she didn't know how. "You should rest now," she said instead, turning toward the door.

"Wait," Aunt Marigold said. She held up the book that had been splayed on her lap. "My eyes are tired. Why don't you stay a minute and read to me?"

"Okay," Georgia replied, taking the book from Aunt Marigold's hands. It felt right somehow, reading to the woman who had once read to Daddy. Like one of the rings Aunt Marigold painted around the edges of her plate. A perfect circle coming to a close.

Chapter Fifty-six

Hank started work on the kitchen the very next day. He insisted he could do the whole job himself, free of charge.

Mama had moved into the locked room for now, which was, of course, no longer locked. She had to drive into town for class a few times a week and always brought dinner back with her. Cooking was tricky without a working stove.

Georgia had taken to going for long walks through the woods every afternoon, wandering through the folds of emerald light and shadow, thinking. She avoided walking the familiar path to the wishing lake. She didn't think she could bear seeing it again with all the magic stripped away.

Some mornings, she was still awoken by a prickling feeling in the pit of her stomach. Fear or sorrow or anger, or all three. A darkness inside her as her thoughts turned to the

Shadow Man pitching her mug against the wall. To wondering how Daddy was and when she would see him again.

Some days, she needed to stomp through the forest with her arms crossed over her chest. Or to cry when she reached the safety of the trees, where the birds would console her with their songs.

On those afternoons, she always found her way into the wishing garden, as she'd come to think of it. She had brought a pair of work gloves and some gardening tools out to the little glade and had begun to tend the patch of flowers. She let their bright colors fight off the darkness inside.

Sometimes, though, she merely sat on her heels and stared at the mossy angel who watched over the garden.

She remembered that day she and Angela had played in the snow. How Angela had made a snow angel, and it had reminded Georgia of this statue. How for a time—until she'd seen the girl at the Boatwright house and mistaken her for Angela—she'd even let herself wonder if her friend might be a ghost.

She knew now that there was no one lying underneath these flowers. No one to haunt this glade. But if she looked closely enough, she could almost see hints of Angela's face in the peace of the angel's eyes, the roundness of her cheeks.

She missed her friend so powerfully that sometimes the longing took up all the room in her chest.

Sometimes, when she was thinking about Angela at dinner or while she was reading in the living room, Angela's beaming face would swim into sight, and Georgia would forget about what she was doing. Then Mama would wrap an arm around her shoulders and say something like, "I know you miss him."

She couldn't tell Mama that she did miss Daddy—of course she did—but that she was thinking of someone else.

As she walked through the forest each day, she played over in her mind every moment she'd spent with Angela.

Angela suddenly appearing that first afternoon when Georgia had fallen, to make sure she was all right.

Angela jumping on the boat, light-footed as a cat.

Angela wishing for an afternoon at Camp Pine Valley so that Georgia could remember what it had been like to be happy. Reminding her that she knew how to be strong without Daddy to make her that way.

Angela encouraging Georgia to write her letter to Daddy. Appearing at the lake on the night they'd hung from the moon.

Angela letting go of the tree branch so she could stop Cole from pulling Georgia away into the air. Making sure she could get back to Aunt Marigold in time.

Everything she had done had been for Georgia.

Maybe the lake wanted to bring us together, she'd said once, when Georgia had asked what she thought the magic was for. *So we could be friends.*

I would have been your friend even if there was no magic, Georgia had replied.

She just hadn't understood then that Angela *was* the magic. *She* had been the very best part, not the lake.

The lake had started out as an escape. It had helped at first. But after Cole arrived, its magic had become something darker. Something Georgia didn't know how to control. Something that nearly controlled *her.* Like the drink that controlled the Shadow Man.

It had never been the wishes that she'd needed but the girl who had made them. Angela had seen all the things in Georgia that Daddy had once seen. Angela had pulled her back from the darkness threatening to swallow her. Angela had loved her—if a girl who came from thin air and disappeared back into it *could* love.

But where had Angela come from? And why had she gone? These things, more than anything, were what Georgia longed to understand.

Had one of Aunt Marigold's buried wishes grown into something more than just a flower? Had her angel grown it into something more beautiful than she could ever have imagined?

I wished that someday I would have a little girl, she'd said, *whose wishes would all come true.*

Hank had said that the magic had come to her for a

346

reason. But what if it hadn't come *to* her at all?

What if it had come *from* her?

She thought back again to the day she'd first met Angela. How before she had even set eyes on the lake, she had wished for someone to help her feel less lonely.

Perhaps you couldn't change everything just by wishing, but could a wish be strong enough to invite something new into the world? To create *magic*, even? To take what had been within Georgia all along and make it come to life?

Hank had also said that when the magic left, that would be for a reason, too.

Angela had stayed with Georgia until the very end. Until Georgia had been able to choose reality over the magic. To stay rather than fly away.

Don't let me go, Angela had said, just before she had faded into the sky.

And Georgia felt she finally understood what her friend had meant.

Because if Georgia had summoned Angela from somewhere within, then Georgia couldn't *really* lose her, could she? Unless she allowed herself to forget. But she would never do that. She would hold her friend inside her, and she would be daring and bold and strong. All the things she was when she was with Angela.

She would not let go.

Georgia didn't think so much about Cole. She didn't like to remember his eyes, hungry and bottomless, as he had disappeared. Because if Angela had come from somewhere inside her, that meant Cole had, too, didn't it? Could she hold on to Angela while letting Cole go? Perhaps they were two sides of the coin. Perhaps a part of him would always be there, watching her from the shadows, beckoning.

One afternoon, she returned to the country house to find Mama and Aunt Marigold sitting at the table, a pitcher of lemonade between them. They were flipping pages in what looked like an old scrapbook.

"Oh, Georgia, you're back," Mama said. "Come and look what I found in the bedroom."

Georgia pulled up a chair and looked over Mama's shoulder at the black-and-white pictures. "It's from when your aunt Marigold was a little girl," she said.

There were photos of curly-haired Aunt Marigold holding a squirming piglet in each arm and of a man and a woman holding up ribbons at some kind of fair, looking proud. Georgia laughed when she caught sight of a familiar face in a line of men standing shoulder-to-shoulder in front of the barn. He was much younger, his face smooth, but she would recognize that round nose anywhere.

"It's Hank!" she said, pointing to the tallest of the men.

Mama turned another page, and a loose picture fell out. Aunt Marigold stooped to pick it up. "Huh," she said. "Not sure what this one is doing with the others. It should be in a different book."

She laid it on the table, and Georgia gasped as she stared down at the photo of the boy, smiling down from the forked branches of a tree.

"Is that—?"

"Your daddy when he was a child," said Aunt Marigold. "Yes, I must have taken this photo when he was about your age. You can see a lot of him in you."

Georgia remembered the first day she had run into the woods, before she had even met Angela. She had imagined a boy running beside her. A boy with dark hair, freckled cheeks, and a mischievous grin. A boy who had once roamed these woods, climbing trees and whistling tunes.

And then one day a boy just like the one she had imagined appeared from the thistly darkness and had nearly convinced Georgia to follow him back into it. A boy at war with himself, like the man Daddy had grown into.

Aunt Marigold was turning to the next page in the scrapbook, pointing out the pictures of Georgia's grandfather being christened.

Georgia watched silently as the pages flipped by, one after another, telling the story of a life. Of many lives, all of them entwined. She paid special attention to her great-grandfather in each photo. His face crinkled with laughter in one, his brow covered in a sweat that spelled hard work in the next. A handsome face, full of pride and promise.

In the last photo, his face was etched in misery as he stood beside Aunt Marigold, outside a church.

"That was the day of my mother's funeral," said Aunt Marigold quietly.

The end of one story and the beginning of another.

Two versions of one man, standing side by side as if they could shake hands with each other.

As if a single person could be split into many people. Their pasts, presents, and futures. Their brightest and darkest selves, all tangled up together. Fighting to see who was strongest.

Everyone startled when the phone suddenly rang. Mama was the first to rise. "I'll get it," she said, sweeping into the living room.

Georgia's eyes never left her as she answered the phone and began talking in a low voice. After a moment, Mama turned to look at Georgia. "Hold on," she said into the receiver. Then, placing it on the little table, she strode back into the kitchen.

"It's your daddy," she said. "He called to check on you. Do you want to talk to him?"

A long moment of silence stretched between them as Georgia considered the answers she could give to Mama's question. Yes, she wanted to talk to Daddy. Of course she did. She ached to hear his voice.

But she didn't know if she wanted to hear the things he

would say. What if he made her more promises he wasn't ready to keep? What if he said he wanted her to come home? Her heart wasn't ready for that. Not yet.

She looked down at the photo of the boy smiling from the tree.

"I can't."

Mama gave a single nod of her head, then went back to the phone.

"Georgia," Aunt Marigold said, seeing Georgia's gaze. "Would you like to see more photos of your daddy as a boy?"

They spent the rest of the afternoon looking through the photo album with pictures of the summers Daddy had spent at the country house. Georgia listened as Aunt Marigold described a boy who was as funny as he was kind, as smart as he was mischievous. A boy Georgia almost felt she knew, and one she would have liked to be friends with.

Looking at those pictures, Georgia felt closer to Daddy than she had in a long time.

Though they looked alike, the smiling boy in those pictures was not, she knew, the grinning boy she had met in the forest. Cole had been a shape-shifter. Something that had formed from the thorns and briars and the darkness inside her.

Something made of shadow.

That night she lay in bed, thinking of her great-grandfather in the photos taken before his wife's death. Would things have turned out differently for him if she hadn't died? Would he have been able to fight the drinking?

And would Daddy?

He loves you very much, came Mama's voice. Or maybe it was Angela's. Sometimes, she could swear she still heard her friend. Reminding her that she wasn't alone.

Aunt Marigold's father had lost his greatest love. His greatest ally. But not Daddy.

Daddy had Mama and Georgia. He had his piano-playing hands. He had his smile.

She knew she couldn't wish this battle away, and she couldn't fight it for him. Nobody could. But Daddy was strong. And he had everything to fight for.

Georgia felt hope creep back into her heart. It didn't shine as brilliantly as a star, but it nestled inside her like a fine blossom.

When Aunt Marigold had been out of the hospital for a week and had begun standing over Mama's shoulder as she cleaned, telling her how to do things "the right way," Mama decided it was time to go home.

Georgia followed her out onto the porch, sat on the stoop as Mama put her suitcase in the trunk of the car.

Mama turned to look at her. Her face fell into a little frown as she placed a hand on each hip.

"Sure you don't want to come?" she asked.

"Sure you don't want to stay?" Georgia returned.

Mama shook her head. "I have to go back," she said. "I have to make sure he's all right."

"Just like I have to make sure Aunt Marigold is."

Mama took a step closer, brushed a few strands of hair from Georgia's eyes. "This summer," she said, "it's changed you, hasn't it? You've grown up so much. I'm sorry if—if you've had to grow up too fast."

Georgia grabbed her hand. "Mama," she said, "don't forget about your studying. You've worked too hard to let anything stop you. Promise me."

Getting her degree was Mama's dream. And this family had buried quite enough dreams already.

"Now I *know* you've grown up too fast," Mama said. "But I promise, Georgia. That's a promise I can keep."

She gave Georgia's hand a firm squeeze. Mama, Georgia thought, was strong, too. Strong enough not to lose herself to Daddy's fight.

It had taken Georgia a long time to really *see* her mother, but she had finally found her. No matter what happened now, they would have each other. Georgia felt a rush of love as she squeezed Mama's hand back.

Then she pulled a folded envelope out of her pocket. "Will you take this to Daddy?"

Inside the envelope was the letter she'd stayed up late the night before writing. A few last things that needed saying.

Dear Daddy,

I wish I could wave a magic wand and make it so you didn't need to drink anymore. But change doesn't happen by magic or by wishing. Aunt Marigold says you're the only one who can decide to change, and I think she's right.

And I just wanted to say that I believe in you. I believe you can change, because I believe you still love me, just like I still love you. I remember you the way you were before, and I'll keep remembering you that way until you come back. I'll be right here, waiting.

Please hurry, Daddy. I miss you.

Love,

Georgia

Mama took the envelope from her and nodded. "I'll be back this weekend," she said. "I love you."

"I love you, too, Mama," said Georgia.

Then she watched as her mother got in the car, honked twice, and waved at the top of the driveway before disappearing down the road.

"Just you and me, then, hmm?"

Georgia turned to see Aunt Marigold standing behind the screen door.

"For now," she said. "Aunt Marigold?"

"Yes?" Aunt Marigold opened the door and came out to the porch to stand.

There was something that had been bothering Georgia, gnawing at the back of her mind. "My daddy and your daddy," she said, "they both ended up the same way."

Her great-aunt nodded. "It's true," she said. "Alcoholism runs in families, same as most other things."

Georgia took a deep breath. She had been expecting this. "So, what about me? Will I, you know, be the same?"

Aunt Marigold didn't answer right away. She looked around, seemed to take in the wind through the trees, the slowly yellowing grass. "You remember what I told you about trying to shape clay?"

"Yes."

"Well, it's the same way with life. Nobody can control it completely. The best we can do is work with what we've got and try to shape it into something beautiful. And I have a feeling you're gonna do that just fine."

"Okay," said Georgia. Her great-aunt believed in her, and she would just have to do the same. "Thanks, Aunt Marigold."

"Well, come on inside, then. Speaking of clay, I've got the studio ready, and that pottery wheel ain't gonna spin itself."

Chapter Fifty-seven

E verything was the way it had been at the beginning of the summer, and yet everything was different, too.

Mornings were for chores, and for helping Hank to paint the new wall once it was finished. Then Georgia would help Aunt Marigold make lunch. Some days, when her great-aunt's hands were giving her too much trouble, Georgia would make the lunch herself. Then they would walk together into the pottery studio.

Georgia never got tired of the slippery cool of the clay between her hands. Never got bored of Aunt Marigold teaching her different firing and glazing techniques. Sitting in the quiet studio, shut away from the rest of the world, was the best part of each day.

Afterward, she would walk in the forest. Sometimes, she would think about Daddy. She would wonder what he'd thought when he had read her second letter. Whether next time Mama came back, it would be to say that Daddy was ready. Really ready this time. To get help. To fight.

But mostly, she tried not to think about him. It was like Aunt Marigold said. She couldn't waste her life waiting.

As she walked, she noticed the way the bark furrowed in different patterns on different trees. The colors of the leaves. The way the light dappled the earth. She did her best to memorize them so that later, in the pottery studio, she could create them again.

One afternoon, she looked down just in time to see half of a bird's egg lying in her path. She remembered the one she'd found the first day she met Angela, broken neatly in two, the baby bird inside it long gone. How she had given one half to Angela and kept the other for herself.

Much better than one of those friendship necklaces. Angela had laughed.

Georgia picked the delicate shell from the ground. As she held it, she thought of how sometimes, things needed to be broken so they could be put right. If an egg never cracked, how could a bird ever take flight?

Maybe some summers *were* just meant to break your heart. But perhaps a single summer could break a heart and start to mend it, too.

Georgia startled when she heard a voice nearby. In the second before she turned, she felt a smile lifting her cheeks.

For just a moment, she was sure she was about to be face-to-face with Angela once more. One last time.

But when she turned, she saw a different girl standing a few paces away, her mouth rounded in surprise. Behind her, a redheaded boy caught sight of Georgia and gasped.

"Who's *that*?" he asked, pointing at her. His sister slapped his hand away.

"Sorry," she said. "You kind of scared us. We didn't know there was anyone else around."

They might not recognize Georgia, but she recognized them. They were the children she had seen in the old Boatwright house. The ones she had once mistaken for Angela and Cole.

"I'm Georgia," she said, waving. "I live with my great-aunt."

The girl's surprise melted into a smile as she waved back. "That's funny," she said. "Not your great-aunt, I mean. Your name. I'm named after a state, too. Dakota. And this is Michael. We just moved here."

They each took a step closer to the other. "Nice to meet you," Georgia said.

"What's in your hand?" Michael asked, lifting his chin to get a better look.

Georgia uncurled her palm to reveal the bird's egg.

"Cool!" cried the boy.

"Do you want it?" Georgia said. "You can have it. As long

as you take good care of it. I have one of my own at home."

Michael grinned, revealing a missing front tooth. "Thanks!" he chirped, taking the egg with surprisingly gentle fingers.

"We were just exploring," Dakota said, pushing her braided hair over her shoulder. "You must know all the good spots out here."

Georgia thought of the wishing lake. Then she shook her head. "Not really," she said. "But maybe . . . maybe we could find some together?"

Dakota's face broke into a grin, the same as her brother's, except for the missing tooth. "Totally," she said. "That sounds like fun."

So they ventured off into the checkered green forest— Michael running ahead while Georgia and Dakota walked behind—to see what there was to see. To find out what more the summer held.

Author's Note

Dear Reader—if your family, like Georgia's, is dealing with addiction, then this letter is for you. First, I want you to know that you are not alone. Countless families have been impacted by drug and alcohol addiction, including my own. I went through some very tough years, and sometimes wondered if I would ever make it through. I did, and you will, too.

Second, I want you to know is that addiction is not your fault. No matter who you are or what your relationship to the addicted person is like, the addiction is *never* your fault. "Fault" is not really a useful word to use when it comes to addiction because addiction is, by definition, something that is out of a person's control. That means it is not in your control, either.

So, if you can't fix someone else's addiction, what can you do? You can care for *you*. Sometimes, when we are hurt, we are tempted to give up on ourselves. We feel unworthy of love. We might do unsafe things to regain the love we've lost. Or we shut ourselves off to other people because we are ashamed or afraid of opening up. Both Georgia and I struggled with those feelings. But those are not ways to take care of yourself.

Instead of giving in to the idea that you are unloved or alone, lean hard on the people you *can* trust—your other family members, friends, teachers, neighbors, etc. Focus on doing the things that make you feel happy. Remember all the awesome things that make you unique and wonderful (and if you can't remember, ask someone to remind you!). And don't be afraid to talk about what you're going through. Chances are the person you reach out to will know someone else who has had to cope with addiction, or might have been through it themselves.

If you feel unsafe in your home or want to connect with someone who understands, but don't know who to reach out to, check out the next page for some resources.

Last, I want you to know that there is hope. People do recover from addictions. But even if your loved one doesn't recover, it doesn't mean that your life will be defined by their addiction. Remember, hearts can be broken, but they can mend, too, if we only give ourselves the permission to heal.

Sending you love and strength,
Ali

Crisis Hotlines

If you feel unsafe in your home, you can always call 911. You can also call any of these numbers free of charge 24 hours a day:

Childhelp®
Phone: 1-800-4-A-CHILD (1-800-422-4453)

National Domestic Violence Hotline
Phone: 1-800-799-SAFE (1-800-799-7233)

For more information on getting help for someone with an addiction, you can call:

National Alcoholism and Substance Abuse Information Center
Phone: 1-800-784-6776

Substance Abuse and Mental Health Service Administration's National Hotline
1-800-662-HELP (4357)

If you just need support, you can call:

Girls & Boys Town National Hotline
1-800-448-3000

If your family is struggling with alcoholism, you can visit www.al-anon.org/newcomers/teen-corner-alateen for support and guidance. If you are 13 and over, you can even connect with other teens whose families are affected by alcoholism.

Ask an adult to help you sign up for the Children's Program offered free of cost through the Hazelden Betty Ford Foundation. You can visit www.hazeldenbettyford.org/treatment/family-children/childrens-program for more information.

If you love camp like Georgia, you may want to check out Camp Mariposa, a camp for kids whose families are impacted by addiction. Find out more at www.elunanetwork.org/camps-programs/camp-mariposa.

Acknowledgments

Thanks to Sarah Davies at Greenhouse for her championing of my work and for all the moral support. To Alyson Day and Megan Ilnitzki for shepherding this book into the world and for their excellent editorial guidance. I am immensely grateful to them and the entire Harper team, including Jon Howard, Emma Meyer, and Aubrey Churchward, for all their hard work on this novel.

To Sarah J. Coleman for her blissfully beautiful cover, and to Laura Mock for her wonderful design.

To my early readers—Kristin Gray, Supriya Kelkar, Jen Petro-Roy, and Nancy Ruth Patterson—for their incredible insights into this shape-shifting story. And to the members of the Cramp for all their feedback and support along the way: Paige Nguyen, Keith Dupuis, Christie-Sue Cheeley, Scott Reintgen, Kwame Mbalia, Jen Perez, and Caitlin Coombs.

To J.B. Lykes and Melissa Nguyen for their medical expertise.

To Aki for always being my biggest fan and being there with me every step of the way. To Luka, who grew right alongside this book and waited to make his entrance to the world after the second draft was done. Good timing, little dude!

Finally, to my mom, dad, and brother for being my original family. Addiction is a complicated beast, and there are innumerable factors that go into how and whether someone can overcome it, many of them outside a person's control. But no matter who you are, recovery takes a lot of hard work and resilience. I am thankful to my father and brother for their strength and determination, and to my mother for holding our family together in our darkest years. The trials we went through together made us stronger as individuals and as a family, and without them I would not have been able to write this story.